Ddraig Chronicles: Reclaim

Ddraig Chronicles: Reclaim

Carmen
Rubino

C. Rubino 8/11/2019

Big Black Dog
Publishing

Ddraig Chronicles: Reclaim is a work of fiction. Names, place, and incidents either are products of the author's imagination or are used fictitiously. Any resemblance to actual events, locales, business establishments, or persons, living or dead, is entirely coincidental.

Cover design by Rachel Foote

Big Black Dog Publishing
PO Box 1886
Longmont, CO 80502

First Edition: August 2019

Hardback ISBN-13: 978-1-7338994-0-6
Ebook ISBN: 978-1-7338994-2-0

To
Thomas Wolfgang Jefferson

Prologue

There were the two – Red and White. And the two went high into the sky. There were shrieks and lightning. The people were afraid.

Mahrah sighed as the memory rose unbidden into her mind. She realized she had retreated into it so shook herself from her head to the end of her tail to bring her back to the present. Gazing at the sky over the hilly region, she spotted a brilliant blue speck, her daughter, Elian. Even from this distance, she could make out her hatchling's distinct almost metallic color. Instead of flying down to the landing courtyard to meet her, Mahrah chose to walk. Her daughter's visit could only mean trouble, and Mahrah wanted as much time as possible to prepare herself.

After the two dragons exchanged greetings, they began to communicate, using images and emotions. It was a telepathic method their kind had developed millions of years ago.

"Mother, I come to bring you news. . ."

Mahrah hissed imperceptibly before her daughter could continue. *"Of your brother,"* she completed.

Elian looked around at the many dragons in the area and understood. Mahrah turned to the large domed structure that was her palace, Elian followed. They spoke of Elian's brother. Once inside, they dropped the pretense of describing the antics of a male dragon.

"Your impatience almost alerted others." Mahrah chastised.

Elian bristled at the reproach. *"You have been concerned for thousands of years. Surely someone has noticed by now."*

Mahrah paused. She did not want to have discord between them, especially at this time. *"I am sorry. I anticipated what you were to tell me, please continue."*

Elian's emotions settled. She straightened up a bit and pushed her wings back to their resting position. *"There has been a draw on the energy source that fuels the Talismans in the First World. Given the amount of energy, I believe the Kinetic Talisman has been used."*

"Then, it is time to act."

"Mother, it is the least dangerous of all the Talismans. I don't know why you are so concerned."

"You do not know those beings' insatiable curiosity. And, I am still unsure of the allegiance of all here. It could be one of our kind helped the two-legged being find and learn how to use the Talisman."

Elian studied her mother for a moment. *"You think someone here may help those in the First World put together all of the Talismans."*

"And, the Amulet."

Elian was shocked at the audacity another dragon would have. She wondered how the two worlds could reconnect. *"How can someone reach a being in the First World?"*

"In the same way I am about to."

Chapter 1

The insistent bark from my dog came moments before the doorbell. Wizard's four paws were much faster than my two feet and he beat me to the front door. Just as I was turning the bolt to unlock the door, I heard the rumble of the delivery truck as it sped off to its next destination.

A small box sat on the porch. That was odd as I had not ordered anything recently. I double checked the name before slicing the tape on the box. Both my PO box and my street address had been listed. Inside the postal package was an old, red, mahogany box. I took it out gingerly and set it on the dining room table. The index card sized box gleamed in the sunlight.

I racked my brain. Maybe it was a late birthday present. Maybe I had won a raffle. I definitely had not ordered this. There was also a card in the package.

When you have a few hours, please go into your beautiful backyard, and sit. Put this on when you are comfortable. – A friend

I unlatched the small hook on the front of the box. Nestled in black velvet was an exquisitely crafted silver bracelet. The bracelet had the design of a dragon - actually, the dragon was the bracelet. The light shimmered off its scales, the wings were pulled back along its body, and its head rested on the end of the tail. It was beautiful. I didn't even like bracelets and I wanted to wear this one. I almost put it on right then, but stopped short when I caught sight of the note again.

I wasn't going anywhere soon. I had just finished my last contract looking for archaeological sites for a road construction project. There were no projects waiting. I had time.

Calling Wizard, I went into the yard. There was a light, early Spring breeze but the morning sun kept me from feeling chilled. The birds had come back in force and were chattering away to attract mates. As I filled Wizard's bowl with water, I noticed the smell of the earth. Winter was losing its hold and the soil was waking up. Wizard pranced around the yard a bit and then laid down to watch the squirrels in the neighbor's tree. He reminded me of a radar dish with his large cupped German Shepherd ears. Instead of panning the area, he would turn his head quickly and refocus his ears on other potential prey. Mostly, they were false alarms.

I sat down with my back against a large stone which radiated warmth. It was at the perfect angle for lounging. I closed my eyes and listened to the songs of the chickadees and white-breasted nuthatch. My reverie was interrupted by a wet slop across my face.

"Wizard," I remonstrated.

He was standing there looking pleased with himself. His black and gold brindle coat both caught and reflected the sunlight. He was smiling. It was hard to be mad at a smiling dog. "Thanks, but I didn't need a bath. Go lay down." Wizard trotted off to another part of the yard, lowered himself to the ground with a grunt of dissatisfaction, and rolled on to his side.

I sat for a little longer taking in the essence of Spring, tucked a lock of my brown, shoulder length hair behind my ear, and opened the box. The bracelet was even more beautiful in the full sunlight. It almost looked like it was breathing. I hesitated. What if this wasn't meant for me? What if it was a hoax? Why was I told to get comfortable in my backyard and then put it on? I moved to put the bracelet back in the box.

Instead of finishing that action, the bracelet ended up on my left wrist. One moment it was headed for the box and the next I had slid my hand through it where it promptly contracted and began to turn the same color as the mahogany box.

"Hey," was all I could say before I could not move. For a moment, I panicked and thought I was having a seizure. But, in my peripheral vision I saw Wizard sunbathing on the other side of the yard. He would have warned me if this was the onset of an episode.

In addition to not being able to move I had the distinct sense that someone was there. I saw my hands in my lap. My eyes said nothing had changed. My brain was setting off alarms that someone else shared my space.

"Who's there?" I noticed this question was mental. I reasoned my lips were part of my non-moving parts. Was I being poisoned?

Greetings.

It was a voice. I was positive I heard a voice. It was an alto voice that was rich and inviting and nothing quite like I had ever heard. I was definitely being poisoned.

You are not being poisoned. You are being contacted by another being.

Not poison. Crazy. I must be going crazy. I finally recalled what I had been told and tried to make sense of it. "You mean you are an alien?"

The chuckle had a rumble to it. *Not precisely. My kind once roamed your world but no longer do.*

Questions poured through my brain: "Who are you? Why can't I move? Why can't I see you?"

Calm. We have much to discuss.

An image of a perfectly still lake came to me. Then, I felt the peace I had just had moments before come back to me. It seeped into the frenzied questions and calmed them.

I can speak your language some, but I also use images. Your words take a while for me to bring together. You are Nadia.

It was a statement, not a question. "Okay. You seem to know who I am, who are you?"

I have many names but the one that was last used by your beings where I lived was Y Ddraig Goch.

Here, the word sounds of 'eh dryg goh' came in the beautiful alto voice.

"Pleased to meet you," said one part of my mind automatically. Another part was wondering what in the breadth and depth of Hades was happening.

Please forgive my way of contacting you. Your kind often has a hard time with my kind.

"What is your kind?" I asked with some trepidation.

The answer is on your wrist.

My eyes fell to my wrist and I saw the bracelet was now entirely a red mahogany color. "You are a dragon?" And then I remembered from my European studies, "Ddraig" was the Welsh word for dragon. "A dragon?" I repeated incredulously.

Yes, it is what your kind calls my kind.

"What does your kind call my kind?"

A chuckle and small rumble again. *We call you Impatient Beings.*

Again, an image came. It was a man pacing. I gave a small sardonic laugh. "You aren't far off the mark." Maybe I was not hallucinating or being poisoned. If so, I was going to relish the experience. "What are you doing here?"

You have been selected to be Chosen. There is need because your world is now in more danger than it has been for a long time.

"No kidding. We have pollution, overpopulation, climate change. . ."

The voice interrupted. *Please explain.*

Reclaim

"Can I send you images like you sent me?"

Yes.

I thought of oil spills, forests being razed, areas parched with drought, poached animals, large urban centers, and people who were diseased. I sent all these images of degradation. It was all happening at the hands of a single species. I began to lose my peace.

I see. This makes our meeting more important. Your kind has created great damage to your world. In addition, some of your beings are about to tip the balance further, threatening the lives of your kind and other beings in your world.

"How can I change that? I can't take control of the world and fix all that."

Truth. You are Chosen to keep power out of the hands of those who will abuse it.

"That sounds ominous."

"Ominous?"

I thought of dark clouds rolling over the countryside and a tornado developing out of them.

"You aren't far off the mark."

"There are a lot of people in this world, why me?"

There are several reasons. First, one of your ancestors was someone I knew.

"How long ago was that?"

That is not easy for me to say. My kind measures time differently than your kind."

I idly wondered how dragons measured time. The dragon continued.

Also, we are convinced you would stay the course even if it meant your actions may cause you injury.

"Um, this sounds a little dangerous. What if I don't want to be chosen?" I didn't realize you could stutter in your thoughts, but I just did.

A sigh. *It is your choice. Being Chosen is between beings. At this point, I have Chosen you. You must also choose. Before you choose, there is much to tell you. Then, you can decide to be Chosen or Not Chosen.*

"And if I decide not to?" Always good to know your options.

I will cease to speak with you. There are other beings in your world who may be able to help - you have been deemed best. You and I need to speak of what happened when my kind meddled in the lives of your kind and why you have been picked to help. Then, you can decide.

Sound filtered in around the conversation. Wizard. He was growling.

You have been interrupted. There is one not far from you who wishes for what you have. Your life will be in jeopardy if it is found that we have met.

Except there was an image of a grave instead of the word "jeopardy". I swallowed hard.

A voice outside the yard was calling hello. "What about the bracelet? I can't take it off."

It will be unseen by others. Your yard is no longer safe for contact. Use another place of nature for us to continue our discussion.

Then, the presence was gone. Wizard was having a barking fit at the gate and a woman called, "Anybody home?" I quickly stuffed the box and note under the mulch by the rock. After calming Wizard and getting him to sit, I opened the gate. A woman stood there smiling. A smile that did not reach her eyes.

Chapter 2

"Can I help you?" I asked. The woman stood slightly shorter than my five feet eight inches. Sun was spilling over her shoulder. It is then I realized it was afternoon, late afternoon. Where did the time go?

The strawberry blonde woman tossed her hair, "Hi! I'm your new neighbor. I moved in down the street last week."

Hospitality took over and I extended my hand, "Hi, I'm Nadia. Good to meet you. How are you finding the neighborhood?" The neighbor reached for my hand. I swore she gave me the once over as she answered. "I love it here. The trees and old homes are so charming."

I looked at her expectantly as I removed my hand. She realized she hadn't given me her name. "I'm Kelly," she added.

"Welcome, Kelly. There are some good people on this block. I hope you get to know them."

"I'm sure we will." When I looked puzzled at the pronoun she added, "My husband Aidan and I." I caught her looking over my shoulder and I turned to see Wizard standing. I surreptitiously made the hand signal to sit. He rested back on his haunches.

I looked back at Kelly and smiled. She smiled back uncertainly, "Is that a wolf? Does he bite?"

Wizard's black muzzle and intense brown eyes often led people to believe he was a wolf. "No, and only if he thinks you are a threat," I answered. I didn't often say the last part, but I also didn't entirely trust my new neighbor.

"Did you need something?" I asked pointedly.

"Right," she replied as she slowly switched her gaze from Wizard to me. "Aidan said he saw a delivery truck come through here today. Did you happen to get a package?" I hoped I didn't look as wary as I felt.

She continued, "I was expecting a small package from my mom and Aidan said a small package was left on your doorstep. I thought maybe the delivery man made a mistake since our addresses are almost the same."

But our names are not, I thought. "I received a package from a friend." The explanation didn't seem to be enough to satisfy her curiosity. Instead of telling her to mind her own business, I added, "It was a late birthday present." I didn't enjoy lying. However, the warning from the dragon, if it was a dragon, was fresh in my mind. Also, there was something unsettling about this woman. Then again, there was something unsettling about this day.

Kelly seemed to realize I wasn't going to tell her anything else. "Okay, I guess I will keep looking for it."

"You could always track it."

"I could," she said as she turned to go, "but my mom threw the information away. She does that." She gave a dismissive wave of her hand. "Thanks, anyway."

"No worries. Have a good day." Another hand wave and Kelly headed back to the street and sashayed down the block. After making sure she left, I turned to go back into the yard. Wizard came and licked my hand. "I'm fine," I told him. I gave him a kiss on the top of his head to convince me more than him.

It took me a long time to fall asleep that night, which was not normal. I kept looking at my wrist. The bracelet was silver. The workmanship was amazing with extremely clear detail and no sharp edges. I tugged on it. It was smaller than when I slipped it over my hand. The bracelet was the only thing keeping me tethered to the idea something actually happened.

When I finally slept, a dream came. I stood by my messenger bag with the box in my hand. As I put it in the bag, it glowed a little bit. I turned to see the card floating in the air right in front of me. As I reached to grab it, it burst into flames and the ash settled into my hands. "*Do so,*" said a voice.

The next dream was a whirlwind of all the places I liked to hike. There were images of the trails near Rocky Mountain National Park, a trail in a wilderness area to the west of Denver, and a few trails in the southwest part of the state. I sighed happily as I remember the hours spent wandering through forests, up mountains and along streams. Scenes from all seasons played across my dreamscape. I relived the snow shoeing of winter, the soaked shoes of spring, the beauty of the flowers from summer, and the golden aspen of fall. Throughout the dream, I found myself revisiting one particular trail.

At 4:00 a.m., my eyes popped open. I knew I was not going to go back to sleep even though it was hours before the time I normally woke. I felt as though I had been up all night. However, two things were quite clear — where I was going to 'find nature' and I was going to light something on fire.

Wizard and I went into the backyard. He snuffled off to take care of business and see if a raccoon had been through his domain. I pulled out the items I had hidden the previous afternoon. Walking over to the chimenea, I tucked the box into my hoodie pocket. The moon had waned and there was little light. I located the matches with a little fumbling, put the card in the chimenea, and lit it on fire. Even the flame had a slight mahogany tinge to it. I turned to go back into the house, but stopped. Just burning the card didn't seem to be enough. I pulled the ashes out and made sure the breeze took them to different parts of the neighborhood.

***

Having lunch with Jannet always lightened my mood. How could it not? She always had a positive, calm demeanor. I smiled even as I saw her sitting under the awning of one of our favorite restaurants. After welcoming hugs and a pat for Wizard we sat and picked up menus.

"See anything different about me?" I queried. Jannet sat up and peered at me closely. Her long blonde hair had been pulled into a pony tail which swept back and forth as she shook her head.

"No," she began hesitantly, "wait, did you cut your bangs? You always tease me that I don't notice when you cut your bangs."

I had carefully put both hands on the table. Even my acquaintances knew that I only wore a watch and only when I needed a timepiece out on a dig. Jannet was an attentive friend and would not have overlooked an unusual accessory on my wrist.

"Did you get a new shirt?" she offered.

I smiled. "No. I thought I would give you a false positive reading."

"I could read your aura." She took one of my hands in both of hers and looked into my eyes. Those clear blue eyes had once caused my heart to skip a beat.

"You are a person who cares deeply and makes bad jokes," she proclaimed. I tried to pull my hand away. "It's true," she said soberly.

"Which?" I asked.

"Both," she smiled. "And, you didn't sleep well last night," she continued, sitting back, and pulling her menu toward her.

"You don't need to read my aura to tell me that. My eyes always look a little bleary after a bad night of sleep."

"I worry when you don't sleep well. It makes you more susceptible to episodes."

"Then, let me put your mind to rest. I haven't even had a tinge of a seizure in six months," I announced. "It is a good thing I really like Wizard or I would see him as an unwieldy accoutrement."

Wizard grunted from under the table as if to object to the comparison.

The waiter came to take our order. I ordered chicken salad and Jannet settled on a Rueben sandwich with sweet potato fries.

"It's odd you didn't sleep last night," she began, "because I didn't either."

"That's unusual for you. You sleep like the dead."

Jannet laughed, "Don't you know it. Ben says I could sleep through a war."

"How is Ben?" I asked just as something caught my attention over Jannet's shoulder. It was a woman and a man walking around the corner somewhat quickly. It seemed almost too quick for such a nice day in such a small town. I was sure the woman had strawberry blonde hair. The man was taller and had dark brown hair like mine.

"He seems to be impressing everyone at the company with his ideas. They are thinking about creating a new department for him," Jannet was saying as I refocused my attention.

"Will he be working away from home more?" I asked.

"I hope not. I do enjoy the time we have apart to do our own things, but I married him because I wanted to spend more time with him, not less."

"Maybe you should travel." When Ben was away, Jannet had the time to travel. Since Ben's company rewarded him handsomely for his ideas, she also had the means.

"Hmmm," she said hesitantly. "I have a better idea. We can travel together. It has been too long since you and I have taken a trip. I'm afraid you are going to turn into a hermit."

"I have Wizard."

Jannet gave me a pained look, "You are a good person. I would love to see you share yourself with someone." The look on my face told her this wasn't open for discussion.

"Very well," she continued in a lighter vein, "I will be your traveling partner for the foreseeable future. I will make sure you have proper accommodations and food while you spend your days wrestling with sun and dirt."

"Which means you will be by the pool while I am out at a site."

"Exactly." We both laughed.

Lunch arrived and I picked up the silverware and prepared to attack my food. I admired people who could eat daintily. I tried but failed miserably.

A sudden gust caught my napkin and I ended up chasing it a couple of tables across the patio. I was about to turn back when I looked at the bench across the road. The dark-haired man from before was there. The intense gaze of his eyes was unsettling. I acted like I didn't notice. Sitting down again, I said quietly, "Jannet, I think there is a guy watching us."

"Where?" As she asked, she didn't change her posture or turn around.

"On the bench, across the road," I said, beginning to eat again.

Jannet waited a bit before turning around. While she waited a bus pulled up in front of the bench. When it pulled away, the man wasn't there.

"Are you being a bit paranoid?" Jannet asked since she saw no one.

"Maybe so," I shrugged, trying to dispel my wariness. Jannet knew me well enough to know that I was really concerned.

Jannet and I met when I had a minor seizure during my third year in college. I was finishing some research in the library when it happened. The other students thought I was drunk or on drugs. Jannet came over and realized it was a medical issue. She stayed with me until my parents showed up at the emergency room. I thought it was the last I would see of her, but she tracked me down the next week and wondered if I wanted to hang out.

I soon found out Jannet was one of two daughters of diplomats. She had lived in ten countries by the time she was eighteen. She was taken with the idea I had spent my whole life in Colorado. We spent many nights swapping stories of growing up and found our experiences to be surprisingly very similar. When I told her I was gay, she didn't bat an eye, and I was able to take my initial feelings of attraction and turn them into a friendship.

The waiter put down the dessert menu at the same time he picked up the plates. He wasn't being presumptuous, we always ate dessert. After deciding on what to share, peach cobbler, we chatted about the rest of the week. I wanted to let her know I was going to be out of town. Jannet was responsible for knowing my exact whereabouts when my parents were traveling.

"I'm going to be gone a couple of days to see about some sites," I said. Mentally I added, "And, talk to a dragon."

"Out of state?"

"No. I want to check an area I haven't seen with low snowpack. I am hoping the dry winter and melting snow will show some boundary markers."

Finding places where people had lived in the past was something I was particularly good at and Jannet found utterly bewildering. The only reason Jannet would know that some ancient people had used an area for habitation was when there was a large interpretive sign. Sometimes, even that didn't work. We once visited Dinosaur Ridge outside of Denver. I was enthralled with the footprints in the rock; Jannet saw a bunch of dents.

"I will think of you when you are freezing and I am very warm under my comforter. Should I have a cup of hot chocolate for you?"

"Yes, please, with a few marshmallows."

Wizard and I set out early the next morning. The trailhead was a few hours from home. When we arrived, there were no other cars in the parking lot since it was in between recreation seasons.

After hiking for a few hours, Wizard and I followed the trail as it dropped down into a meadow. The meadow rose slightly as it went west. The stream I had heard for the last half hour as we crossed the top of a cliff lay on the south side of the meadow. I had been in this area many times. Of all the hikes in this part of the world, it was my favorite. Even now, I looked forward to the turn in the stream which left a nice flat spot. I sat down under a pine and looked at the bare aspen on the other side of the brook.

But, now I was here, I realized I didn't know what else to do. The instructions had been to find a nature spot. I sat down and leaned against the tree. Nothing. I closed my eyes. Still nothing happened. I tried closing my eyes as if I were meditating. The brook skipped over the rocks and a few pine siskins were chirping in the tree tops. I felt too anxious to be meditating.

I tried being more assertive. "Hello? Dragon? I'm here," I said out loud. Wizard picked up his head from between his paws and looked at me quizzically. Okay, the direct approach wasn't working either.

It was time for Plan B. I had not been kidding about trying to find some sites in the area. It was a long meadow with small ponds where beavers had dammed up the water. There was lots of water and animals to hunt. Besides Jannet, who wouldn't want to spend a summer here?

After setting up the tent not far from a rock outcropping on the north side of the meadow, I tossed our packs into the tent. Wizard seemed happy to get rid of the dog pack he wore, but concerned that his food was no longer on his back. He took one last, longing look and then bounded after me as I began to explore the meadow more methodically. He enjoyed the afternoon. Free from his service dog vest, he snuffled at logs and marked territory, but never out of sight.

We spent the afternoon in the meadow and the draws leading down to it. I mapped several potential sites. The snow was a little deeper than I had expected in some of the meadow and the shady part of the draws. I made plans to come back in the summer to get a more thorough look at one or two places I thought were warm weather camp sites for the Ute tribe. As the shadows lengthened, I rehydrated a meal pack and gave Wizard his kibble. Later, the stars found me drinking a cup of hot chocolate with no marshmallows.

Before falling asleep, I pulled out Wizard's pink pig toy. It was my signal to him that I wanted to go to sleep. He took it gently from my hand, dropped it on the floor of the tent and then put his head on top of it. The sight of a dog who looked like a wolf with a pink stuffed animal between its paws always made me giggle.

I was a touch disappointed when I woke early the next morning and realized I had slept soundly through the whole night. I had expected lucid dreams telling me what to do next, but there were none. Maybe I had imagined the whole thing. Except, there was still a dragon bracelet on my wrist.

To shake off the cold after breakfast, Wizard and I climbed a draw running north out of the meadow. It was tougher going than I had realized it would be, and we reached the top of the rock bench forming the edge of it an hour later. Just as I was about to walk into the forest, a ground squirrel skittered between my feet. Startled, I picked up one leg and jumped to the side. Wizard went into protective mode and chased what he believed was a life-threatening rodent.

As he rushed past me, he knocked me off balance and I fell forward. For a moment, I thought I was headed right back down the rock face. Out of instinct, I grabbed the nearest thing — the exposed root of the nearby pine tree. It kept me from sliding back down the steep rock face. I took off the small pack I had donned and rolled on to my back. I could feel a scrape and a couple of bruises but nothing worse. I stayed on my back and took time to look up. The sun was filtering through the tree branches and warming the rock. There was a brilliant blue sky, a sky which then turned a reddish mahogany.

Chapter 3

"*Greetings,*" came the same rich voice I had heard days before, "*You return.*"

"Yes, but I wasn't sure how to get in contact with you again. You didn't exactly leave me a phone number," I spoke mentally.

There was a moment of confusion. *It was important to not be discovered.*

"You said something about being chosen and the world being in peril. I have a whole lot of questions about what you meant. And, I have questions about you being in this world before but not now."

Yes. There is much to discuss.

"You were also going to tell me why I have been selected. I have questions about that too."

There was a pause. I thought I heard a sigh of exasperation.

I will start with who we are; who I am. Please, describe what you see as I send images.

I was confused about that request, "Why?"

For me to learn your language more. It is better to close your eyes. This set of images comes from one of my kind of long ago. I will relay it to you.

In my mind's eye, a scene played. I saw a rainforest. The foliage was massive and dense. The humidity was oppressive. Before I could get a thorough grasp of the surrounding, the view began to bob up and down. After a minute of the motion, the forest thinned ahead. Suddenly, the forest dropped away and a hazy, light blue sky came into view. The trees fell away further and hills on the horizon could be distinguished. Lakes dotted the landscape here and there. A few breaks in the forest below revealed large meadows, animals moving in them. It was difficult to know exactly types of animals since they were almost the same color as their surroundings. I started with the realization that the beings were some of the dinosaurs I had seen in museums. I tried to form a question but found that it was impossible to put together mental speech beyond the travelogue I was relaying to the dragon.

A screech sounded and the view shifted to one side. A pterodactyl was approaching quickly, intent on interception. At the same time, I saw the wings of the dragon to which this view belonged. They were large and a beautiful emerald color.

Without warning, the world began to spin. The sky and forest traded places. There was a thud which shuddered the dragon, followed by a roar. Two more pterodactyls came into view. A long, spiked tail swiped at one of the pterodactyls and it peeled off. The other two kept following. The sensation of falling came with the image of a dive. The trees came closer and closer and then, when it seemed a crash was certain, the view leveled. The being leveled out above the trees. With a look up and back, I saw that the pterodactyls had stopped pursuit and were returning the way they came.

This flight pattern continued for a time. The thick, massive greenery was broken up by meadows and lakes. After a bit, I became aware I could feel the sensation of the beating wings. The sensation of the being's body followed shortly after. I felt the length of the tail, the four legs being held tight to allow for efficient flight, and the air buffing the nose and face. From nose to tail, I could sense the being was enormous.

I was still marveling at the feeling when there was a change in the beating of the wings. The dragon had caught a rising air mass and was using it to get higher than the cliff which had risen in front of it. Once high enough, it left the warm air and glided to a large open space on the top of the cliff. I felt, more than saw, the landing.

There were almost twenty dragons on the butte. Most of them had four legs of equal length. A few had shorter forelegs and stood more upright. There were various colors and sizes. There was no speech, but it was apparent they were communicating. Some of the dragons would nod or swing their head to the side. Sometimes there would be a low rumble or a swish of a tail.

The dragon whose memories I shared focused on one of the beings. It was a cherry color with four legs of the same length. The two dragons approached each other. They reached out with their necks until their faces were next to each other and one eye could look into the other. They both rumbled with contentment. I realized they were mates.

The scene faded. Then the voice of the mahogany dragon began.

"You now know who we were."

"You lived during the time of the dinosaurs?"

"Yes."

"Where have you been? Why haven't we found you?"

The reply came more in images than words. *The answers to your questions form the next part of what we need to discuss.*

Everything grew dim. Initially, I thought the darkness was because the memories were taking time to unfold. However, I noticed movement. This scene was taking place at night. Adjusting my internal vision, I saw a large ring of stone slabs. The dragons were changing where they sat. One would move it a bit towards one side. Others would look at it and either bob to shake their head. The inner faces of the rock pillars had been shorn vertical. The ring was about a hundred feet across. I was aware of a crowd of beings, all dragons.

I heard and felt thuds. Logs were being dropped from above by flying dragons. As soon as the tree trunk rolled to a stop, one or more of the dragons would take the log and place it against the outside of the ring of stones. I thought they were creating a fence. Over time, the fence turned more into a heap. I had seen heaps like these at bonfires.

A crescent moon rose. The emerald dragon looked at it and then turned and looked to another part of the sky. Stars gleamed in an inky sky. There was a sudden brightness near the horizon. It was hundreds of times brighter than any falling star.

A surge of something close to panic mixed with determination went through the emerald dragon. The other dragons turned and looked at the unnatural brightness. They radiated the same emotions. Quickly, a ring of dragons formed outside of the stones and logs. As one, they set the logs on fire with their breath. A small inferno started and continued to grow as the dragons breathed fire on the rocks. As a result, some of the rocks began to glow in the heat.

As the temperature around the rocks climbed, a horde of dragons had left the ground. They were circling above the enclosure. Though it was hard to see, I noticed that many smaller ones followed one big dragon. The rising light from the fire glinted off their scales as they climbed. Then, the large dragon dove straight for the center of the circle. The flames lit its yellow eyes as it careened to the ground. The smaller dragons formed two lines straight behind each wing of the large dragon. I felt a panic rise in me as the dragon's nose touched the earth.

Instead of collapsing into one big heap, the dragons passed through the ground. It was as if they were going through a gateway. The emerald dragon was relieved. It roared at the success and others replied. A second group of dragons flew up and circled until they were high above the circle.

As each wave of dragons passed through, a new group would launch and climb. When the dragons heating the stones became tired, other dragons took their place. Slowly, the crowds of beasts dwindled down. Dawn approached and there were only a small remnant of the multitude left. A bank of coals had formed over the hours of the evening. The remaining dragons put more wood on them causing flames to erupt from the smolders.

Just as the last group of dragons were getting ready to take off, the flames were snuffed out by a great gust of air. The emerald dragon looked to the west. The sky was lit up not with the sun but with fire. A moment later, the air grew extremely still. All the dragons realized the shockwave from the meteor hitting the earth was about to sweep over them. The emerald dragon and cherry dragon communicated with each other. Heat was needed to help the gateway stay viable. They would stay and relight the fire as the last group got into position.

Twenty-four dragons took off as one. They strained to gain height as quickly as possible. The two remaining dragons relit the fires. Their fatigue meant their streams of fire were not as large or intense. They looked up to see the last formation get into position as the wind began to strengthen. The group of dragons formed one long line; each one slightly biting the tail of the dragon in front of it. The smaller ones were in between the larger ones, hoping to keep the smaller dragons from being blown off course. They began their headlong decent.

Just as they reached the gateway, the last two dragons took to the air. The emerald dragon was knocked into a tree by a strong gust. The right wing was in pain but intact. The cherry dragon trumpeted in alarm. The emerald dragon gave a reassuring thought and gained altitude.

The gut-wrenching, panicked cries of other animals in the forest reached the two dragons as they climbed. Herds of dinosaurs could be seen stampeding away from the oncoming fury. Pterodactyls screeched in alarm as they careened east.

The sky was growing red in both the east and the west and the air was heating up. The cherry dragon reached the dive point. It hesitated. Its mate was not yet at the right height. It reluctantly began its descent at the urging of the emerald dragon.

As the emerald dragon finished gaining the height it needed, it saw the earth undulate like the sea. If the ripple reached the circle before the emerald dragon reached the gateway, it would snap closed and there would be no escape.

The emerald dragon saw its mate pass through the gateway and began its own desperate dive. A pang of regret echoed through its being at the inability to get any of the other beings to join the dragons. They had been too afraid of the beasts who could communicate. Their fear sealed their fate. The emerald dragon felt a deep loss for the others, certain most of them would not live.

Halfway to the ground, a group of terrified pterodactyls bowled into the dragon and knocked it off course. At the same time, the wind began to howl. If the dragon opened its wings it would be blown completely off course. If it kept them closed, the dragon would miss the target.

Thinking quickly, the emerald dragon adjusted its trajectory using its tail and the slightest unfolding of its wings. As it reached tree level, it saw in its peripheral vision the pitching of the forest just outside of the circle. One of the trees rolled towards the stones just as the dragon's nose hit the trigger. The emerald dragon slid into the gateway and into another universe. Behind it, the world succumbed to the devastating impact, changing the planet forever.

Chapter 4

My eyes fluttered open. The birds were singing and puffy clouds scudded across the sky.

I became aware of Wizard's head on my stomach. It was heavy since he was sound asleep. I was finding it hard to breathe. "Do you mind?" I asked aloud. He snuffled, moved his head between his paws, and fell back asleep.

I had just seen how the world ended. Only, it was still here with birds, sunlight, and trees. I reached out with a mental question, "Did they all die?"

Your world still has life in it which means not all life died.

"How could you leave them?" I asked growing angry as I grappled with the immense loss of life long ago, "Why didn't your kind try harder to get the others to come with you?"

It was a great regret we dealt with for a long time. We did not believe in forcing other beings to our will. After arriving here, we were not sure we made the right decision.

"How did you know about the gateway to the other world?"

I will tell you another time. I sense you need nourishment. It has been some time since we began.

I really looked around and was surprised by two things. First, I could move my head. Second, the sun's position indicated it was early afternoon.

"I am able to move some now."

It has to do with the energy I am using to contact you. I can focus on you and the bracelet more.

I realized I was hungry, thirsty, and surprisingly tired. "Okay, I will take a break. How do I find you again?"

Come back to the same spot when you are ready.

I got up and stretched thoroughly. I felt like I had been working all morning instead of sitting in a type of trance. Instead of sitting back down to eat, I grabbed an apple and a protein bar from my pack. Wizard was instantly on his feet and we meandered through the forest that lead away from the rock edge. After about one hundred feet, the trees thinned. A ridge rose above the western side of the clearing. Some trees on the north side of the clearing provided shelter from the wind I heard blowing over the top of the ridge. It was surreal to be looking at such a beautiful landscape while the scenes of the previous devastation replayed in my mind.

I wandered back leisurely. Before sitting down, I pulled out Wizard's bowl. My eyes fell to the dragon bracelet as I filled it. The back of the dragon on the bracelet was now tinged mahogany. Wizard nuzzled my other hand, he did so when he wanted a treat, so I dug a few out of my pack. I made myself comfortable near the same place I was before. There was a smooth round rock on which to lean and I looked down the draw and across the valley, at the trees on the next mountain over.

Mentally, I reached out with a greeting.

Welcome back.

"What should I call you? It seems odd to just sit down and expect you to be there."

We do not often use names.

There was a short pause. *You may call me Mahrah.*

"Are you. . ." I trailed off because I was embarrassed this had been my next question.

I sense you have another question.

"Are you male or female?"

Female.

"Mahrah," I mentally said, rehearsing her name, "The bracelet had some mahogany on it even though we were not talking."

I expected so after you told me you could move while communicating. Our connection is growing. Soon, you will be able to contact me without the energy of rock and will be able to move more freely.

The comment caused a few things to click into place. I had not been able to chat with Mahrah the day before because I had been on a stream bank which was all dirt. It also meant that the rocks I saw in the dragons' flight from the planet were more than symbolic. Another instance of the same formation came to mind, but before I had much time to think about it, Mahrah began again.

It is time to begin the tale of why you have been contacted and asked to be Chosen. After I finish, you will need to decide if you will accept.

Reclaim

I held my breath expectantly.

You have seen that we were in your world and we left. The world changed and the gateway closed. After a time, your world shifted and the gateway opened again. We returned.

"You came back? When? Why? What happened?"

A small chuckle. *You have many questions. Your kind asks many of those. I will show you memories to answer as well as I can. Close your eyes.*

There was a moment of darkness and then stunning sunlight. The deep blue sky glistened overhead. Mahrah, for the memory was hers, arced up into the azure and then came down on a plain. She landed and thumped her tail in gladness. Five other dragons landed around her. Three of them were four footed. Two had shortened front legs. One was much smaller than the others. It was one-fourth of the length of the largest and stood slightly taller than the long grass. After finding it could not see clearly on the ground, it hovered for a bit before settling on the shoulder of one of the other dragons. All their scales glistened in the sunlight — yellow, white, blue, iridescent green, and black. They formed a circle and checked on each other's well-being. The dragons communicated primarily with images and it took a little bit for me to understand the conversation.

Before long, a decision was made to pair up and look around the area for whatever beings were now on the earth. They went three directions with the understanding they would meet back at night and an alarm would be raised for the others to come if the beings were dangerous.

Mahrah and the white dragon flew southeast. They searched for the large two-legged and four-legged animals who had been there when their ancestors left the world. Instead of pterodactyls, there were many very small winged beings with soft coverings. The small ones travelled in groups. A few of the larger ones, but not nearly as large as the pesky pterodactyls, travelled by ones or twos. All of them fled when they sensed the dragons overhead.

The two dragons exchanged glances as they glided over a field and a small heard of fuzzy four-footed beings stampeded. The soft covering of the deer instead of iron plates or tough hides puzzled them. The dragons reasoned the abundant smaller species were food for the larger predators they would soon find.

Many wingbeats later, the dragons still saw none of the large scaly creatures they had expected. This puzzled them.

The horizon turned blue signaling a large body of water. The dragons glided down to the choppy waves and landed. Mahrah took a drink of the abundant resource and then immediately blew it out. The unexpected saltiness was more than a surprise, it was an omen.

In the memories of the dragons from the escape of long ago, there had been no water with this quality. The two explorers knew this meant the planet had changed significantly after the tragedy it endured.

Flocks of terrified birds began diving at the two enormous creatures. The white dragon tried to communicate with them and they went bezerk. Mahrah chided her companion for inciting the chaos.

Leaving the churning sky of birds, the two began to fly along the coastline. They played in the breeze coming off the water. Following the coast into an inlet, they discovered a ribbon of water flowing into the bay. Wondering if it would also be salty, they decided to follow it inland and then land in it. When they did, the water was fresh and refreshing. Both were relieved to find that not all the water on the planet was salty.

As they were sharing ideas about what they had seen, a motion in the trees caught their attention. The two dragons had been so absorbed in their conversation, they had ceased being vigilant. They realized with some concern it would take a couple of wingbeats to lift off the river. A large predator would do some damage before they could fly to safety.

Instead of a large beast, a small herd of upright, two-legged beings came out of the trees to the edge of the river. Their light-colored limbs were not protected with any hide or scale. The dragons realized the soft covering on the rest of their body was not their own, but the hides of other animals. Some of them had other coverings which smelled of plants.

The hominids were not large. They brandished rocks and sticks menacingly. The dragons looked at them quizzically. Then, one of the beings threw what it was holding at the dragons. It was a stick as long as the being was tall, tipped with a pointed rock. It bounced off Mahrah's scales.

Upon seeing this, more of the beings threw their long, pointed objects. A couple splashed in the river. The rest harmlessly hit the dragons. The white dragon sighed contemptuously and then used its wings to splash the beings with water, causing them to retreat quickly.

Exasperated, Mahrah reproached the other dragon. She reminded the white dragon they had agreed to do reconnaissance before interacting. Twice her companion had not kept to the agreement. The white dragon did not reply.

Before the two-legged beings returned from their scare, the dragons decided they could learn nothing new. They took off and flew back to the gateway.

As they travelled, the others sent communications that other two-legged beings were at the arrival place and were not friendly. The images they sent confirmed the defensive beings were like the ones who had thrown objects at the river. It was decided to meet a bit to the northeast of the gateway, by a stream.

Once they convened, all six dragons were at a loss to explain the foreign world. Before coming to this world, there had been speculation among their kind of change but not to this extent. The lack of lush vegetation, large animals, and dense air was surprising. The decision made at the end of the reports and consultation was to look for the expected flora and fauna in other places.

Mahrah stopped sending memories to me.

The next things we did took some time. I will reveal only bits of the memories.

She began showing the dragons traveling the globe. They checked each continent. Some animals were larger than others but there was nothing to rival the size of the beings the dragons' ancestors reported. The dragons had a spike of hope when they found herds of elephants in Africa. Tentatively, the dragons contacted the lumbering animals. The elephants were bewildered at first, but came to understand the communication of the ancient species and did not fear them.

When the oldest elephant indicated there were no larger land animals in the area they roamed, the dragons' hopes fell.

As they circled they earth, they also checked the oceans. When they found the whales, they again hoped some of the ancient species had survived. However, the large sea mammals indicated they were the largest being in the ocean. They also gave the dragons information about the land masses of the world - how the continents connected, Australia, the larger islands, and the ice at the poles.

The global search came to an end after many years. From what I could determine, they were in Europe. At this point, Mahrah communicated more directly with me.

I think I can translate the next conversation we had because of all you have been describing.

I saw the circle of dragons once again. The blue dragon began, *"This is truly not the planet our ancestors left. It has changed much."*

Mahrah replied, *"We were to reach out to those who survived and help them if we could. Our goal was to do what we could to create balance in the world, to make sure life will go on for the most number of species. The task will be different from we imagined.*

"What seems to have survived and risen to prominence is the two-legged beings with no fur or scales. Somehow, they have prospered across the whole planet," Mahrah said. The other dragons agreed.

"They are quite impatient," said the iridescent green dragon.

"And hostile," added the yellow dragon who had more than a few objects hurled at her.

"Yes. I am not sure they are good for the balance of this world," Mahrah said.

"We could kill them all and let the rest of the world maintain balance," suggested the black dragon.

"I do not think doing so will cause the world to be in balance," replied the yellow dragon, *"Besides, I think whatever processes happened to bring these beings to their place will only act again."*

"We could bring our kind back and rule them," said the white dragon. *"The gateway is still open."*

"It may not stay open. Once it closes, it may be many trips around the sun before we are able to use it," the blue dragon stated.

"Then, whoever is here can stay. Think of it, two worlds where we thrive!" the white dragon said.

"It is not our goal." Mahrah disputed, *"We are looking to set right things our ancestors felt they did wrong by not intervening before. Entire clans of beings that used to live before are no more. Our ancestors anticipated some of the changes, but not all. They tasked us with helping this world when we could return because they believed they were responsible for those kinds perishing. We must decide if we should act and what should be done if we do."*

The green dragon had listened to all that was said and now spoke. *"I believe we should choose to act. The two-legged beings have the most potential. They have minds closest to ours. We could speak with those who do not attack us in hordes. If we helped them, they may be able to develop themselves and create a way of life which will protect and sustain the world."*

"These beings also have great fear. I think they will only run from us and our ideas. They are too simple," countered the white dragon with ardor.

Such open dissent was a signal for a raging debate in dragon culture. There was a congregation of voices as each dragon tried to speak about what to do. Mahrah chose to remain silent.

A thump of the tail or exhalation of steam was present when a dragon countered another's ideas. With such a commotion, Mahrah hoped the two-legged beings were not close. She conceded they were quick to fear and then violence. Finally, the other dragons realized Mahrah was not participating in the clamor. They became quiet.

"You all make important points," she said. *"It is why you were each asked to come. Your combined wisdom was needed to make the best decision for our mission. I do not know how often we will be able to traverse between the*

worlds. If this is our last time, we should leave this world with the benefit of our knowledge and abilities. I will take all your counsel and let you know my decision."

It was after these words an idea I had been forming for the better part of the day became clear to me. Mahrah was the leader. She ran the expedition and had final say. I wondered if she was picked just to lead this expedition or if she maintained a similar role on her own world.

I do.

Her response surprised me because I didn't realize I had made my thoughts available.

I am considered ruler of my kind. I am descended from the last two dragons who left your world all those years ago. I am the oldest female of the brood of my parents. Therefore, I am required to rule.

"Wasn't it risky to send the ruler of your kind to this world?"

It was necessary. At the time of these events, I was not the ruler, but the next in line to rule. My mother was still leader of my kind.

My female ancestor, the emerald dragon, felt she had failed this world. It was determined, if there was ever a chance, one of her descendants would try to make things right. When the energy fields had realigned and the gateway opened, we took the opportunity. It did not matter if I was unable to return or died trying. What mattered was honoring the edict of my ancestors.

"Is the reason you haven't come back because the energy fields have not allowed the gateway to open?"

It is one of several reasons. The alignment requires the interior tides of your planet to be in the right place along with its place in your planetary system. It has not happened since we left.

Mahrah paused. *I now realize how weary I am. You must be also. It currently takes great energy for me to communicate with you. I need to rest before I can tell you more.*

"But," I began.

A tired laugh. *Impatient One, we both need rest. I can tell you need sustenance also as your energy is low. I now remember your kind needs to eat more often than my kind does.*

"Okay," I agreed with dismay. "I will call Jannet and let her know I am going to be here longer than I anticipated." I don't know why I told Mahrah this, it seemed important.

Make your arrangements. Caution – do not tell anyone where you are. This is for your safety. I sense another has tried to listen on our conversation since I used a larger area of the earth than I would have liked. I do not know what has been heard or where the being is. I know it would be dangerous for you if you were found. Eat. Drink. Rest. Return when you have done so.

I became more aware of my surroundings as the connection faded. The shadows were long. I had spent most of the day sitting or lying on the rock ledge and I was sore. My stomach rumbled. I pulled out some food and a satellite phone from my daypack. The phone was a necessary expense since many of the sites I worked at were far away from cell towers. As the phone booted up, I gnawed on some biscuits and cheese.

Jannet picked up after a couple of rings. "Good news?" she answered.

"Some promising beginnings. I am going to be out an extra day or two. Can you let me know what type of weather to expect?"

"Sure. What area of the state should I tell you about?"

I thought of Mahrah's warning. "How about the high and low systems expected the next two days? I can usually tell what is going to happen anywhere between Utah and Kansas with the information."

Jannet was a little perplexed at the vagueness, but read off the official weather report like it was a child's book. She even changed voices when she switched days. She had never done this and I had to stifle a giggle. "The End," she said with a flourish and then inquired innocently, "Anything else?"

"You are a nut and my mother was right to put you as point person." My parents were out of the country fulfilling my father's dream of seeing every bird he possibly could before he died. Whenever they traveled, Jannet was the person who made sure I didn't disappear into a ruin or fall off the map entirely.

"Right on both counts. See you in a couple of days?"

"Tell Ben hello for me. Ringing off."

After a good stretch and some more food, I clambered back down to my tent. Wizard seemed happy to finally go somewhere. When we reached the tent, I felt uneasy about how exposed it was and decided to strike camp. It was true I was away from the most popular trail, but I was fairly near the trail running through the meadow. As I packed the tent and sleeping bag, I was glad there would not be a fire ring to indicate where I had been.

Twilight came as I reset the tent under a tree on the western edge of the clearing I had seen earlier in the day. The ridge above would protect me from any strong winds from the incoming weather system. Dinner was red beans and rice with some bread I had brought with me. I sat with a hot cup of tea as the temperature began to drop.

Right before settling in for the night, I pulled Wizard's toy pig from the pack. He took it, laid it between his paws, and settled down next to me. The sleeping bag and Wizard's warm mass were welcome as the temperature continued to fall. I fell asleep almost immediately.

Chapter 5

The birds started chirping gleefully at 4:30 a.m. I rolled over, pulled my hoodie over my eyes, and tried to ignore them. They were persistent and loud. After about twenty minutes, I decided to give up sleeping any longer. It was still frosty as I made a breakfast of oatmeal. I looked forward to getting home and making pancakes or biscuits.

As the sky grew bright, I made sure I had all the necessities for the day in my small pack. Wizard nosed around the short grass as I started back to the ledge. Right before I stepped clear of the trees, I looked down into the draw and saw movement.

Two people stepped clear of the bushes and into the meadow below me. They both wore dark coats and hats, blue and red. The one with the blue hat had a daypack. The lack of backpacking gear and time of year gave me the impression that these two were not here to enjoy some time away from civilization.

Wizard was off to my left. I caught his attention, and gave him the signal for laying down. Hiding behind a scraggly bush, I peered over the ledge.

When the two walked to the place I had pitched the tent the night before, I became more uneasy. The crisp morning air carried their voices up the draw.

"There was a camp made here recently. Whoever it was probably went further to the west" said the one in the blue hat, gesturing the length of the meadow. The other man, with his back still to the ledge, looked to where the first man pointed.

"Are you sure she is here? There are a lot of places she could have gone," the man in the blue hat continued.

"I am sure," the man in the red hat said. "Do not question me about it again." His speech was accented.

I pulled out a small pair of binoculars to get a closer look. As I raised them to my eyes, the man in the blue hat looked up into the draw and pointed, "Then again, she could have gone up this draw."

When the other turned around, I was startled to see the intense gaze of the dark-haired man who had been at the bus stop. I held my breath because it felt like he was looking right at me. After a moment of staring at the rock ledge, he shook his head and turned. The two of them then headed west along the meadow. They were soon out of sight around a copse of trees.

I let out the breath I had been holding. I was uncertain what to do next. I knew I was virtually unaware of my surroundings when speaking with Mahrah. If these men decided to come up the draw, how would I keep them from finding me? But, where else could I finish the conversation with her?

I hoped their path would keep them away from the draw for at least a half hour. I sat on the uphill side of the same rock I had leaned against the day before. I was more certain about reaching Mahrah. She was waiting for me and we exchanged greetings.

"There are a couple of people in the meadow below me. It worries me because it is unusual for this time of year."

Silence. "Mahrah?" A flame of worry flared up.

Yes. I am here. I was speaking with my Watchers. We believe the others are beings who are looking for you. It would be wise to move to somewhere you believe safe from their presence.

"Does it need to have a lot of rock?"

It does not. I am familiar with your energy and can find you more easily. After yesterday, I can focus on a smaller area.

"I think I can find a place soon. I am going to take my camp with me." This brought about confusion. "I am going to pack my belongings and take them with me," I restated.

I have been too patient. By the end of our conversation today, I will tell you what we did and why we need your help.

A little over an hour later, I was up and over the ridge to the east. I then scuttled down it and found a rocky overhang. Since most of my hike had been over rock, it would be hard to track me. I connected with Mahrah almost as soon as I sat down.

Is your companion with you?

I was surprised. "You mean my dog? Yes, he is always with me."

Please put your arm on him so your bracelet touches him. I will communicate with him.

"You can talk to my dog?" I asked draping my arm over Wizard's back.

He took that as a sign that he was about to get a belly rub and rolled over, putting his forepaws in the air.

Not with language, with images. Please think of the others you saw not long ago. Since I will use your images, you will see some of the communication.

As I did, the very images began to be edited. The men were in the meadow but then they were also right in front of me. Then, they looked like they were being pushed away.

Your companion now knows to be aware for these beings. He will alert you if he senses them.

Some questions came to mind, but I figured now was not the time for satisfying curiosity. I was getting very nervous that somebody was looking for me and had gotten close enough to know where in this set of mountains I was.

Mahrah was aware of my thoughts.

I have been a bit careless. I will confine the energy of our connection to as small a space as possible. We are speaking across worlds and it takes much energy to accomplish. That is why you are so tired when we finish. But now, we must finish talking so you may choose.

***

The dragons reconvened the next morning. Mahrah was at the top of a small hill and welcomed the warmth of the rising sun. She had been in a state between sleep and awake to allow her mind to be active enough to ponder.

"I have taken your counsel and selected," she began as the other dragons gathered around, *"We will work with the two-legged beings."*

Two of the dragons began to object. Mahrah blew out a puff of smoke. It was a sign the decision was final.

"First, we will address their fears. I believe we are safe traveling alone. Each of us will go to a different part of this world, contact one or more of them, and find out what they fear. Then, we will create devices to help them overcome those things. This will allow them to focus on protecting other beings on this world."

The dragons accepted the decision.

"It is unwise to put such power in their hands without guidance," Mahrah continued. *"We will also help them develop so they may use the devices in the best interest of all."*

Turning to the iridescent green dragon, she said, *"You are the smallest and wisest among us. In addition to finding a source of their fear, you will find clans of these beings ready for counsel on keeping their planet in balance.*

"You will also need to be the most careful. They may decide you can be

caught or tamed and not realize how dangerous you can be to them. Hurting them may make them afraid of our help."

Mahrah's memory skipped to where four of the dragons took off for different parts of the world. Mahrah and the green dragon traveled together for a time. As they did, they discussed Mahrah's plan of helping humans.

"The devices of which you speak will require some craft," This was the green dragon's way of asking Mahrah about her plan.

"We will use some energy elements from ourselves. Since it is from another world and is sensitive to the matter in both worlds, it should create power to help the two-legged beings with the things they fear."

With this memory, Mahrah sent me an image. I had seen the cellular structure before in Jannet's textbooks. Mahrah was referencing mitochondria.

She continued, *"Our bioalloy will not be a sufficient energy source for the device to accomplish its task. It will also need energy from the two-legged being activating it. We will need to warn them that using it will make them tired and even weak."*

"I believe it would be wise for them to record the instructions we give them. They are inclined to storytelling. We could use that and encourage them to create glyphs. By writing they could communicate about the devices and their use in helping all kinds on this world," the iridescent green dragon stated.

Mahrah thought about the suggestion. *"Some of them have begun the process of writing. I agree it would be wise to encourage more clans to do so. As they read each other's stories, they can come to see that they are more similar than different, as we have. Once they stop fighting among themselves, they can help all on the planet."*

After some time, the group reconvened. Each dragon spoke of the things humans feared because they caused death or destruction. The dragons chose a few of those fears to mitigate — being hunted, attacks by other clans, wildfire, poison by ingestion or bite, and flood or avalanche.

The dragons came back together and discussed how the devices would keep those things from harming the humans. They agreed giving a species early in its development something which could kill beings easily was unwise. They decided to construct the Talismans to act only on nonliving matter.

Five Talismans were crafted from silver and coupled with the dragons' mitochondria. Each dragon focused on one ability when distilling its mitochondria and placing it into the silver. Once made, the devices could not be destroyed without consequences to the energy flow in the two worlds.

The Talismans would be given to a member of one of the clans on five different continents. The dragons would observe the bearers of the Talismans and intervene if it became necessary. The intervention would be to hide the Talisman if humans became unable to use them wisely.

The black dragon made the first Talisman to create a concealment which fooled all other beings' senses. Humans had been hunted by animals who could see, hear, smell, and sense better than they could. The Conceal Talisman would not remove the bearer's presence, but would keep the human from being discovered.

Some clans were more concerned with death by weapons or stones. They had been the first to develop objects allowing a human to kill more easily. Often, those objects were used on each other. The clans lived in fear of each other. The white dragon created a Kinetic Talisman which would redirect the force intended to harm the Bearer.

The third Talisman was more difficult to create and use. In some places of the world there were many other beings who could kill them with a bite or a sting. The green dragon studied many of the molecules and put the knowledge into the Venom Talisman. It was designed to find the substance poisoning a person and neutralize it.

In places, fires raged across forest and plain. The conflagration would overwhelm entire clans with smoke or flame. The yellow dragon crafted the Torch Talisman to push the fire to where the user wanted it. It could be gathered into a smaller area or pushed away so a circle of protection could be created around a clan.

The last, the Weir Talisman, took the most energy to create and use. It would redirect a flood or avalanche. This meant a larger area needed to be affected by the device. The blue dragon amplified the energy in the Weir Talisman by using some of the water's own kinetic energy. Even with that, the draw on the bearer's energy would be considerable, possibly harming the Bearer.

Mahrah hoped there would come a time that all the clans would come together and work in one accord. So, she created her own device. The Amulet was an energy consolidator designed to fuse the abilities of the Talismans. The one who possessed the Amulet would have the ability, and responsibility, to avert disasters using the fullness of the dragons' power.

Where the Talismans were small tiles of silver with designs etched into them, the Amulet was a curved plate of silver with the figurine of a dragon sculpted onto it, hung with a silver chain. Stone beads flanked the silver plate on either side. Mahrah put her own full mitochondria into the Amulet.

After the Talismans had been created, each dragon went back to a part of the earth where it would help the most. Each dragon watched the clans and connected with one of the humans who appeared to be able to handle the responsibility. Once the human agreed to be the Bearer, the dragon taught the Bearer how to activate and use the Talisman. Early on, some of the recruits passed out from exhaustion. The dragons continued to meet with the Bearer until the person was adept at using the Talisman. A pact was then made with the dragon to use it for good and the Talisman was given to the human.

Initially, there was little to no change in the villages with the Talisman. The Bearer had been warned by its dragon not to reveal the existence of the Talisman. However, others in the village began to notice the Bearer had a type of power, which was called 'magic'. Songs and stories were created about the Bearer and the unnatural events that happened. Word traveled to other villages about people not dying from bites of vipers or of fires going around a village instead of through it.

Wanting to benefit from whatever power there was creating these happenings, clans began to join each other and work together. It seemed the humans would overcome their fears and begin the road to promote balance in their world.

With the original Bearers chosen by the dragons and honoring their pact, Mahrah began to look for a human who would be worthy to handle the power and responsibilities of the Amulet.

After a few decades, the first Bearers bequeathed their Talisman to another in their village before dying. Each time the dragon who had picked the original Bearer approved. The new Bearers did not see the dragons but did not doubt their existence. The oaths continued to be honored and the clans in the area continued to grow and flourish.

When the devices were handed to the third generation, there were instances of the Bearers using the Talismans for their own benefit. One directed fire to burn down the empty house of a clan member who had stolen a blanket from her. Another concealed himself and then took food from a nearby village.

Generations continued to pass. With each, the Bearers showed even more of a schism between the intent of the Talismans and their use. One Bearer creatively manipulated the Kinetic Talisman so it could be used to help kill another by luring enemies to cliff edge. When the enemy struck, the rebounded energy pushed the person over the cliff. The Torch Talisman Bearer had its own clan set fire to another village and then made sure the flames burned all the structures in the settlement.

The dragons, now disheartened, met to discuss the humans' actions.

"It is as I thought, the humans have not risen above their fears. They have even used the Talismans to create fear," the white dragon said.

"The Talisman I created to save them from wildfires is being used to burn down the houses of people the Bearer dislikes," the yellow dragon lamented.

"I stopped the current Bearer from putting fire all around a person to kill him."

"Certainly, the Torch Talisman cannot burn a being," the small green dragon said with alarm.

"No, it cannot. But, the fire can surround a being and suffocate it."

The dragons discussed how greed and lust for control were motivating the two-legged beings. They wondered if it was simply the clans they had chosen or something more widespread in the entire species.

"How is the training of the Amulet wearer going?" the black dragon asked Mahrah, for Mahrah had finally chosen a bearer the previous decade.

"It is almost finished. I chose a woman who was a leader and warrior among her tribe and respected in her part of the world. She possesses strength, honor, and intelligence. She is now adept at working with the power of the Amulet. I believe she could wield the full power we possess if...," here Mahrah paused. She thought of all the humans who began fulfilling their oath and then acting differently when they found out what power they had. She believed her Chosen would not do so.

Mahrah continued, *"She has four Watchers with her. They have been trained in their duties."*

"You trained Watchers?" the white dragon asked lifting her wings to communicate her disapproval. *"You did not consult us."*

"I did not have to," Mahrah said with a rumble and authoritative thrash of her tail. *"As you have reported misuse of the gifts over these last few years, I began to fear the person using the Amulet would be vulnerable to attack by some others who wanted the power for themselves. I still hoped we could find enough humans who would use our gifts to benefit this planet."*

The iridescent green dragon spoke what they were all thinking. *"The two-legged beings do not seem to have the same goals for this world that we do. It is difficult to find ones who think beyond their own time and species."*

Mahrah closed her eyes and slowly blew out a column of smoke. She had wanted this intervention to work. She had fervently hoped to correct the lack of action of her ancestors with an action which would rectify the wrong.

"I think we did our best; the humans are unable to rise above their fear or desire for more," she replied sadly. All the other dragons agreed.

"Then, we must undo what we have done." Mahrah looked at the assembly, *"You each must tell each Bearer to hide the Talisman. We can only hope the humans will forget their existence. Their ability to record events and thoughts is still young and they tend to fanciful tales. Maybe they will come to believe the Talismans are imaginary."*

"They have recorded stories about us also," the green dragon said with a

chuckle.

"Let's hope they believe we too are imaginary," the yellow dragon said dejectedly.

Each dragon found the Bearer of its Talisman. When the human was confronted with the irrevocable and terrible truth of the existence of the beast, the person was easily convinced to hide the Talisman. Mahrah waited for the dragons to return before giving up her last hope of helping restore balance. Once the dragons reconvened, she would tell the warrior woman to hide the Amulet.

The timing favored the dragons. The tides in the molten core of the earth shifted and the gateway began to open, which had closed a century before. However, there was something different this time. The opening was smaller on some days. Since Mahrah did not know how long the portal would stay open, she was unsure if she had the time to fly to the Chosen and get back to the gateway before it closed. If she missed this opening, she and the others would have to wait, possibly for the rest of their lives. All the dragons, Mahrah included, wanted their mission to be over and to return to their own world.

However, the white and black dragon were uneasy about the Amulet still being in the possession of a human. Since the Amulet did not have the ability to manipulate matter on its own, the dragons agreed Mahrah could send a message to the warrior woman. Mahrah did so via the Amulet.

The dragons arced up into the sky and passed through the gateway. I opened my eyes as the last memory faded.

***

Now, you have seen what we have done. We created Talismans to help humans. They used them not for helping the beings around them, but for their own benefit.

"But, they have all been hidden. Why do you need me?" I asked.

One of them has recently been used.

Chapter 6

I was so astonished I could not say anything for a time. My mind whirled with possibilities. I finally corralled my thoughts, "How do you know?"

Since the energy in the Talisman is linked to our world, we know when it is being used.

"Now, I know what you want done. But, why are you asking me to help?" I put the emphasis on "me".

You have been asked to be Chosen for many reasons. I will reveal two more at this time. First, you are gifted with the art of finding that which was. Second, your brain processes energy in a way which allows you the use of the bracelet and will allow you to use the Talismans very well. These reasons are in addition to the two I told you already — you have been deemed honorable among your kind and you are the descendent of the first one Chosen to bear the amulet.

"Seriously? I am descended from a queen?"

I assure you, I am serious. There was a huff of indignation.

"Um, it is an expression when people are surprised. It just seems a bit incredulous."

I am sorry for the error in understanding. I had relied more on the words you sent than the images. I was overconfident in my ability to understand.

After a moment, she followed up on her statement about my ancestor. *I can show you her if you would like.*

Not wanting to confuse Mahrah anymore, I replied simply, "I would like that."

Mahrah's memory began with a group of riders seen from overhead. There were about twelve of them mounted on horses. They all wore pants, a long-sleeved shirt, and a vest. Many held bows and all had swords. Their heads were covered with woven hats, including ear flaps. A couple of the hats looked like they had poms on the end of the straps. I was reminded of toddlers in snowsuits with similar hats pulled so low they could hardly see. But, the look on these faces showed they meant business.

As Mahrah landed, the group came to a halt and spread into an attack formation. The horses danced and whinnied when the wind shifted and they caught the odor of the beast in front of them. The bows were ready with knocked arrows. The lead rider was a woman and she drew her sword. Her deeply tanned face spoke of hours spent hunting and gathering. Her dark brown eyes revealed a deep intelligence.

She bade the rest of the company to stay with a hand signal and urged her steed forward a few paces. It shied and snorted at the command. After she patted its neck, the horse settled and took tentative steps in the direction of the danger it sensed. It tossed its head a couple of times to communicate its unease, but did not buck.

The woman's grip on her hilt tightened when Mahrah reached out mentally. The warrior woman looked at the other warriors in her party and then back at Mahrah. Her dark eyes narrowed and she raised her sword. A tattoo of a snake with stars adorned her wrist. Mahrah readied herself to retreat. Instead of attacking, the leader mentally returned the salutation.

Mahrah knelt on one knee and bent her head down to the ground, keeping her eyes on the uneasy warriors. The woman who led them dismounted when she was ten feet from Mahrah. Scarcely had she taken a step away from her mount when an arrow flew. Mahrah moved slightly so it harmlessly hit the scales between her eyes.

The warrior woman, enraged, turned around and yelled at the young warrior who had let the arrow loose. I did not know the language but the meaning was clear. The young warrior accepted the berating with an acquiescing nod and shrank into her saddle.

The leader turned back to Mahrah. The woman's muscles were taut with anticipation of defending herself, but she did not attack. She took tentative steps until she was within arm's length of Mahrah.

This was a test of trust on both sides. Tooth and sword could be used to cause injury to the other and they both knew it. When the woman could feel Mahrah's breath, she held her sword high and behind her, reached out, and put her hand lightly, even reverently, on the dragon's nose.

Mahrah was impressed with this human. She had not attacked impulsively but had approached and assessed the situation. This restraint was not common in the two-legged beings Mahrah had met.

I was memorizing my ancestor's appearance when her picture faded.

A dozen questions came to mind. As I was about to ask them, Mahrah spoke.

Those may be answered at another time. Now, it is time for me to pose the Challenge.

Mahrah's voice became even more majestic as she continued.

My kind tried to help your world. It did not work. One of the Talismans has been found. If one can be found, so can the others. They can be used in ways which will harm your kind and other kinds in your world. We offer you the appointment of Chosen to help us and to help your world.

As Chosen, you will have tools at your disposal no other human has. In exchange, you will be asked to live your life to ensure the devices we left are not used for harm. You will have the space of one of your nights to consider your answer.

"What if I say no?"

A heavy sigh. *No harm will come to you if you do not accept. There are others in your world that carry your ancestor's energy. We have considered what to do when you decide; whatever you decide.*

"Does this mean you asked someone else and I am Plan B or C?"

That is not important. Consider the Challenge. I will be ready for your answer in your morning.

Mahrah withdrew her presence. Again, my surroundings became vivid. I stretched as much as I could while staying seated. Wizard got up, shook himself, and sniffed around some trees. I looked up at the bit of rock over my head. There was soot on it from campfires. Those fires could have happened last year, last decade, or last millennium.

Just as the times of the inhabitants of this shelter had been compressed into layers of carbon on a rock, events from millions of years ago and thousands of years ago had been pressed on me in the space of a couple of days. Now, I had been given one night to make a decision, one which could impact the rest of my life. At least, I thought it would be the rest of my life. There was a lot Mahrah said; there was a lot she didn't say.

I had the notion I should sit there all afternoon and ponder. Since meditation was the most prudent course of action, I chose to wander.

Wizard and I put on our packs and headed away from the ridge, through the trees. I knew we were traveling parallel to a stream a mile to our right. This would put us far from any trails. I hoped it would keep anybody from finding us easily.

The two men from the morning still worried me. Their presence added another layer to the Challenge. Would being Chosen mean I would need to start looking over my shoulder because of other people and their desires for the Talismans? That and a legion of other questions blasted through my consciousness all afternoon.

The next morning, I packed up camp and got everything ready for the hike out. After making sure all was in order, I was ready to have the culminating conversation.

I knew I didn't understand all the implications of my decision, which was typical of decisions. My mother had told me we make the best decision with the information we have at the moment. I knew what the best decision was for me. I sat down on an expanse of rock. Wizard came and added warmth to the cool morning by lying next to me. I reached out to Mahrah.

Good morning.

"Good morning, Mahrah" I returned.

We are ready to hear your answer.

She was straight to the point. Who was being impatient now?

"Is there a way it should be phrased?" I asked wanting to make a good impression.

Our kind does have formalities. We rarely make terse statements in these situations like your kind does.

I became aware of more than one consciousness. It was like knowing someone has come in behind you when you are in a coffee shop or bookstore. "Are there others listening?"

Yes. I have included my Watchers.

Great. An entire dragon audience. I became extremely nervous. Despite the chill, my face grew hot. I put together what I hoped was a reasonable response.

"Of the Challenge to be Chosen to help your kind keep my kind from destroying the planet, I accept."

I heard a rumble of what I hoped was approval.

On behalf of the beings who once were in your world, who returned to help, and who now are moved to remedy the help they rendered, I accept being Chosen to assist you.

This puzzled me a bit. "I thought you were just asking me to help."

Being Chosen is for two beings to commit to each other. We will work together as we are able.

"Did I just marry a dragon?" I quipped.

"Marry?" Mahrah said, puzzled.

I reconsidered my levity and chose not to explain. After a few moments, Mahrah continued.

It would be helpful if our communication could happen more fluidly.

Currently, I can find you because of your particular energy, but need the earth to magnify my communication. If you wish to communicate without the aid of the earth's energy, I can make it happen. The bracelet would still be needed, but you would be much less limited as we conversed. Let me know what you wish.

This was something I hadn't expected. Did it mean she would be able to read my every thought? The times she had heard the mental questions before I had pushed them out to her already unsettled me. I wasn't sure how I felt about somebody else living in my head.

"I hesitate because it seems very invasive. Would there be any way I could close the door?" With the question, I made sure to send a mental image.

Yes. You will be in control of what is shared. I too will want to 'close the door' on many of my thoughts.

I was relieved because there were some things I didn't want anybody to know. Stealing the pack of gum when I was six ranked high among them. "Sure. I mean, it would be good to connect more easily."

Look at your bracelet.

"Pardon?" I had been so busy thinking what a dragon might want to hide that I wasn't really focused on our conversation.

Look at the bracelet and show me what you see.

The entire bracelet now shone with a reddish mahogany hue. There was the faintest hint of silver on the edge of the claws and tip of the tail. The silver of the tail outlined the detail of the face. As I watched, a very small bead rolled out of the mouth. In surprise, I almost dropped it.

Swallow it.

I was not okay with swallowing something which had just rolled out of a bracelet of unknown origins. I went back to my original thought of this whole escapade. I was being poisoned.

You are not being poisoned. Mahrah was exasperated.

"Can I save it for later?"

No. The energy will dissipate. Your decision must be made now.

As a child, my mother often told me not to put things in my mouth if I didn't know what they were. I now did exactly what I always did as a kid, I popped the bead into my mouth.

The aftertaste was something like fish, asparagus, mustard, and barbecue sauce. I disconnected from Mahrah and took a drink of water. It helped but didn't entirely get rid of the repulsive taste. I took another swig, reconnected, and asked, "What was that?"

A piece of myself.

The water spewed from my mouth and I started coughing. I was trying to decide if I should take more evasive maneuvers.

"I just ate some of you? Dragon?"

It contains my own energy. It will bind with yours and make our connection possible at any time.

"It won't harm me?"

There may be some impact on your system; it should be small.

"Haven't you done this before?"

For this, we have worked out the theory and all should be well.

I thought some very vulgar words at that point. I hoped they didn't get past my personal mental space.

"You mean I am a guinea pig?"

You are human, are you not?

"It's a figure of speech. We say it when someone experiments and the results may not be favorable."

What is a guinea pig?

I sent a picture of the family guinea pig from years ago.

Your kind experiments on these beings? No wonder you have damaged your world.

"In our defense, they can bite pretty ferociously. My brother found that out when he was using it as a duster."

I am not sure I understand all you said.

She paused.

You are upset. This was not meant to distress you. I would not have asked this of you if I did not think it was safe for you.

I calmed down after she spoke.

I expected to feel something as a result of the dollop. If this was the movies, I would have felt something by now. I was hoping for extra sight or the ability to fly. But, the world was exactly as it was before.

"I don't think it is working."

A chuckle with a rumble. *You are impatient. It takes time for the energy to merge.*

"When will I know it has happened?"

This has never been done before so I do not know how long it will take.

"Thank you. I hope it does all work out," I said sincerely. "What is next? Do I need to go somewhere? Do you have a mission briefing ready for me?"

Before action, you need to gather your Watchers.

"What are Watchers?" This had been one of the questions in the back of my mind.

Who are Watchers? Mahrah corrected. *They are beings who will watch for those who wish to stop you from your tasks as Chosen. They will protect you and help you.*

"Were the people I saw with my ancestor her Watchers?"

No. Those were members of her tribe. Two of them became her Watchers. There were two other Watchers not of her tribe.

"I am supposed to have a small group of people with me all the time? Who am I going to ask?"

We have already selected your Watchers. Watchers are not always of your kind. In times of peace, they do not always need to be always present.

I thought on Mahrah's words for a minute. I was uneasy I did not get to choose the Watchers. I looked at Wizard thoughtfully. He looked back at me with a wagging tail.

"Wizard is one of my Watchers?"

Truth.

"When did you pick him?"

He was picked for you some time ago. I asked him if he wished to be a Watcher when we spoke of the intruders. He agreed.

Others were also picked as you were picked for Chosen. They will be asked to make their decision soon. If they all agree, there will be four.

"Are they going to be perfect strangers? It seems a bit odd to have someone I don't know guarding my back."

They will not guard just your back. Many times, they will create a circle around you, forming a ring of energy to defend against others. Any Watcher may be touched but the field among them will be very difficult to pass through.

"How is the energy created?"

Four bands with signets have been made. They must not be worn by any until all four Watchers are together. This is to make sure the energy is connected correctly.

"They need to synchronize first before they can be used?"

I believe those are your words for what must happen.

"Where is Wizard's band? Also, he doesn't have any fingers. How is he going to wear a ring?"

I could sense Mahrah was a little aggravated, but her voice stayed even. *You ask many questions. You will see Wizard's band in a short time. We have considered his kind and how it might be worn. It has been altered accordingly.*

I started to ask another question. Mahrah stopped me.

Calm. There are many things of which we still need to speak. But, I am uneasy about your safety here. Before you chose, those who wished to interfere saw you as a nuisance. Being Chosen, you are now an obstruction to their goals. I think the other humans have not given up looking for you in this place. If your other tasks are finished here, return home.

I agreed that was a good idea and assured her I was hiking back to the car. Besides, Wizard was low on food. He made me feel very guilty with flopping on the ground and sighing when he didn't get a full meal.

It took a little more time to get to the trailhead because I wasn't in a hurry and was bushwhacking my way back. I didn't dare go back over the ridge and through the meadow. Using the surrounding mountain tops and rivers as landmarks, I found my way to more familiar territory.

Cheeky squirrels derided us from the trees, birds expertly navigated a sea of limbs at high velocity, and the warmth of the sun was welcomed when its rays broke through the canopy. It was a good day to be hiking in Colorado.

We were a few hundred yards from the car when Wizard stopped in front of me. Since I was looking at yet another squirrel, I almost went right over the top of him. I took a couple of steps around him only to find him blocking my path again. He looked down the path and then at me meaningfully. He wasn't growling, but his tail wasn't wagging either. I got the hint.

Instead of continuing along the trail, we climbed the hillside overlooking the parking lot. There was a dense thicket of pines and junipers so it was easy to stay hidden. The hard part was finding a place to see the parking lot the, now below us. I dropped my pack to be able to maneuver among the branches.

When I was finally able to see through the greenery, I found my jeep wasn't the only vehicle in the lot. There were a couple of other empty cars. However, next to mine was a silver SUV with someone in the passenger's seat. Across the parking area, in the lot for horse trailers, was a forest ranger's vehicle. The ranger was standing in between the two vehicles talking to someone.

I shifted a little in my natural blind to see the other person in the conversation. I gasped. It was the dark-haired man.

Chapter 7

This guy was starting to get on my nerves. It was one thing to have him show up in one of my favorite places in the mountains. Now, it was obvious he was not going to leave me alone. I wondered how long the conversation with the ranger was going to last when the dark-haired man spun on his heel and stomped back to his vehicle. He communicated his rage further by slamming the car door and driving away at a speed that caused his car to buck over the rutted road.

I expected the ranger to leave. Instead, he sauntered over to his truck, climbed in, and took out a notebook. I waited ten minutes. The ranger was still there, the other car did not come back, and I was getting tired of peeking through the trees. I gave up my surveillance and went down to the lot.

The ranger came over as I loaded my bag and Wizard into my jeep. We said hello to each other.

"How was your time? Did you find any archaeological sites?" he asked.

"Nothing definitive. I will need to check with the registry and see if anyone else has filed sites for the area," I replied while changing out of my hiking boots.

"You were back there longer than you told me you were going to be."

"I decided to look at some of the overhangs to check for possible rock shelters. It took another day or two to see if the habitation was more recent."

"You probably saw that guy I was talking to."

I froze in the middle of tying my shoe. This ranger knew I had been watching. "Yes, I did. Is he also looking for sites?"

"No. He was looking for you. Said he was your dad."

I shot the ranger a look. His expression was neutral.

"I would have believed him if you hadn't stopped and chatted a few days ago. It was lucky you mentioned your dad was a bird lover and out of the country."

The ranger looked at me in a fatherly way. "I hope you aren't in some kind of trouble. I suspect that man is going to be sitting at the highway waiting for you."

I had thought the same thing. "I have no idea who he is, and I don't know why he wanted to find me."

The ranger looked up the trail for a while as I finished changing out of my boots and clipping Wizard into his travel harness.

"Thanks for letting me know about the guy," I said lamely and moved to get into the driver's seat.

"You really don't know him?" The ranger looked me in the eye.

I held his gaze, "I really don't."

"He doesn't seem the type that is going to make somebody's day better." The ranger pulled out a stick of gum, slowly unwrapped it, and folded it into his mouth.

"I don't like it when people lie to me." He folded the wrapper back up and put it in his shirt pocket.

He took off his hat and passed a large rough hand through his wavy graying hair. By the time he replaced his hat, he had a conspiratorial look in his eye.

"By the way, did you know there is another way back to the highway beside the one road most people take?" he asked grinning.

"I didn't," I said turning to him with interest. "How would I go about finding it?"

"You would need to get permission from a ranger to use the road." He winked. "It is an old jeep trail. It is usually locked this time of year, but the low snow pack has kept it traversable and I was just getting ready to open it up. Are you up for a little four-wheeling?"

***

I pulled into my driveway just after the sun set. After stowing my gear, taking a shower, and feeding Wizard, we headed over to Jannet's house. She lived a mile away on an acre in the old part of town.

The two-story, beige sandstone house was a welcome sight after a few days in the back country. I parked outside the three-car garage behind the house. Wizard was happy to be released from his car harness and did a full body shake after jumping out of the back seat.

After emerging from my alternate route to the highway, I had texted Jannet. She figured, accurately, I had nothing at my house for dinner and invited me over. Since both Jannet and Ben liked to cook and were quite good at it, I rarely declined an invitation.

I let myself in the side yard door which led into the kitchen. An aroma of lemon, basil, and shrimp made my mouth water. Wizard trotted over to his corner and sank onto a dog bed. He promptly closed his eyes.

"Hi, Rascal," Ben greeted me with his normal term of endearment, in front of the gas stove. His button-down shirt was untucked over his jeans and he was barefoot. "Seems your dog is used to plush living." He glanced at Wizard as he stirred the food in the pan.

I sat on one of the cushioned chairs at the small, light, wood table and sighed in agreement. "He isn't the only one. I wonder how long it will be before I won't enjoy sleeping a half inch from the ground."

Jannet came into the kitchen area from the butler's pantry, "I have a remedy for that. How about a glass of wine?"

"I drove."

"How about a glass of wine and a night in our guest room?"

"That sounds like a winning combination." I replied with a grin.

Jannet handed me a glass of Tempranillo. It was tasty and not to light. "Thanks. What's for dinner?"

"Just a quick dish with shrimp and pasta," Ben replied.

Knowing Ben, it wasn't a quick dish at all and something way beyond my culinary expertise.

The table had already been set with blue-banded stoneware dishes and rough linen napkins. A lit pillar candle stood in the middle of the table. In addition to the main dish, there was a Caesar salad and fresh-baked rustic French bread. Conversation meandered among topics from computers to gardens. Ben's sandy brown hair was unusually out of place. The longer top stuck out at various angles. His mussed hair was completely at odds with his clean-shaven jaw and heavy rimmed glasses. I thought again that he and Jannet made a good pair both in looks and in personality. Jannet pulled him out of his shell and he provided a calm retreat for her.

After dessert of peach pie, Ben reached over to Jannet. She took his hand and squeezed it briefly. I tried to ignore the look of affection they exchanged.

"I am going to check on some things since people are starting to go to work on the other side of the world." He stood and nodded at me, "You two don't stay up too late talking."

His warning was well justified. Jannet and I had the ability to have marathon conversations. We often said we were trying to solve the problems of the world when we were really trying to figure out something more trivial like how to tie a shoe with one hand.

Our friendship had a rocky start since I had a significant crush on her after we met in college. Instead of walking away from an uncomfortable situation, she used her kindness and tact to help our friendship grow. I was so glad she did since she was what I imagined a sister to be.

Jannet and I cleaned up from dinner and then settled in the den on the soft couches with cups of chamomile tea. No sooner had I gotten comfortable when she rounded on me, "Okay, spill it."

"What do you mean?"

"There is something that is worrying you. Ben knows also. He doesn't have any work to do."

"How do you know something is bothering me?"

"You should never play poker. Your face telegraphs everything."

I couldn't deny that having someone track me into the mountains was worrisome. I just didn't realize I was being so transparent about it. But, I had a problem. I didn't know how to tell Jannet about what was going on when I wasn't supposed to tell Jannet what was going on.

I looked into her eyes and blew out my cheeks with uncertainty, "I am not sure what to say. Something did happen." I combed my fingers through my bangs. Jannet watched me for a moment. Her gaze fell to my exposed wrist. I looked down at the bracelet. When I looked back, she met my gaze.

"I think I can help you with what to say." She hooked a thumb under the silver chain around her neck so the pendants which had been hidden by her shirt became visible. Only, they weren't pendants. They were two identical silver bands, one larger than the other. On the flat part at the top of the band they had a mahogany imprint of a dragon.

I stared at them and then at her. My mouth opened and closed a few times. Then, I lifted my arm and pointed at the bracelet. Jannet giggled.

"I saw it when we had lunch the other day, but was told not to say anything to you until you had a different color bracelet," she revealed.

"You talk to Mahrah too?" I felt a little disappointed.

"Who? No, I received a box about a week ago. There was a note in it which had quite a few instructions on it. At first, I thought it was a practical joke; I went along with it. When you showed up with the bracelet at lunch, I still thought it was a practical joke.

"Can I see the box?"

Jannet went to her study and brought back a cardboard box almost identical to the one I had received. Even the hand writing for the address was the same. There was nothing inside but a black velvet cloth bag.

"What exactly did the note say?" I asked, puzzled when I shook out the bag and there was nothing there.

"It said not to put either ring on but to keep them very safe. Like I said, it indicated you had a bracelet with a dragon, but I was to not discuss it until you were wearing a bracelet which was not silver. I noticed at dinner that you have a different one on today." Her last sentence had a question in it.

"It is the same bracelet," I said. Jannet looked like she didn't believe it. I followed up with, "I need to tell you what has happened the last few days."

After I finished my tale, Jannet sat back, pursed her lips, and touched the end of her nose with an index finger. She did that when she was thinking. I had first noticed it during a test in one of our classes. She held the pose for a couple of minutes while staring at a picture on the opposite wall.

"The first answer is yes," she finally said.

"What was the first question?"

"Whether I would serve as one of your Watchers."

"Oh, I thought it was whether I was off my rocker or not."

"No," she drew the word out. "There is too much physical evidence; this is not a delusion or a practical joke."

I was not sure I wanted to drag somebody who was important in my life into what looked to be lots of trouble. "Are you sure you want to commit to being a Watcher? I don't even know exactly what you are supposed to do. If I already have someone following me around and I know next to nothing, I think it is going to be risky."

"Even more reason for me to tag along. I trust Wizard, but he isn't very good at communication. And, he doesn't have a credit card," she winked.

Wizard picked up his head at the mention of his name. When there was no other attention directed toward him, he went back to sleep.

"That takes care of the first question," I said. "What do you think the next question is?"

"Who is this dark-haired man?"

"I don't think we will be able to answer that question. I didn't get a close look at him any of the times I saw him."

"What about the car he was driving?"

"It was a rental. I could tell from the color of the plates."

Jannet swished her hand through the air as if brushing it aside, "Then, that will have to stay unanswered for a while. My guess is he will show up again before too long. I think the dark-haired man needs a name. That moniker seems ominous. I am not into ominous."

"How about Reginald?" I ventured. It was the first name that came to mind. "I am not looking forward to him popping up again."

"All the more reason for you and I to be best buddies." She paused. "My third question – When will this transformation occur so you can communicate more freely with Mahrah?"

"I have been wondering myself. If it is something that is happening at the cellular level, it may take days or even weeks."

"It will be less time if it acts more like bacteria. I wonder if there is a critical threshold for the effect. I wish I knew more about the genetic material and the replication method."

Jannet had an advanced degree in molecular biology and was still dabbling in genetics. She loved the field because it was a puzzle to her. I could tell she thought this would be a fabulous research project for her.

"I am more concerned about what is going to happen to me," I said with concern. "What if I get super sick or grow another arm?"

"Be serious, you won't grow another arm."

"How about horns?" I got a pillow thrown at me for that comment. "Okay, how about a question we might be able to answer?"

Jannet looked at me inquisitively. "Which Talisman has been discovered?" I asked as I tossed the pillow back.

"What is your plan for coming up with an answer?"

"I think we should look at the news. We know what each Talisman does. We should look for an unusual event or set of events which would match to the use of one of them."

"How about we do it in the morning?" Jannet asked with a yawn.

I looked at the digital clock on one of the entertainment devices. It was after ten. I had been up since five but wasn't the least bit sleepy.

"Deal. What are you going to tell Ben?"

"I probably won't need to tell him anything because he is probably asleep. He has a flight tomorrow."

I instantly felt guilty. "He is leaving tomorrow and I kept you from spending time with him this evening?"

"No worries. We already decided what to do if you came back today. It's why he didn't mention it at dinner."

She stood and gathered our mugs, "I know you feel guilty. You shouldn't. We have had a wonderful time the last few days."

We went back to the kitchen. Wizard reluctantly followed and went outside. After he came back in, I began to head to the staircase while Jannet finished in the kitchen. "One last question," I called turning to her. "What happened to the note?"

She dried her hands on a towel as she faced me. "That night I told you I didn't sleep well, I had a dream about the box, the rings and the note. When I woke up, I knew that the note needed to be destroyed. So, I...,"

"Burned it," we said together.

Chapter 8

When I came down the next morning, Jannet wasn't in the kitchen, but there was a pot of coffee. I poured myself a cup, fed the hound, and began wandering around the house looking for her.

I found her on the porch attached to the South side of the house. Sometime in the last century, the porch had been screened in to keep out the few bugs in this part of the world. There was a nip in the air, but the promise of a warm spring day. Jannet sat cross-legged on one of the outdoor couches with her laptop. Her hair hung over her shoulder in a long braid, which she played with. I sat in a chair facing her. Wizard padded in after finishing his breakfast. He sniffed around the edges of the porch and then chose a spot in the sun for his morning nap.

"Ben get out okay?" I asked taking a chair across from her.

"I think so. He left at o'dark thirty. I got up a half hour ago." She took a deep sip of her coffee, "I don't know how I pulled those all-nighters in college."

"A sign of your age," I teased.

"And yours since you are only one year younger."

She patted the seat next to her. "Come see what we can discover about events in the world."

We spent the next forty-five minutes looking at news articles from around our country and across the world. It was hard not to get side tracked. As usual, there were a handful of countries calling for sanctions against a handful of other countries. Nothing popped out as being connected to one of the Talismans.

"Let's make some breakfast," Jannet said closing the laptop.

"I have been wanting biscuits and gravy. How about I make the biscuits and you make the gravy?

"Deal."

Jannet decided we needed omelets to go with the biscuits and gravy. "What do you know about dragons?" she asked as she was cooking the fluffy egg crepes.

I thought through things I had seen and heard as I finished setting the table. "I don't know much. I think myths about them are common. Right now, I can't think of a single continent without a myth about dragons."

We sat and began eating. "I agree. They seemed to be in the cultures of all the countries I have lived," Jannet said.

I began to pull together things I remembered, "In the Chinese culture, dragons are honored. There is the plumed serpent of Central and South America – I suppose serpents count. In Europe, there are lots of stories about knights killing dragons."

"Humankind seems to have some sort of fetish with them. We have games, books, movies, and songs about them. Do you think anybody else has thought they could have been real?" she asked and then ate some omelet.

I shook my head. "We are convinced with facts. There haven't been any fossils of the types of beast most cultures call dragons. Most anthropologists consider the cause of the legends to be crocodiles and other large reptiles."

"If those are the origins, it doesn't explain why dragons fly in all those stories."

"You're right. I didn't think much about the flight of the animals."

Jannet bounced up. "I just remembered that Ben has a book about dragons." She strode purposefully out of the room and came back a few moments later. We looked through the slim volume, which indicated stories of dragons did exist on every continent. The summary pointed out most dragons of Eastern cultures were portrayed benefiting humanity. Conversely, Western cultures had a plethora of stories of dragons who were evil, spiteful, or just in a very bad mood - they were all dispatched.

By the time we finished, it was an hour later. Jannet peered analytically at me over her now empty coffee cup.

"How are you feeling?"

"Full."

"I mean…"

"I know what you mean. I don't think anything is happening. Maybe the change Mahrah expects won't happen."

A non-comital sound was Jannet's reply. She followed up with, "What do you need to do today?"

Reclaim

"I would like to go to the state history museum and find out if there are any sites listed where I was."

"How long do you think you will be?"

"About an hour; not too many people are around."

"I can keep myself occupied for an hour. Can you handle some shopping?" Jannet knew I did not share her enjoyment of shopping.

"You are asking a lot of me," I teased.

"How about I throw in a trip to the independent bookstore you like?"

She hit my weak spot. "Deal."

The three of us piled into Jannet's car. The trip to the Archaeological Office in the history museum didn't take long. Most people were wrapped up in finishing documents or cataloguing inventory. It was eerily quiet. Jannet wandered through an exhibit or two while I chatted with a person who had specialized in the geographic area I visited. I could have checked the catalogues online, but they often were not as informative.

I met Jannet by an exhibit about the history of the state. "I'm finished," I announced. "Time to pay the piper."

Instead of responding jovially, Jannet spoke in a low voice, "I think Reginald is here. Don't look around; let's see if we can find a way for you to catch a glimpse of him."

"Let's go to the coffee shop down the hall from the exhibits. When we order at the counter, he will be in sight if he follows us."

We ordered some drinks and a brownie. As Jannet was paying, I meandered around the corner. Wizard's body tensed and then he pulled. I stepped up to reign him in and almost ran into Reginald. He took a quick step around me, crossed the coffee shop in a couple of strides, and went out the street door. He stopped at the far edge of the last window of the storefront and pulled out a cigarette. Wizard watched him all the way out the door.

"Yep, it's him," I said quietly to Jannet as we waited for our drinks to be made.

"I think he has a friend," Jannet said with a discrete glance over my shoulder.

"Think they know we have an idea we know they are here?"

"Hard to know since you haven't been close to Reginald."

"What should we call his friend?"

"Buttercup." Jannet said this with a straight face and I sputtered in amusement as she smiled innocently.

We spent the next hour playing hide-and-go-seek with Reginald and Buttercup as we shopped. Their tactic on this venture was to follow and not confront. We played along but tested their abilities by going into stores which had multiple exits, some leading onto busy streets.

Our last stop was the bookstore, one of my favorite places in the city. Decades ago, it was a warehouse. The owner bought it and slowly turned it into one of the largest independent bookstores in the region. I loved all the nooks and crannies of the three-story structure, the large staircase, and the smell of books. It also had four exits. Our tails followed us into the establishment so not to lose us.

After a half hour of browsing for books we didn't need, we finally decided we were done with the game.

"Where do you think we should confront them?" I asked.

"We need to pick a place with some visibility but also a bit of privacy," Jannet replied as she put her books on the counter.

"Do you think outside one of the exits would work?"

"Only if no one else comes out right after they do. How about we go out the door which has the ramp and the stairs. You go one direction and I will use the door to keep them from spotting me going the other."

As we exited, I went right and started down the ramp. Jannet slipped around the edge of the door to the left and immediately stepped in behind it.

Reginald and Buttercup had already hastily made their way through the door and down the ramp when they realized Jannet was right behind them. They both turned to reenter the store. Jannet boldly shut the door and stepped in front of it.

"Good afternoon, gentlemen," she said coolly. "Might I inquire as to why you are following us?"

Reginald looked at Jannet, at me, and at Wizard. Wizard's hackles were raised. I put a hand on him and told him to stay quiet. Reginald replied to Jannet, in German.

Jannet also switched to German, "I understand you may not speak English. Let me ask you again, why are you following us?"

Reginald then began speaking in French. He said he did not know German well and could only converse in French. Switching to flawless French, she repeated her question one more time. Reginald's jaw clenched and Buttercup coughed uneasily. Wizard was pulling on his harness.

Jannet told the men to stop following us or we would call the police. Reginald became livid, "Your police can do nothing to me. I have diplomatic immunity," he continued in French.

"That may be," Jannet replied evenly, "But diplomatic immunity doesn't give you permission to commit a crime or to harass American citizens. We will call the police and let you sort it out with them if we see you again." She had a pleasant but stiff smile.

While they were speaking, I assessed Reginald. His clothes were neatly tailored and he wore two rings on his left hand. His thick wavy hair gave him a friendlier look than his hostile eyes.

It was harder to get a look at Buttercup since he was partially behind Reginald. His straight blonde hair was cut evenly and had a windblown look about it. Where Reginald wore slacks and leather dress shoes, Buttercup wore jeans and sneakers.

In response to Jannet's edict, Reginald clenched his jaw so hard I thought he was going to grind his teeth. He motioned to Buttercup and they walked past Jannet, down the stairs, and around the corner. We both let out a breath we had been holding when they were out of sight.

"They never thought an American would be able to speak another language, much less two," I said giving her a high five.

"Never mess with a diplomat's daughter," she intoned.

Jannet's father had served in many countries around the world. As a result, she was fluent in six languages and could make herself understood in six more. Reginald had picked two of her favorite languages. He hadn't stood a chance.

I sobered quickly, "Jannet, you probably didn't get a chance to look; Reginald had on two rings."

"Even dolts can be married," she replied nonchalantly watching the corner a bit longer.

"Marriage may be the reason for one of his rings. The other ring had an imprinted dragon, much like yours."

Before we could talk any more, my stomach lurched. Immediately after, it felt like somebody had hit me between the eyes with a post. I staggered back against the building. Jannet caught me by the elbow.

"Seizure?" she asked.

Wizard had not given the signal. I shook my head slightly, even the small motion caused the world to spin.

"We need to get you somewhere to sit or lay down," Jannet said looking around. "I have a friend who has a loft not far from here. Think you can make it?"

My stomach felt like someone was trying to turn my guts inside out. "I think so," I said through gritted teeth.

One text, two blocks, and three floors later we were in the loft of Jannet's friend. I sat back on the couch and tried to stay calm amid the pain. The noise in the apartment suddenly grew very loud. I could hear the refrigerator running, a high pitch coming from the vicinity of the computer, and all the traffic outside. Then, the light became weird. The flowers in a nearby vase suddenly had florescent streaks, light seemed to seep from Wizard and Jannet, and the screen across the room looked like it was a headlight. Jannet sat on the coffee table in front of the couch. She was biting her lip in worry.

"Nadia, can you hear me? Are you okay?" I think she was trying to whisper, but it sounded like she was using a megaphone. Wizard's breathing sounded like a freight train. I clapped my hands over my ears and closed my eyes. There was one more lurch in my stomach and then all went black.

When I woke up, I was on a bed. I rolled over to look straight into Wizard's face. I reached out to scratch behind his ears. He settled on the floor and I rolled back on to my back. As I was watching the ceiling fan, I felt a presence.

"Greetings, Chosen. The integration has finished."

"The end of the process was much rougher than I would have liked. What was up with all the light and sound?"

"The change in cell structure included a change in perception. My kind sees a wider array of light and hears much more than your kind. I believe your brain now filters out what it normally does not perceive."

"The men from the mountains showed up again. One of them was wearing a ring with a dragon imprinted on it."

"There should be no more bands than the ones for your Watchers. Maybe you were mistaken."

I sent the memory to Mahrah. In return, I sensed apprehension. It seemed our connection allowed me access to more of her emotions.

"This is a grave thing. Another from our world has contacted another one of your kind." Mahrah wasn't just apprehensive, she was alarmed. *"When you were found in the mountains, I wondered and started searching for other signals from this world. I will make sure my inquiry is pursued with more diligence."*

"What does this mean for me and the Watchers?"

"It means we need to collect your Watchers quickly. It means you have much to learn quickly. It means what I have hoped would never happen is possible."

"I was actually hoping more for hiding out until the storm passed."

"This storm is just beginning. There are some abilities you now have that I want you to know how to use. Up to now I have started our conversations. It is time for you to try to reach me."

"How should I reach you? You probably don't have a cellphone."

Mahrah ignored my quip and centered on my question. *"Create an image of me and then send a greeting."*

I saw a few problems with this process. "I don't know what you look like.

I know you won't hear me if I yell. How will you hear me?"

Mahrah rumbled with exasperation. *"I am sending you an image of myself. Think of it then reach out with your mental voice."*

The dragon which appeared in my mind's eye was one of the most majestic beings I had ever seen. Her brawny body was covered in dark reddish mahogany scales except along her throat and underside where they were beige. She stood on all fours with sharp claws at the end of her feet. She held her lithe head regally. Large teeth protruded down from her upper lip and fangs were at the front of her jaw. Her emerald eyes gleamed with intelligence and fierceness. She did not have horns. Virtually every picture of a dragon I had ever seen had horns. The thought slipped through.

"I cannot believe your kind believes we are horned like the grass grazers." she said with scorn.

"It seems natural," I offered feebly.

"We are one of the ancient beings of your world. Surely you know they did not have horns."

I thought back to all the elementary field trips I had taken to see dinosaur exhibits. "Mostly not."

"Yet, you say it is natural for my kind to have horns. Your kind must not think highly of my kind to portray us with such traits. This is not expected."

Mahrah was taking offense. A redirect was needed. "So, now I know what you look like, I am to call to you mentally?"

"Yes," she calmed a bit, *"I will stop creating the link and wait for you to establish it."*

Mahrah's presence disappeared. I always hated it when someone hung up on me. It seemed worse when it was a being in another world.

I revisited the image of Mahrah and made it as tangible as possible. Then, I tried a greeting. Nothing. Maybe I wasn't remembering her correctly. I took a deep breath, focused intently on the image, and tried again.

"Well done. You now know how to establish communication when you need to do so. If I need to do so, you will feel a stirring in your consciousness. The image I sent you should come to mind at the same time."

Like caller ID, I thought bemusedly.

It was then I realized our current communication was almost completely without images. "Have you learned to speak English?"

"In a manner. When our connection opened earlier, I was able to learn much from your language faculties."

"What else did you learn?" I asked apprehensively.

"I assure you, I kept my access to a minimum. I wanted to be able to communicate more like your kind does. If there were memories or other

connections to words, I retreated."

I hoped she was telling the truth. I was not comfortable baring my soul to another being. I had hardly done it with the people in my life. I did not want to start with someone who wasn't even human.

"Is the Watcher with the bands close?"

"I think so. She is probably in the other room."

"Form an image of her and you will get a sense of how far she is from you."

As I thought about Jannet, it was as if I had activated a GPS sensor. I don't know how I could tell; she was twenty feet to my right. I didn't have x-ray vision through the walls, just a sense of where she was in space in relationship to where I was.

"You are sensing the energy of the bands. It is why you are able to determine her place. The bands have an energy which matches yours. Hold her image and reach out again with your mental voice."

I tried. And, I tried again. After a couple of minutes, I had a slight headache from the intense concentration and was ready to give up.

"I don't think it is going to work."

"May I observe your mind as you try?"

"Sure." After trying again, Mahrah made some suggestions on how I was thinking about Jannet and how I was creating the imperative. Ten seconds later, Jannet opened the door to the bedroom. She stepped over Wizard's mass, sat on the bed, and felt my forehead.

"How are you feeling?" she asked sitting back.

I found I could not focus on speaking with Jannet and Mahrah at the same time. "I haven't gotten up, but I think I am fine," I said to Jannet.

"Did you have an episode?"

"Did Wizard give the signal or did I have spasms?" Jannet shook her head.

"Then, I think I blacked out because of the pain. I thought my guts were going to come out of my body."

Before she could speak again, I asked, "Jannet, why did you come into the room just now?"

"You called me."

"You heard me call your name?"

"Yes. Wait," she paused, puzzled. "It sounded clearer than it should have been with you in here. You did call me, didn't you?"

I ignored the slight headache I had and sat up quickly. "I did, but I didn't say anything." I put emphasis on the word 'say'.

Understanding flashed in her eyes. "You are able to talk to Mahrah more directly?"

"Yes." I could tell I was beaming.

I felt a nudge on the edge of my consciousness. Mahrah's image came to mind.

"We have much to do."

Chapter 9

I spent the next few days working in the backyard. It was a very different kind of work than any I had ever done. Instead of pulling up dandelions and trimming back plants, I was learning how much energy there was in the world. It made sense energy often can be sensed by touch, sight, or hearing. But, I didn't realize how much energy was in constant ebb and flow around me.

The first few lessons were about sensing forces around me. I hypothesized, with my rudimentary understanding of physics, I was sensing photons and electrons. After becoming conscious of the currents, Mahrah wanted me to collect some of the particles and create a flow between my two hands.

After two full days, I could create a very weak current. It was a great victory for me. To Mahrah, I knew it was just a beginning, and a slow beginning at that. Still, she encouraged me.

At dinner that evening, Jannet announced, "I think I found the Talisman."

"How?" I asked around the bite of a taco.

"I finally just put the words 'weird news' into a search engine and hit a website which reports on odd happenings. In a small French village, the police were perplexed by a car which flipped and landed upside down in a field. The driver was a thirty-eight-year-old man who tested negative for any substance. Also, he had a perfect driving record."

"Maybe he blacked out for some medical reason?"

"He indicated he was alert during the whole episode. When he drove around a bend in the road he saw someone standing directly in front of him. The lane was narrow and there were dense bushes on either side so he didn't have anywhere to turn. As he braked, the person bent down. He closed his eyes because he didn't want to see himself hitting someone and felt his car go flying. The car landed on its side. When the driver climbed out of the car, and went back to the road, nobody was there. He was relieved; he thought he had killed someone."

"Incredible. My bet is on the Kinetic Talisman. Bending over could have made the person act like a ramp. How fast was the car going?"

"About twenty miles per hour. It was a small car."

"I wonder how much force the Talisman can deflect. Do you think it is a force field of some sort?"

"I don't know, I'm just a DNA person," Jannet said with a shrug.

I finished off the taco and reached for another. Jannet had marinated the chicken filling with lime and chilies. She added some corn and black beans to the mix, topped off with fresh cilantro. I took a moment to admire her ability to turn something I found mundane into a meal full of nuanced flavors.

"The fact this took place in France cannot be a coincidence," I stated.

"I do find it awfully odd it happened there and Reginald claimed he was most fluent in French. His pronunciation indicated he has either spent a lot of time in the country or it was his first language."

"Did he have a regional accent?"

Jannet scooped up some guacamole with a chip and ate it. She chewed thoughtfully. "I would say Parisian. But, his German accent was from Rhineland."

"He only spoke a couple of sentences in German," I said amazed.

"The people from that region have a very distinct way of saying 'I' and Reginald was all about himself," she said flatly.

The next morning, Jannet announced she was going to go work out and do a couple of errands. I worked on creating a stronger energy flow. When I took a break, I went over to the rock I had been sitting against when the whole thing started and leaned against it. My back tingled a bit and I sensed the latent energy in the rock. Newton wasn't far off with the inertia idea, I thought.

Suddenly, the light tingle turned into a burning sensation. "Ouch!" I exclaimed jumping up. I looked at the rock suspiciously.

"My apologies."

"You did that? What did you do?"

"I tried to send a bit of energy from this world. I did not think it would transfer with such force."

"Well, it did. Maybe you should warn me next time. I am okay being Chosen. I am not okay being a . . ."

"Guinea pig," Mahrah finished. *"I will ask next time I wish to try something. Especially if it involves possible force."*

"Speaking of force, I think we found out something about the Talisman used." Sensing a heightened awareness from Mahrah, I told her about Jannet's discovery.

"Why did you not tell me when you spoke of it with the Watcher?"

"I didn't think it changed anything. And, her name is Jannet."

"This use is not as I suspected. We believed the Talisman was accidentally used. What you speak of indicates someone knows what it is. The person also knows how to create the buffer before it is needed. If so, much more has been communicated about the activities of our last visit than we believed."

"And the world is in even more danger than before?" I thought I knew the pattern to Mahrah's thinking.

"I believe affairs are the same as they were when you told me of the other being with the band."

"Care to tell me why?"

"Because of the band, we thought the information passed on was about gathering Watchers. We also believed the Talisman had been discovered by a different being of your kind, not the one with the band. It now seems the two are connected. This means some of the information communicated was about the Kinetic Talisman."

"We need to find this person. When will it be time for me to go find the other Watchers?"

"It has always been time."

I was a bit perplexed at the statement.

"You must also choose to go. It is the nature of the pact between us. I can let you know what is wise to do, but I cannot command."

"Mahrah, when you want someone to do something, you ask a question. That is how it works with words."

A feeling of sheepishness and ire came through. *"It is not our way of communication. I am a being who is just beginning to learn how to transmit information as your kind does."*

"I'm sorry," I said back. "We will probably run into a few more of these communication differences. I hope it doesn't happen at a critical moment."

"Now I understand your torrent of questions. Chosen, are you ready to gather your other Watchers?"

"Yes. Have they been informed?"

"As clearly as was able. They will understand more when you arrive."

"If it is their decision, I am ready to go ask them. Though, I am not sure how many people will sign up for this ride."

"Your words do not make sense for the situation; I assume it is a figure of speech."

"It is. If we have time, I am going to have to work on those with you." Schooling a dragon was both intriguing and terrifying. "Where do I need to go?"

"You and the two Watchers will go to a tall mountain in a land with large animals."

"That description doesn't really narrow it down much. You wouldn't happen to have an image, would you?"

Mahrah sent more memories. I saw a large savannah. Extensive herds of elephants and giraffe meandered through the grassland. A herd of zebra took off when a large shadow passed over them. Africa. But, Africa was an awfully large place.

"The animals help a little bit, but I really need some landscape features to know on which part of the continent to look."

"I can only show you what was seen. This is the memory of another."

I was dependent on the whims of a dragon out for an afternoon glide.

The dragon wasn't just gliding, it was joy riding. I could think of no other reason it would repeatedly scare up herds of zebra, gazelles, and giraffe. Finally, a large body of water came into view. The other side was quite distant. The dragon dove and swam for a little bit. When it came to the surface, the sun was low on the horizon. The dragon flew opposite the setting sun. A large snow-capped mountain came into view on its right. The dragon turned and flew towards it. The memory stopped.

"Isn't there anything more?" I asked.

"What you have seen is all the memory the being left. We do not know why he did not leave more."

"Is he dead?"

"He still lives. All beings on the journey we made left memories for the possibility that they might be needed."

"Left them where?"

"Your kind leaves memories on surfaces or in verbal stories. How my kind leaves them is difficult to explain. Was it enough to direct you?"

"It gives me a general idea. I believe it is Mount Kilimanjaro. However, that is a sizable mountain. How will I find the Watcher there?"

"The Watcher will also be looking for you. Approach the peak with the rising sun to your left."

"Can the Watcher come here? It seems much more efficient."

"It is not the way of it. You must go to the Watcher."

I walked through the back door. I had been moving while speaking with

Mahrah. And, I hadn't walked into the door off the breezeway. I grinned, elated. Mahrah must have sensed my emotion.

"Is the approach to mountains I told you comical for your kind?"

"Not at all. I just realized I have been in motion while speaking with you. I guess I am getting the hang of communicating without it tying me down."

A moment later, I tripped over the leg of a dining room chair and went sprawling. "Okay, maybe not."

"All is well?"

I replayed the memory for Mahrah. She made a sound I deduced to be a snicker. I was going to take offense, but realized how funny I must have looked so started chuckling. Wizard took my laugh as permission to give me a wet-willy. When I sat up to escape him, he promptly laid down in my lap. This made me laugh even more. Jannet, back from her outing, came into the dining room looking for the cause of amusement. I asked Mahrah if I could talk more with her later.

"All is well. I will rest."

Jannet and I took Wizard for a walk. He bounded out of the door, happy to be able to stretch his legs. He was used to walking in the morning with me, but I had neglected our ritual the last few mornings. Last night, he had brought me a ball every two hours. I got the message.

These walks were when Wizard was off duty, so I took off his vest. He was allowed to stop and sniff. Sometimes his meanderings tried my patience; it was a small price to pay for the service he did.

"We need to go to Mount Kilimanjaro from the Kenyan side?" Jannet asked after I finished what I had learned about where to find the Watcher.

"Only if you want to. I am not comfortable with you putting your life on hold for me."

"I am not doing this just for you. There is something bigger at stake here and I would like to know what it is."

Wizard darted from one side of the sidewalk to the other to sniff, stopping me suddenly. It was an ideal Spring afternoon. The trees were beginning to bud. A few crocus and tulips were blooming. I could hardly wait for the perfume of lilacs which would bloom in a couple of weeks. Only, now it seemed I wasn't going to be around for the event. The consequences of my decision started sinking in.

"I don't know much more about the trip than our initial destination. I don't know how long we will stay or if we are coming directly back. It may be weeks or even a month before we make it back to the States."

"Ben is okay with whatever time it takes to do this."

I stopped and looked at her. "Jannet, you didn't tell him, did you?"

"I did." She held up a hand as I started to object. "While you were hanging out in the backyard, I let him know we needed a very secure connection. He worked on it for a couple of hours and then called me. He said he used four different protocols and assured me there were only a dozen people in the world who could get through the security he put in place. I told him what had happened and how I had been asked to help."

I believed in Ben's assessment of his digital security abilities. From what I could tell, there were less than a dozen people in the world who did what he did. "What was his opinion?"

"He is concerned. He is unsure about the credibility of the whole thing; he believes it far more than he disbelieves it. We discussed what this would mean for us as a couple over the next bit of time. On one hand, he is relieved because he was asked to set up a couple of work stations in other countries and was feeling guilty about the time away. On the other hand, he is concerned about the ramifications for my safety. Either way, he agrees I should be with you since someone who knows better has asked me to do so."

"He is a very understanding man. Please thank him for me." I paused. "He is going to keep this to himself, right?"

"He is. You must admit any one else would think we are mad. At least you and I have physical evidence. And, he is intellectually curious. He thinks your bracelet acts as a type of receiver."

I then realized she wasn't wearing the necklace. I should have noticed earlier since she was wearing a V-neck shirt. "Where did the rings go?"

"I fastened them to the key clip in my pocket. I didn't want anybody to see them. From what I gather, only I can see your bracelet. Since Ben was surprised when I told him about your bracelet, I am certain he cannot see it."

"Does Ben have an idea what the rings do?"

"He says," Jannet said chuckling a little bit, "That he has to wait to see how they function and then he will do a little reverse engineering." It was a typical statement from my engineering geek friend.

As we walked back to the house from the top of the hill in the neighborhood, Jannet called her travel agent. I wasn't sure we would be able to get flights anytime in the next week, but Jannet indicated there were plenty of business class seats available. She was finishing up the arrangements when we turned the corner near my house.

Someone was sitting on the front porch and she had strawberry blonde hair.

Chapter 10

I tried not to change my pace, but I must have slowed. "What's wrong?" Jannet asked.

She followed my gaze. "Oh good," she said discreetly, "I have been wanting to meet her ever since you told me about her."

We got to the end of the sidewalk and Kelly stood up and brushed off the skirt of her floral sundress. She had the same unconvincing smile from our first meeting. Jannet slowed her pace to make sure I would be the first to reach Kelly.

"I hope you don't mind me waiting for you to get home," she said. Then, she took a quick step onto the grass because Wizard growled with warning.

"What did you need?" I asked as I nudged Wizard toward the door with my knee. He didn't get the hint and tried to stay rooted to the spot.

"I thought I would ask to see if my package showed up here."

"It hasn't. Sorry to hear you haven't found it yet. I hope it wasn't anything valuable." I said dismissively. I was thinking she had a bad alibi for camping out on the porch.

As I wrestled Wizard up the front steps, Kelly turned her attention to Jannet, "Hi, I'm Kelly Devlin. Who are you?"

"I'm a friend," Jannet said.

"Do you have a name?"

"Yvonne," Jannet lied.

"Yvonne…?" Kelly was fishing for her last name.

Jannet appeared obtuse by saying, "Yes, Yvonne."

"Do you live around here?" Kelly gestured vaguely with a float of her hand.

"Not too close," Jannet said. I hastened to unlock the door before Kelly's interrogation could go much further. I wasn't afraid for Jannet. I was afraid I was going to blow her cover.

I looked out the screen door after I hauled Wizard into the house. Kelly had stepped back onto the sidewalk and was between Jannet and the door. I had seen Jannet in situations like this before. It was usually a guy at a party who wanted her number. Wizard's growls turned to sharp barks so I lead him away from the front door, to the den. He stopped barking once we were there. We watched without being seen through the sheer curtain.

Kelly stood with arms akimbo on the sidewalk. Jannet's body language was arranged to intentionally deceived. To the casual observer, she looked completely relaxed and even submissive.

Jannet must have asked about where Kelly lived. As Kelly turned and pointed, Jannet deftly repositioned herself. Kelly stiffened a bit when she realized she was no longer directly between Jannet and the door. After another half minute of conversation and maneuvering, Jannet was the one closest to the door. She said her farewell, turned, and lightly took the steps two at a time. Kelly's expression soured. Turning on a heel, she stalked away. I heard Jannet close the door and lock it.

She found me in the den. Before she could sit down, Wizard decided to give her a sniff over to make sure she had all her body parts. "What did you two discuss, Yvonne?" I tried to ask with a straight face and failed.

Jannet smiled ruefully. "Thanks for playing along. I got the sense I would regret telling her anything about myself."

"I understand completely. Nice job with the conversation dance." This is what we had named the moves she made to get out of being trapped in conversations. Jannet was a pro at it. She said she picked it up from watching her parents at dinners and other functions.

Jannet flopped into the arm chair. "She asked questions about you. Some of them were the neighbor kind of questions like how long you had lived here. But, then she tried to ask questions about where your family was from and what your ethnicity was. I told her I thought your family was from South America."

I shook my head in disbelief. "Did she buy it?"

"I don't think so. It was almost as if she already knew your last name."

"I wonder if she is going to search for families with the last name Kokinidis in South America. At least you gave her an entire continent to consider."

"I try to be helpful," Jannet said facetiously.

She sat up and continued, "What was up with Wizard? I have never heard him bark so aggressively. If I didn't know him, I would have thought he was going to attack."

"I think he shares our distrust of the new neighbor. Though, I don't know exactly why he was so upset."

"Do you think Mahrah could find out for us? It would be interesting to know if it is something he senses from her. I have always wondered if dogs just know when someone is a bad egg."

"I could. But, I don't want to do it now. I think she is taking a nap."

"A nap?" Jannet was incredulous. "Dragons take naps?"

"She said she wanted to rest. I interpreted that as taking a nap." I could tell Jannet had not considered that Mahrah's kind slept. It reminded me of the shocking realization I had when I first saw my third-grade teacher at the grocery store.

"What do you say we sleep at my house tonight?" Jannet asked. "Now I have met Miss Nosey, I am not sure I want to be near her after sunset."

"Works for me," I replied.

After that, we discussed what to pack. Jannet had told the travel agent to get round-trip tickets with the return three weeks after we arrived, knowing we could always change the tickets. The harder part was knowing what to take. We decided to pack light and pick up other essentials as we traveled. Jannet was less okay with roughing it so I was sure her luggage would have some amenities mine didn't.

I decided to wait until the next morning to contact Mahrah. After brewing a cup of coffee, I sat at the kitchen window and looked into Jannet's backyard. The coffee smelled earthy and I was grateful for living in an age that had plenty of it. Before I had time to reach out to Mahrah, I sensed her. The first thing I did was bring her up to date on the meeting with Kelly.

"I am not sure if she is the one who wishes for what you have or if it is the man with the band who wants it."

"I think she knows about the bracelet but doesn't know if I have received it. She definitely wants to get her hands on the package. Who else in your world knows what you are doing?"

"My Watchers know. There are few others who know, and I am sure they will keep the information to themselves."

"You have Watchers?"

A chuckle with the characteristic rumble. *"You are surprised? The idea of Watchers is an old one in my world. It was started a long time ago after the first rebellion."* I waited for more but Mahrah became silent.

"It is not fair to hint at something so interesting and then to say nothing more."

Reclaim

"It may seem unfair because your kind is impatient to hear stories. I never fully understood the need."

"Now you are changing the subject," I said a bit irritated. "What happened at the first rebellion?"

Mahrah relented with a light sigh. *"After my kind came to this world, there was harmony for many generations. We were grateful we had escaped the fallout from the meteor. We focused on learning about this world and about the connection which had allowed us to travel here. As we learned, we also forgot about the agreements we made to each other after possible extinction. There came a generation with a few individuals who wanted power over my kind, a power which was not theirs by agreement.*

"They attacked the ruler while she was deep in thought about the energy construct of the gateway. When dragons think so deeply, they do not sense the world around them. She was badly hurt, but was saved by four dragons who were loyal to her. However, one of her offspring was killed.

It was then decreed that those who ruled or studied should have Watchers. During a time of rebellion, the ruler and the sages would be protected."

"You said this happened during the first rebellion. What happened during the second?"

"There hasn't been another rebellion."

"Then, why do you call it the first?" I was puzzled.

"Because, we know if something happens once, it will probably happen again."

This information helped other things make sense. "Do you think you are at the beginning of another rebellion?"

"Truth." With that one word came an overwhelmingly sadness and weariness.

"It has been proven one of my kind is communicating with one of your kind. We cannot yet determine which of dragon it is. The being would do this only if it sought power. It seems both our worlds have challenges in our near futures."

"If there is a rebellion in your world, what will happen to the Talismans here?"

"They will stay active. What is more important to determine is what another of my kind will incite your kind to do with them."

"Do you think someone there wants to destroy this world?"

"Either destroy it or rule it."

I invoked a deity or two. "But, the gateway is closed. How could they rule it?"

"I do not wish to find out. This is why we, you and I, are working on

reclaiming the discovered Talisman. As you work to keep your world balanced, I will do the same in my world. The last bit of time has shown me there is much more happening than a relic of our previous visit falling innocently into the hands of a human."

I pondered for a moment. After another sip of coffee, I asked, "Why did you contact me this morning?"

"I wanted to know when you will be in the place of the next Watcher."

"We leave tomorrow and will be in that country within about two days."

"It is good you travel quickly. Since you do not leave now, you have time to extend your abilities with energy"

"Certainly. Will I need both Watchers close?"

"Do they not stay with you?"

"Jannet told me last night she has some errands to run today. She hasn't left yet so I can still ask her to stay. I would rather not."

Mahrah wasn't pleased, but she wasn't objecting. *"Make sure your companion is with you. He will be enough for this time. You will also need the bands the other Watcher has."*

"Her name is Jannet," I objected. "What are you going to call the others when we get together? It will be a little confusing to call them Watcher One and Watcher Two." Not to mention lengthy, I added to myself mentally. At least, I hoped it was just to myself.

"I remember now, your kind is also very dedicated to names. Very well, you will need to get the bands from Jannet." Her voice sounded just like a parent who is humoring their child.

Jannet barely had her eyes open when I knocked on her bedroom door. She reluctantly gave up the chain with the two rings. I waited until I finished going down the stairs before focusing again on Mahrah.

"Since your ability is still rudimentary, you will need a smooth surface."

I spied the enormous oak dining room table. "I think I found just the place."

Mahrah gave me instructions. I took the smaller of the two bands off of the chain and placed it on the table just further than I could reach. Sitting on the edge of the chair, more from my nervousness than need, I closed my eyes and pictured the band on the table. I tried to visualize energy moving between the band and my now outstretched left arm. I kept thinking back to science class and the whirling electrons of an atom. After a minute of nothing happening, I opened my eyes. I had only thought nothing had happened. The band was spinning.

"That's pretty cool," I said self-congratulatory.

"I believe you are using the word to describe a state other than the

temperature. I find your extremely varied uses for the same word perplexing." She continued, *"It is not what you were asked to do. Try again."*

"Way to pop my balloon," I said fully aware Mahrah would have to work on the meaning. I closed my eyes again and thought of illustrations of energy particles. I pictured them creating a stream. I thought about that stream like a rope and began to envision pulling the rope. Before too long, I felt the band touch the edge of my fingers. Mahrah knew when it happened.

"Now, place the band further."

We did this half a dozen more times with the band being placed further each time. Finally, I was at one end of the long table and the band was at the other. My back and shoulders ached as if I had been tugging on a real rope for the last half hour. My stomach growled; I had forgotten to follow up my coffee with breakfast. Mahrah sensed this.

"I need to remember your kind needs nourishment more often and that you tire more quickly. You do not need to finish. You may go eat."

I wasn't about to be called a wimp by a dragon. "I'll do this task and then grab some food."

As the distance had grown larger, the feeling between me and the band was more like a tether. It was harder to get the ring moving from a distance but it came more quickly as it got closer. I learned I needed to focus on the energy trail with my eyes closed. When I opened them, the ring stopped. I felt accomplished when the ring finally slid into my fingertips a minute later. Opening my eyes, I saw Jannet was standing at the far end of the table.

She had frozen in the middle of drying her hair. The towel she was using was over her shoulders and one hand held it to the side of her head. "Not even Ben is going to believe this. How are you able to move the ring?"

"The ring must also have some dragon mitochondria. I can create a type of link because of it."

"Where is all the mitochondria coming from?"

"I don't know. Mahrah hasn't told me."

Jannet looked suspicious. "Is it just the little ring?"

I sat back and rubbed the sides of my face. The last task had taken a lot out of me. I was either out of shape or this was hard work. "I think it will work on either, but I really need breakfast before trying." My stomach chose that moment to audibly growl. "It might almost be an emergency," I said lightly.

Jannet made sure I was well-fed with bacon, eggs, hash browns, and toast before she left. I spent the time she was running errands looking through books and websites. First, I learned more about dragon lore in different cultures. Virtually every culture on every continent had some myth about dragons and their interaction with humans. I wondered if this was the result of the dragons traveling the world.

Next, using Mahrah's memories as evidence of my ancestor's time, I spent time poring over the dress and weapon styles of late Bronze age people. I narrowed down the possibilities for where she lived and was just beginning to investigate some of the archaeological sites in the area when Jannet came back.

She came into the den and sat in one of the wingback chairs. She looked a little miffed. "Ever feel like you have been followed?"

I put my finger on the place I was reading and looked at her cynically. She caught the meaning of my gaze.

"I mean when it is not obvious. Reginald and Buttercup are two of the worst tails I have ever seen in my life. The only way they could have been more obvious was to wear yellow safety vests."

I realized I wasn't going to get any more reading done. I made note of the page and shut the book. "You think someone else was watching you?"

"There was a car I could swear I had seen in three different parking lots. Either we had exactly the same type of shopping to do or someone wanted to know what toiletries, make up, and undergarments I needed."

"Did you write down the license plate?"

"I guess that would have been helpful. I was too busy trying to see the person inside. I couldn't see much because the windows were tinted."

"Did you see the car when you returned to the neighborhood?"

"I'm not sure. Nobody was directly behind me. I went around a few random blocks and came in the back way just in case. I think I will have the security service drive by a few extra times tonight."

Ben dealt with sensitive processes and information. Jannet's family had been in a few unfriendly countries. The couple didn't want to live in a gated community so felt a security service would be a nice compromise. Ben joked it was to keep the wine cellar safe.

Jannet made the call and told the dispatcher to send any updates to her and Ben. We ate a light supper and went to bed early since our flight was 6:00 the next morning.

Chapter 11

The Red and the White grappled in the sky. In the midst of the battle, the air churned with the heat of their fire. A rancid breeze brought rain and burned all it touched. The world below waited breathlessly on the outcome of the battle.

***

I practically tasted the air in Nairobi when we deplaned. After almost thirty hours of recycled or mechanically cooled air, it was both refreshing and muggy.

After customs, we looked for a cab. Since the airport was on the outskirts of the city and we were staying more towards the middle of the capital, transportation was a must. Jannet ignored the men who quoted outrageous prices. They were looking for a large fare from a couple of supposedly naïve American tourists.

A few drivers were reasonable. However, when they realized Wizard was part of the package, many of them either bowed out or tripled the fare. The conversation among the drivers was quick, but I caught enough of it to know what was being said. Jannet and I both knew enough Swahili to get around and had practiced as we traveled. By listening to the banter, we discovered an individual among them who wanted an honest fare and was chiding the others for the prices they were quoting. We decided to ride with him.

The hotel was quiet and just north of the city center. It was an oasis of calm in the middle of a large, busy, and sometimes messy city. The hotel building encircled a large garden. Jannet thought it would give us a place to reset our internal clocks and adjust to the country's rhythms.

I had forgotten how much other cultures shy away from having animals in human living areas. It took a conversation with the manager of the hotel and all of Wizard's printed credentials to get the hotel to even consider the request. It was difficult for me to stay level-headed when I had spent the last forty hours hurtling through space. Jannet seemed unaffected by our travels and was able to get the manager to nominally commit to Wizard staying in the room. When I pulled Wizard's bedding out of my own bag, the manager was assured Wizard wouldn't be sleeping in the bed and had no bugs. He consented.

We woke late the next morning. It was amazing what a good night of sleep did for my perspective. To dress appropriately for the culture, we donned cotton blouses and light but long skirts then headed to the dining room. The fresh fruit was fragrant and juicy. The mangoes and pineapple practically melted in my mouth in sweet goodness. I knew, as a result, store-bought fruit was going to be a disappointment for the foreseeable future.

Jannet wanted to stop by the American Embassy before we wandered around the shops and stalls. I watched her bearing transform as we entered the building. I called it going into diplomat mode. She took on an air of being confident, yet detached.

It was a good thing she was in charge of this part of the venture. The high-ceilinged entry with guards, tellers, and shut doors was intimidating to me. Jannet strode over to the receptionist and spoke with her briefly. We were taken to a waiting room until the person she came to see was free. After a short wait, a door opened and Jannet was ushered into the office area. She told me she would be back in twenty minutes.

I wandered around the room. The paint on the walls was peeling with the constant humidity. Photos and pictures by local artists were on display. Brochures for different trips and places to stay lay on the small tables between some of the chairs. I glanced over them and wrote down a few names of hotels and safari companies operating on the south-side of the country.

Jannet popped her head back in the room a half hour later; she didn't come all the way through the door. It was a sign her meeting wasn't over.

"I need to check with you about something," she said as I wandered over. "I think we can get close to Kilimanjaro without hiring transportation."

"That's good news," I said happily. Transportation could be difficult to get and was often crowded in this part of the world.

The mischievous expression on her face made me suspicious. "But, there's a catch," I said slowly.

"We have been asked to attend a dinner this evening. I know how you feel about such events. My friend was excited to hear you were an archaeologist. Part of the dinner is to address creating archaeological sites in Kenya."

Reclaim

I was indecisive. I hated formal dinners. I felt like I belonged at such events as much as Jannet belonged on a dig. "Let me guess - no dinner, no ride.

"That is putting it without tact," Jannet said blandly.

I scratched Wizard's head, which drew Jannet's attention to him. I read her thought. "You know he has to come," I said defensively.

"I do," she said with resignation. "It is going to take all my persuasive powers to get permission for him to attend."

"A challenge for you," I replied with a slight smile. "I promise to go and be an intriguing guest, if he joins us."

"Challenge accepted. But, it will probably take at least half an hour. Do you need anything?"

"No. I will take the time to get in touch with Mahrah."

Mahrah made it clear she had been worried about my silence.

"I tried to reach you but could not find you."

"I wonder if it had anything to do with the fact I was stuck in a metal canister high in the atmosphere." I sent images of airplanes at the same time.

"An interesting idea; I will ponder it."

Before she could continue, I remembered the question Jannet had about Wizard. "Wizard, my companion, was acting aggressive toward Kelly. If I put the bracelet on him, can you communicate with him and find out why?"

"Yes."

With Wizard sitting in front of me, I leaned over and buried my bracelet in his fur. I was disappointed when I wasn't included in the conversation. I could tell he was communicating by his change in body posture. His ears rotated as if he were trying to figure out which direction to turn so he could hear better. At one point, he cocked his head to one side. I wish I knew what was being communicated.

I let my gaze drift to a picture of Mount Kilimanjaro on the wall. I thought it would be an interesting experience to talk to my dog. About then, he licked my nose, and I quickly swiped at the slobber with the back of my hand.

As Wizard settled back to the floor, Mahrah began. *"Some of his aggressiveness may have been my fault. Earlier, I asked him to protect you against the ones who were searching for you. The person at your house had the same scent. He was warning her to leave you alone."*

"We are now in a place not as welcoming of him among my kind. If he behaves aggressively, the authorities may ask us to leave or take him from me."

"I will communicate the information to him."

I leaned over and made the connection again. After a minute, Wizard harrumphed. He continued to express his disapproval of the current situation by groaning as he stretched out on the floor.

"It is not in his nature to be quiet when danger is close; he will find a way to let you know when those beings are near." Mahrah continued, *"Since you are in a different place, I assume you will be to the large mountain with snow soon."*

"We should be able to get there in the next day or two." I realized I had forgotten to ask Jannet about exactly when we would be going.

"Your land vehicles are much slower than the air ones."

I laughed. "No, Jannet is arranging a ride for us, but we won't leave for at least a day."

Mahrah was anxious. *"I wish it would be sooner. However, we can use the time to work more on your abilities to direct energy."*

"We can't right now. I am in a public building and Jannet is in a meeting."

Mahrah's harrumph matched Wizard's from minutes earlier.

"Let me know when you can do so," she said curtly. Instantly, she was gone.

I chuckled at *her* impatience. Then, I sobered as I realized there was probably a good reason for her urgency. She hinted at other happenings but never told me the details. I wondered, not for the first time, what she knew but wasn't telling me. It made me feel like I couldn't be trusted with anything other than what was needed at the moment. This didn't feel like a partnership.

Jannet came back into the room. She looked me over and said, "How many skirts did you bring?"

"Just this one."

She smiled, not unkindly. "I thought so. We need to get you another skirt and possibly another blouse."

I knew better than to argue with her on matters of dress, especially for dinners that were part of embassy affairs. I resigned myself to an afternoon of clothes shopping. We spent the first part of the excursion picking out fabric from one of the many vendors in the area. For the skirt, Jannet picked a beige linen. She pored over many batiks for the shirt and settled on one with greens and blues swirled through it. We spent another hour with a tailor and her employees. The tailor was happy to have some business and I gave her a little extra to have the clothing delivered to our hotel by evening.

After a short nap, I tentatively reached out to Mahrah. I wasn't exactly sure how to talk to a miffed dragon. I hoped it would be easier than talking to a miffed person. When we connected, she seemed to have forgotten her curtness from earlier. I wondered if I had misinterpreted her actions.

The tasks she had for me dealt with moving the larger ring; the size of the ring did not present much more of a challenge than the little one did. Mahrah then had me work through a set of tasks that became gradually harder. I went from moving the ring along smooth surfaces to pulling them over bumpy surfaces. It took more concentration than I thought I could muster with jet lag, but I did it. Mahrah was patient through the session and encouraged me when I had difficulties. We stopped shortly before dinner and I realized I was tired enough for another nap. Not having time for that luxury, I took a shower and a quick walk around the gardens with Wizard.

Jannet pronounced my attire passable when I donned the clothes that had been delivered while I was showering. Where I was passable, Jannet was elegant. She had an off the shoulder, long, sapphire blue evening gown. The décolletage accentuated her buxom figure. She wore a gold chain with a teardrop pearl that fell right above her low collar. She had matching pearl earrings.

"How do I look?" she asked with genuine concern holding her clutch purse to the side.

"Stunning."

Jannet smiled at the compliment.

"Where are the rings?" I asked suddenly aware of their absence.

"Somewhere safe," she said conspiratorially with the briefest of glances down.

The dinner was more enjoyable than I thought it would be. I spent most of the night chatting with a Kenyan archaeologist who was torn between excavating and preserving. We discussed options for sites which had been used for centuries. An excavation of such a site would not be a dig which would last a few seasons and then be done - it had the potential to last a generation. The logistics of securing funding, protecting the site, and analyzing the data were overwhelming. We debated the merits of leaving the site undisturbed, partially excavating it, or fully excavating it. The conversation drew to a close with a discussion on coordinating research throughout the country.

Before I knew it, the evening was over. We tried to take our leave to walk the short distance back, but one of the staffers insisted on taking us back in his car. It took more time to locate the car and drive through traffic than it would have for us to walk the half mile. When I finally landed in bed, I was so very thankful for a soft horizontal surface. I rolled over hoping for a long, hard sleep.

Instead, I woke suddenly and completely right before dawn. I was halfway out from under the mosquito net before I realized what I was doing. My heart was pounding and I was breathing hard. Around me, Jannet was snoring and Wizard had just shaken himself awake and was stretching. Nothing was out of the ordinary, it was even peaceful. But, every nerve said I was in danger, and I was incredibly afraid. The darkness seemed electric around me. I told myself there was no reason for my fear. Still, I could not shake the feeling. Not wanting to wake Jannet, I brought Mahrah's image to mind and reached out to her. She was there and listened as I poured out words and feelings.

"Calm." That one word in her rich voice had an immediate effect. I was able to take a deeper breath.

"You have your two Watchers with you?"

"Yes."

"It is time to keep them very close constantly. Your one companion may not be enough. Please do not let Jannet go to meetings without you." If I didn't know better, I would have thought Mahrah was being snarky.

"What do you think happened?"

A sigh of resignation. *"I think the one here who has communicated with another of your kind, the one who is rebelling, has tried to reach you. The being knows who you are and where you are. Can you tell me the color you perceived as you woke?"*

I thought hard, but came up with very little. "It was just dark. The darkness seemed to be pushing in around me. I'm sorry I can't help you any more than that."

"It is sufficient."

I sensed she wanted to withdraw. "Mahrah, what is going on? I need more information than the vague directions you are giving me. Aren't we partners in this?"

There was a pause. *"Yes, we are both Chosen."*

Another pause and then, *"I have feared our connection was being observed by another, especially after you told me about the band on the man's hand. What happened this evening confirms the other of my kind knows about you. I have said less to protect you. I do not want to send you to a place and have those who are opposed be there waiting for you."*

"We call that an ambush."

"Yes. I want to keep you safe from an unforeseen attack."

"Two things there. First, I think I need to know what I am up against to keep myself safe. Second, will there ever be a time that we can communicate without others eaves-dropping?"

"I have been working toward unobserved communication. I am close to succeeding. The other made a mistake in trying to reach you. I can now work on blocking our connection from him."

"Him? You know who it is?"

"Yes. You know him also. It is the black dragon."

"The one who travelled here with you?"

"Truth."

It was time to invoke a deity and a very hot underworld. "I am up against another dragon?"

"We. We are opposed by another of my kind. I have long suspected and so planned thoroughly. I have given you abilities no other of your kind has ever had. You, also, are one of the few humans ever to have Watchers. The beings with whom he works will not be able to hurt you unless they ambush you."

"And, they will have a hard time catching me unawares if they don't know where I am. I see why you have kept your cards close to your vest." I sensed Mahrah was perplexed. "It means that you have revealed very little."

"It will not be long before I can tell you more. The lack of information was not to limit or deceive you. Once you told me members of your kind knew exactly where you were, I realized I needed to be even more careful. It is the reason I have not spoken of where to find your fourth Watcher." This surprised me since I had assumed there were only going to be three. *"It will not be long before I can reveal more."*

I felt like this was getting things back on track. "Thank you. I will ask Jannet to stay close for the next bit of time."

"Be ready. I think the humans will find you again before long."

Mahrah didn't know how right she was.

After breakfast, we decided to go to some of the curio shops and make a trip to a bookstore. My conversation with the archaeologist the night before had stirred my interest in some of the prehistory of the country. Jannet and I were chatting about the evening meal when Wizard stopped dead in his tracks. Since I wasn't paying attention to him, I found myself almost pitching forward from the sudden halt, spinning me around.

Wizard's hackles were up. He growled only loud enough for me to hear. I followed the direction of his gaze behind us. Kelly promenaded down the block toward us. Jannet caught sight of her the same time I did.

"Holy cows and all other manner of creatures," she said.

Kelly's self-satisfied smile grew broader when she stopped before us. She was extremely pleased with the shocked looks on our faces. "Hello, Nadia and Jannet Goodwin." She emphasized Jannet's name.

"Kelly," I said with a curt nod as a greeting. Jannet had crossed her arms which she only did when she could think of nothing to say. It looked like I was going to be Kelly's conversation partner.

"How interesting to have run into you here," she said as if we were only fifty miles from home.

"Somehow, I think you didn't just run into us. What are you doing here?"

"Trying to keep you from destroying the world."

"And, how exactly would I possibly do that?" I asked with a scoff.

"By working with an alien life form who wants to annihilate life on this planet," she said smugly.

I had to hand it to her, she had managed to shock me and to put Jannet on her heels. I figured the best way to keep this conversational skirmish from being a total rout was to give her as little information as possible.

"I think you have read too many tabloids," I said derisively.

"You deny you have been in communication with a being not from this planet?"

Instead of answering, I followed up with my own question, "You know there are other beings in this universe?"

"Not in this one." Kelly stopped. Her smile faded and her eyes narrowed as she realized she had told us some of what she knew. She took a step closer.

"Look," she said menacingly, "You have no idea what you are getting yourself into. You are messing around with power you cannot control and will end up gravely harming this world. My brother and I came here to stop you."

"Your brother?"

Just as I asked, a man stepped out from the shop we were in front of and stood off Kelly's shoulder. It was Buttercup.

Chapter 12

I had been shocked before. Now, I was flabbergasted. Before I could stop myself, I blurted, "Buttercup is your brother?"

Jannet snorted and Kelly's face instantly showed confusion. "What are you talking about? My brother's name is Bryce."

"I like Buttercup better," Jannet said with amusement. She had come out of her stupor.

Feeling like she was losing her advantage, Kelly turned on her angrily. "I know you know what is going on here. You lied to me about your name. You are covering something up. I am warning you along with your friend here." She was practically poking Jannet in the chest with a pointed finger, which she then wagged between us. "You both need to stop playing around with fire and go home. Forget whatever quest you think you are on."

"Or?" Jannet asked coolly.

"Or, we will. . ." Suddenly, she hopped back with disgust on her face. I looked down and saw moisture on her shoe, a small puddle, and Wizard. Kelly was now outraged.

"You! Your dog!" she sputtered. "You will pay for this."

As she began to back away, Bryce took a menacing step forward. I now saw a gun-shaped bulk under his light jacket. Wizard's hackles went up along his entire back; he bared his teeth and growled. Bryce put both hands up with palms out as if surrendering and stepped back to join his sister. They turned and retreated down the street. Kelly shook her foot every few steps. It was an inglorious exit.

A quick look around let us know we had drawn some attention. Some people were smiling, others had looks of consternation. "Let's go get some tea," I said quietly. We walked the opposite way of the siblings.

After a few blocks, we found a small eatery and sat with two hot cups of milky chai. The smell of cardamom, cinnamon, and other spices hung over the table. We also had a couple of Kenyan donuts called maandazi.

Jannet began. "That woman has gone from annoying to creepy."

"Agreed. How do you think she found out your name?"

"I am not sure and it really bothers me. I will call Ben when we get back to the hotel."

"Do you think they know where we are staying?"

"Since they tracked us to Nairobi, my gut says they do. The good news is we are going to be there just one more night."

"And, the hotel has quite a bit of security." I continued, "They must be the ones Mahrah warned me about."

I saw a question on Jannet's face. She couldn't express it since she had just taken a bite of maandazi.

"Last night, I woke from a deep sleep. There was nothing physically in the room, but it felt like someone or something else was there. Mahrah told me it was another dragon who was trying to reach me. She said the other dragon was also working with someone here.

"Jannet, this is spinning into something more than just taking a relic from someone who shouldn't have it. I am not comfortable with you risking your life. If those two creepers turn out to be dangerous, this could get beyond what I can handle."

"What is the alternative, Nadia? Should I go back to my nice little house in a nice little town and act shocked when bad things begin to happen?"

I could see she was committed to continuing. There was no reason to try to dissuade her. So, I changed the subject. "Wizard did find a very effective way to get her to stop." I started chuckling remembering the look on Kelly's face.

Jannet joined me. "It was the least tactful thing I have ever seen, but sometimes you just need to let a dog solve the problem."

The staffer from the embassy picked us up early the next morning. As we drove south out of Nairobi, I saw the gamut of housing Kenya had to offer. In one neighborhood, there was a high rise with pools on every balcony; on the other side of its perimeter wall, metal-roofed shacks. In such close proximity, the disparity was heart-rending.

We drove south through the country and along the eastern edge of the Great Rift Valley. There were herds of wildebeest grazing the grass and giraffe grazing the banyan trees. The earth smelled alive and vibrant. The car's motion over the rolling hills lulled me to sleep.

Reclaim

It was late afternoon when we reached our relay point, the last Kenyan city before the Tanzanian border. We had arranged for a shuttle to pick us up and take us to the hotel just north of Mount Kilimanjaro, inside Tanzania. The staffer told us where to find him if the shuttle never came, something entirely possible.

After fending off numerous street vendors, we sat on a bench to wait. A few puffy clouds had drifted overhead. We hoped it did not mean rain. With dirt all around us, a downpour would only create mud. The temperature was comfortable for our short sleeves and light travel pants; we snacked on a rice dish and fruit we had brought from Nairobi.

"Tell me again how you found this place?" Jannet asked.

"While you were chatting with your friends, I was doing reconnaissance in the waiting room."

"The waiting room of a foreign embassy would be the first place I would go to scope out a country," Jannet said jokingly.

"You are lucky I did because this is the only place to stay on the north side of the mountain. I am glad you lowered your standards to a tent hotel with no spa," I joked back.

"You will make it up to me someday. For instance, I am tagging along if you have to look at possible burial sites on a Pacific island."

"Oh, the sacrifices you make for our friendship."

Just then, a minibus pulled up. The man in the passenger seat, the conductor, opened the door to the back seats. Before we could even get to our feet, ten people with baskets and chickens materialized out of nowhere and began climbing into the van. I was unsure this was our transport even though the name of our accommodation, Hoteli ya Hema, was on a magnetic sign attached to the door.

The conductor came over to us and asked in lilting English, "Are you going to Hoteli ya Hema?"

I was going to answer, but Jannet beat me to it. "Who are you supposed to be picking up?" she asked in Swahili, not wanting to be taken for a ride by imposters.

The tall man smiled. His two front teeth were gapped and it gave him a slightly boyish look. He gave us our names and then asked, in Swahili, "Is the dog coming too?"

"Yes, he is," Jannet said firmly but not unkindly.

"He looks like wolf. He bites?"

"Only if you make him angry."

"I see," the man said. His smile was not quite as large. He looked at the van and then back at us. "Does he like chickens?"

Jannet answered with a grin of her own, "I don't think chickens like him."

The driver began yelling from the minibus at the conductor in Swahili, "Kaka, let us go. Leave the white women and their dog. We can say we did not find them. Then we can find other people to pay us for a ride."

Kaka stiffened. He walked over to the minibus and said something to the driver. He must have told the driver the white women spoke Swahili. The driver's eyes got big; he raised his hand in apology.

Kaka came back to us, "I apologize for my friend. He wants to be a good capitalist." Then he picked up both of our bags, took two quick strides back to the minibus, and tossed our bags onto the rooftop luggage rack. At the same time, he ordered the people out of the front bench seat so Wizard could sit on the floor between the bench and the front seats. Even though we had the most legroom in the vehicle, it was still a very cramped ride.

We were on the road for the next hour and a half with between eight and fourteen other riders. At one point, one patron tried to get aboard with his goat. The goat took one look at Wizard and adamantly refused. During the whole trip, the driver and conductor spoke to each other in a language we did not know. Jannet and I privately guessed it was Maa.

We were finally delivered to the building which served as the Front Desk of Hoteli ya Hema. It was a building with two conical thatched roofs. Its walls were permanent instead of being the sides of a tent. The clerk knew to expect the three of us and made no objections to Wizard's presence. He quickly showed us to our hut. It too had a conical roof. The large tent rested on a wood floor and had two full beds in it. A separate bathroom area could be reached through the back door of the tent. The clerk let us know that we could still get something to eat. His one warning was about being careful of animals as we passed between huts since the sun was setting.

We washed off the dust from our travels and then followed the pathway illuminated by lanterns to the building housing the kitchen and guest common area. There was a simple dinner waiting for us. We made quick work of it and walked back under a curtain of stars. The light to the south was blocked out by the hulk of Mount Kilimanjaro. It was nice to be away from urbanity.

I woke when the sky was turning a husky rose. Wizard and I stepped onto the porch. A herd of zebras who had been grazing between the huts snapped their heads up and sniffed, their ears twitching. Wizard sniffed the air, went down the steps, and walked in the opposite direction. When we came back into the tent, the herd had moved off and Jannet was awake.

"I need a run," I said.

Jannet stood and looked out the screened window. "I think you might find a place out here," she said gesturing to the plains. "I am tired of being cooped up too. Why don't you run and I will work out?"

We both pulled on some light sweatpants and a t-shirt. My shirt advertised a national park in the US; hers advertised a local brewery in Longmont. I went to the Front Desk to ask about where to run. The clerk did not respond immediately. I was about to try the request in Swahili when he called over his shoulder.

"Kaka, go with the white woman and her dog so they do not get into trouble," he said in Swahili.

"I will not cause trouble," I answered haltingly in Swahili.

The clerk's jaw dropped. "I apologize." Then, he switched to English, "Because of the animals, we ask you take someone with you when you leave the compound."

I wanted a run to move and to get some time to think alone. It looked like I was not going to have the luxury of solitude.

Kaka came around the desk and smiled. He was dressed in a light shirt and cargo shorts. He had a wide multi-colored beaded bracelet on one wrist and a round red beaded bracelet on his other wrist. His feet were bare. "You want to run? Many Americans run and think. You wish so, yes?"

It was almost as if he had read my mind. I nodded.

As we left the compound, Kaka indicated he would run ahead of me. He was far enough to stay out of my space but not so far that he could not be back if trouble presented itself. I appreciated his consideration as I loped through the early morning. It was cool and the sky was a vault of light blue above me. My mind was just beginning to unclench when Kaka stopped. I jogged up to him.

"Why are we stopping?"

"This is five kilometers. We go back now." I again noticed the lyrical way he spoke. He had said Jannet's name correctly, with the two n's, and today he drew out all the syllables of 'kilometer'. His phrasing was choppy, not uncommon for people learning to speak English. Jannet indicated it was from Swahili not having as many connections words.

On the way back, I began to feel my thoughts settle. When I agreed to being Chosen, I did not expect being pursued by two people across an ocean. It was disturbing. I was also uneasy about the possibility of Mahrah having problems in her world.

A dark thought came. I wondered if I had been deceived and was just a pawn in the dragons' game for power.

I was still deep in thought when we jogged up to the Front Desk. Kaka went to the common area. Wizard and I went to our tent. Jannet was sitting in a chair on the porch. With one hand, she was aimlessly spinning a two-foot long rod. She had a bottle of water in the other hand.

"Are you trying to keep the flies away?" I asked climbing the three stairs to the platform.

She grinned, rose fluidly to her feet, and flicked her wrist. The rod transformed into a five-foot long bo staff. She spun it while taking a sip of water.

"Show off," I said sinking into the facing chair.

Jannet laughed. To be truthful, she was modest about how skilled she was. I had never gotten a straight answer about what she could do. Since she was so demure about it, I found myself forgetting about her abilities. She had not only not forgotten; she had planned on using them if needed.

"Your workout was a kata?"

"Yes, I thought it might be time to let anyone who might be watching know I may be more than they bargained for. I think a series of martial arts movements will alert people the two of us can protect ourselves."

"Do you think we have gotten ourselves into something more than we bargained for?"

Jannet looked out over the plains. "No," she said looking back, "I think we are at the intersection of two sets of events. The Talisman was found and somebody wants to use it. Mahrah's goal was to keep it from being abused."

"But, she suspected something else."

"She did. I don't know if the other dragon is taking advantage of her being distracted with the events around the Talisman or is orchestrating them. He may sense this is an opportunity for him."

"Whichever it is, I hope we don't have to wait long for the Watcher to find us."

"Let's get in touch with Ben. He said he would be able to mask the signal from your satellite phone. He said he was going to look into a few things when I mentioned we had unwanted friends."

"I will touch base with Mahrah." I realized at that moment that I had not connected with her since Nairobi. Granted, I had not reached out to her, but she had not initiated a conversation with me either. A worry crossed my mind.

After setting up the satellite phone for Jannet, I went onto the hotel grounds and sat facing Mount Kilimanjaro. The top of the mountain was covered in snow, with the green of the forest on its lower range. It was beautiful. I reached out and sensed Mahrah, aware her attention was divided.

"Chosen, I cannot speak much now. There are matters here requiring my concentration."

My nascent worry bloomed. Was she okay? What was happening?

Reclaim

"The events are manageable. Facts have been learned about another Talisman."

"The others found a second one?"

"They did not. But, you are to look for it. It is near you."

"Where is it?" I had a sinking feeling I already knew the answer to the question.

"It is on the mountain. I must go."

Mahrah had hung up on me, again. I looked at the mountain. "It's an awfully big mountain," I said out loud.

"Yes, it is," came a voice off my right elbow. I whipped my head around to see Kaka standing there. He was looking at the mountain and petting Wizard. I gave Wizard an accusing glare. He lolled his tongue at me in reply.

"I am sorry. I do not mean to disturb," Kaka said when he realized he had startled me.

"I was just thinking."

"There is much you need to think?"

"Enough for two worlds," I said flatly.

"I see," he said and put his hand out to help me up. "I am here to give invitation. My father is head man of my village. He would like you to come meet the village. It is an honor."

"I cannot leave my friend alone."

"Sorry, invitation is for all in your group," he gestured to Wizard and back to the hut in which we were staying.

"When?"

"This evening's meal, please."

"I am not sure how we will get there."

"The village owns a car. We drive you."

I felt like declining would be discourteous. However, I was also wary for our safety. "May I answer after speaking with the Front Desk?"

Kaka was taken aback, but recovered. "It is good. I think you will say yes. You will be safe from all in my village."

He gave Wizard a final pat, turned, and walked back down the path toward the main building. I watched as he climbed into a waiting minibus which drove down the dusty track I had just run. How did he know I had safety in mind? Maybe it was common for most tourists.

The Front Desk assured me the village was safe and it was a great honor to be invited to visit. They rarely let outsiders come and share a meal with them. With my mind at ease, I went to speak with Jannet.

She was still on the phone with Ben. I showered. The humidity meant my hair wouldn't really dry most of the day. As I finished dressing, my stomach growled, reminding me about Wizard. When I came back into the bedroom, he had his bowl between his paws. His look was recriminating.

As Wizard ate breakfast, I relayed the dinner invitation to Jannet. She agreed we should stay alert; she thought it was probably safe. The call for breakfast came across the compound as Jannet finished her shower.

I was very curious about what Ben and Jannet discussed. I thought we could be discreet speaking at breakfast.

However, there was a general buzz over some breaking news. One of the other guests had internet via a satellite. They had just learned of a terrible accident in Nairobi. An overfilled bus had unexplainably flipped. There were many injured and several fatalities.

Chapter 13

No one could agree on how it happened. One man said the bus hit a hole and tipped. Another eyewitness said they were standing on the corner when a white man ran in front of the bus. A woman on the opposite corner confirmed there was a man but said he dove under the front of the bus. The reporter dismissed most of the reports because no man was found after the accident.

However it happened, the result was that the crowded bus flipped on its side and skidded into the pedestrians waiting to cross. Jannet and I were as shocked as the others. The two of us wordlessly confirmed we were thinking the same thing. The Kinetic Talisman had been used, again.

We finished eating breakfast even though the food now tasted like paste. People had died because of the use of the Talisman, a device I had pledged to reclaim. If I had been more prompt in finding the Watcher, would these people still be alive? On one hand, I knew it was a fruitless question to ask. However, my emotions roiled with the possibility that it was, in part, my fault.

We changed our plans of going on a morning hike along the lower flanks of Mount Kilimanjaro. I left Jannet and Wizard behind as I practically fled back to our hut. Instead of going on to the porch, I went around to the far side where I couldn't be seen. I picked up a rock and threw it as hard as I possibly could. I did this over and over until there were no more stones nearby. Then, I wept. Jannet had arrived and stood next to me. We didn't say anything for some time.

Finally, I turned to her. "Those people," I choked, "Those innocent people were hurt and killed. It was my responsibility to keep people safe. I blew it."

Jannet said nothing. Her jaw was set. It made me realize how hard I was clenching my own. "We need to get the Talisman away from them. I hope there is a plan to put it somewhere it will never be seen again," she said.

"I want to do more than take an artifact from them." I was surprised at the dark thoughts that swirled as I thought of Kelly and Bryce.

"I know," Jannet said quietly. "I just have one question."

"What?"

"Have you ever thrown rocks that far before?" I could tell she was completely serious by the look on her face. My thoughts of retribution faded.

I tried to find the rocks I had chucked. I couldn't see them from where I was so we walked into the field to see where they landed. They were about one hundred yards from where I had been standing.

It was time to invoke a deity. So, I invoked four.

"Nadia, you didn't just throw those rocks. When I came around the corner, I saw the rock go to the top of its arc and then keep going like something was pushing it. Did you know you were doing that?"

"No. I was just so distraught I wanted to toss something as far as I possibly could."

"I think your ability to use forces is extending beyond the bracelet." I could see a look of uncertainty cross Jannet's face.

"I would make a great newspaper deliverer." I joked, trying to dispel my ease.

"Maybe," she had not been truly listening and missed my attempt at humor. "Let's try something. Can you still throw a rock that far?"

"I don't know I want to try. What if I throw it through the side of the tent?"

We picked up several rocks and walked back to where I had stood before. I threw one and it went a fraction of the distance. I concentrated on it going further. The next rock landed close to the one I had just thrown. After seven throws, I stopped trying. "I don't know why they went further. Maybe it has something to do with raw emotion."

"It was impressive and daunting," she said tucking her arm in mine. Leading me back to the porch she said, "Let's talk this through."

When we were sure there was no one around to overhear our conversation, we discussed the bus, Jannet's phone call to Ben, the other Talisman on the mountain, the missing Watchers, and our dinner plans.

Ben told Jannet that both their credit card and mine had an inquiry placed to it in the last few days. "It is how they found us," Jannet said, "They figured out what plane ticket you had purchased and then looked for someone who booked at the same time to the same destination."

"Which means they are able to get information from financial institutions." I sat up suddenly. "What about this place? How did we book and pay for it?"

"It will be harder for them to trace us here. The reservation was made by the embassy and will be charged to them." I was very confused. Jannet continued, "Part of my meeting in Nairobi was to find out if there were any people in the area that our government wanted to contact. It turns out they have wanted to discuss environmental and human rights issues with the Maasai villages in this area. I told them I would deliver the invitation to have a conversation."

"You will be bringing your own agenda to our dinner this evening. I wonder if we will still be welcomed after they hear what you have to say."

"You have no faith in me. I think I can manage to deliver an invitation without creating an international incident," she said, smiling winsomely.

I looked up and saw someone coming toward our hut. After a moment, I realized it was Kaka.

"I am going to ask him about his name," I said lifting my chin in Kaka's direction. Jannet followed my gaze.

"Good, I had been wondering why everybody calls him 'Brother'. Jannet gave the English translation of his name. "Do you think he is a monk?"

I was still giggling when Brother approached the hut. He stopped at the bottom of the stairs. I invited him on to the porch. Before he could begin a conversation, I sprung my question, "Why does everyone call you Brother?"

He smiled his gap-toothed smile. "Because I am so very nice to all around me. They say I remind them of their brother."

"When we go to your village this evening, should we call you Brother or something else?" I inquired.

"My tribal name is Ntrikana Zakia Azima Athumani." He pronounced his name as if it were a song. Jannet and I looked at each other. "I am not sure I can say that correctly," she admitted.

The man brightened, "You do not need to. I wish to be called by another name."

"Which would be what?" I asked.

"Joe."

"Joe?" I tried not to laugh at the absurdity of such an ordinary name after the richness of his tribal name. "Should we call you Joseph?" I tried.

"No. Please just call me Joe. I wish this to be the name you use."

Jannet stood, "Joe, it is a pleasure to meet you. You may call me Jannet.

My response was less diplomatic, "Why 'Joe'?"

"My name has set me apart my whole life. I would like to blend in a little more with English speakers.

Before I could say anything else, Jannet asked, "Can I ask why you came to our hut?"

"I would like to ask if you want to hike on the great mountain. My people have been here for thousands of years and have always thought the mountain sacred. We have many holy sites on it. Would you like to walk one of the sacred paths?"

The thousands of years comment caught my attention. I quickly figured that this was the best bet we had of figuring out where people had been on this mountain during the time the dragons were here. "Why do you offer us such an honor?" I asked.

"Because I can tell you are different."

I wasn't sure what to make of his last comment. Jannet nodded slightly, telling me she thought it was a good idea. We agreed to meet Joe in the parking lot in a half hour. We both put together a day pack. I also put some essentials in Wizard's pack and put it on him.

We met Joe at the four-wheeler, parked in front of the main area. He sauntered up with a basket of food, indicating it was our lunch. I was happy to hear that since breakfast was already starting to wear thin. After making sure we were settled, Joe jumped into the driver's seat. He looked a little too enthusiastic.

I was nervous when we turned off the main road and began driving cross-country. I quietly asked Jannet if she had her staff. She nodded and said, "I am fully prepared for any social situation." I rolled my eyes.

After eating lunch, we began walking a footpath with lush vegetation around it. We saw fern, thick bush, and flowers which looked like fireworks. The rich aroma of flowers hung in the warm air. After about an hour, the trail began to climb. The vegetation slowly stretched upward into a forest of sycamore and juniper trees. A different set of bird and animal sounds accompanied the veld.

Joe pointed to places where his people had built temporary settlements as they foraged or fought battles with the invading Maasai. He spoke of the vital land and the life it suckled. He had picked up a large stick and used it as a pointer while describing some of the landmarks of the dormant volcano.

After a few miles, conversation lapsed. We all become absorbed in our own internal focus as we continued to hike. Suddenly, I felt a strange prickling along my left hand and wrist. I stopped and looked at the bracelet. I couldn't tell if the light in the forest was diffused or if it was giving off a glow.

Jannet, who was ahead a few paces, came back to me. "Are you okay?"

I hadn't realized I had stopped or that Wizard had taken the opportunity to flop on the ground. "Do you feel it?" I asked uncertainly.

"If you mean the almost oppressive humidity, yes, I do." She wiped her brow.

"No, there is something else." I now noticed a very low hum. The bracelet was resonating it.

Jannet, focusing on the sounds around her, heard it too and gave me a sharp look. She looked at my bracelet. I cast a glance over her shoulder at Joe. He had stopped on the trail about fifteen feet away, and was looking up into the trees nonchalantly. "What if the bracelet and the Talisman are somehow synced?" I whispered. "What if an energy connection links them when they are close enough together?"

"How close?" she said quietly.

"I don't really know. I hope it isn't on the summit. It would be a ridiculously long way to create a connection."

Joe glanced back at us. "Joe, did you say your ancestors came up here to worship?"

Joe discarded the stick he had been swinging idly and sauntered back toward us. "They did. It is a place not far, but is mostly unknown to any outside of our tribe."

"If someone outside of your clan found it on their own, would they be welcomed to honor your people by paying a visit?"

"They would be welcomed to pay respect. Our customs forbid us from bringing foreigners to it, but we will allow any who find it to visit. We believe it means they have been asked to do so by our god."

While Joe was speaking, I began to look up and down the trail. There were no posts or paths indicating an offshoot from the main trail. I walked down the trail about twenty yards and slowly came back up it. My fingers trailed along the branches of each tree as I walked by it. When I was a little further around the bend the clue clicked in my mind. I spun around, walked back about ten yards, and peered into the forest. What I saw confirmed my hunch.

Jannet and Joe were watching me and chatting as if it was natural to see someone wander over the same stretch of trail several times.

"It's this way," I said pointing into a thicket.

Jannet looked skeptical. Joe's brow furrowed. "How do you know? It is only bushes." He said aloud what Jannet was thinking.

"Because, all the trees along this stretch are the same except for this one," I said pointing at the tree directly off the trail, "and if you look into the forest, there is a line of these trees. Which means, they were put here intentionally."

Joe smiled and bowed slightly, "Welcome to our sacred place."

We skirted the thicket and followed the line of trees. After climbing over some boulders and winding around a rock face, an established path followed the trees. It entered directly into a thicket. Joe stepped forward and pulled a piece of the thicket away; it was a gate woven from the branches. We stepped into a small clearing.

The air in the clearing was cool. There was a rock face on one side of it with a small stream of water trickling down it. The water continued a few feet across the clearing and then dropped into a small fissure. The rest of the clearing was a garden with grass and flowers. There were one or two stones with chiseled surfaces around the edge of the clearing. The prickling sensation had grown much stronger.

I knew Wizard wanted a drink. I checked with Joe to make sure it would not be dishonorable to have an animal drink from the spring.

As Wizard lapped, Joe looked at my wrist. I wondered if he could see the bracelet or was looking at it just because I had been shaking my hand. He caught my eye and then looked meaningfully at the fissure.

I understood the significance of his glance; Jannet did too. "How far down is the Talisman?" I asked Joe.

"Much further than a man can reach with a spear," he answered. "No one can see it. It was placed there long ago."

"Then, how do you know it is there?" Jannet asked.

"The stories from our ancestors tell us of a powerful gift from the god of the sky. It allowed my ancestors to hunt without being hunted. After many years, the god asked for it to be hidden. This is where we hid it."

"Why are you okay with me finding it?"

"The grandfather of my grandfather had a vision. In the vision, the sky turned red. My ancestor saw two people who had skin like the clouds come from the north. He was shocked because they were female. They had a lone painted wolf with them. He then saw one of the women with the Talisman in her hand. My ancestor felt peace. When he came out of his vision, he knew that the Talisman was to be given to the woman with the light skin."

I turned to Jannet and said, "Which means Mahrah can manipulate time."

"Or, she has been planning this for a very long time," Jannet completed my thought.

Joe continued, "In my village, the third born of the head elder is the one who is told this story. It is the person's responsibility to watch for the visitors and to bring them to the mountain. If the women can find the place of the Talisman on the mountain, we know they are the ones chosen by our god to take it."

I went over to the fissure and knelt down beside it. It was about a hand breadth at its widest point and about three feet long. After a foot down, there was nothing to be seen. I was about to put my hand into it when a thought crossed my mind, "Are there any poisonous snakes or spiders in this area?"

Joe shook his head. I put my hand into the crack and closed my eyes. In my mind, I created an energy rope. I was surprised when I felt the stream stop and an almost palpable attachment. Then, I began to pull. About ten minutes later, I felt a cool rectangular metal object touch my palm. I wrapped my fingers around it and sat back.

Jannet caught me before I pitched over. She sat down next to me and put an arm around my shoulders. It was then I noticed I was sweating profusely and my arms ached as if I had just spent the last ten minutes digging a trench. Wizard walked over to me and dumped a mouthful of water in my lap.

"That wasn't exactly what I needed," I said. He followed up with a wet tongue across my face.

"Well done, Chosen," Joe said.

Jannet and I looked at him inquiringly, surprised. In response, he took off his wide beaded bracelet and turned it inside out. Woven into the underside was a ring with the signet of a red dragon.

Chapter 14

"Score," I cried hoarsely.

Now, it was Jannet and Joe's turn to stare at me. I followed up with, "A Talisman and a Watcher at the same time."

I sobered when I realized I had assumed. "You do want to be a Watcher, right?" I asked.

"I, too, had a vision," Joe began.

Joe was stopped short by Jannet. "Is this going to be a long story? Because, Nadia needs something to eat. Oh, and I am hungry too."

Leave it to Jannet to make sure we were comfortable. However, in my case, it was more than being comfortable. Jannet knew that I needed to eat after exerting myself to keep from having a seizure. We dug some energy bars out of our packs and offered one to Joe. He accepted; I could tell he was eating it just to be courteous.

Joe continued his story.

"I was in this place when I had my vision. I came to settle the matter of how to spend my future. My father told me he wanted to send me to school in England. I wanted to be a warrior. This is not the Maasai warriors the world knows today. Our tribe was absorbed by the Maasai when they moved into this area. We keep some of their traditions and we keep traditions of our own.

"If I left my village and joined another, it would bring dishonor to my father. Going to University would honor my father, but I would give up what I had trained myself to become. I came here to think and pray.

"My vision began exactly as my ancestor's vision did. Only, now I saw the women for who they were, white women. The vision did not show their faces plainly. The animal was much like a painted wolf except it had pointed ears. I had seen pictures of dogs from around the world at in a book at primary school. The animal in the vision reminded me of German Shepherds.

"I saw, as my ancestor did, the Talisman in the hand of the white woman. In the vision, we were all then transported to a different land. There were other white people and they attacked us. I knew in my vision they wanted the Talisman.

"The white women, wolf, and I fought together as a group to keep the Talisman out of their hands. I could tell there was one more who fought with us, though, I never saw that person. I just saw men who would be clutching their head or arm because of his attacks.

"I understood that this was my calling. I was to be a warrior and defend the Talisman when it was passed to another for protection. Since my vision included other countries, I determined I needed an education. So, I went to school in England and then came back here to wait for the one Chosen to protect the Talisman."

"When did you have this vision?" I asked.

"Almost five years ago." Joe looked at me with a serious expression, "I was afraid you would come when I was at University."

Jannet looked at Joe thoughtfully, "You keep other people from knowing about your education by appearing to be less fluent in English than you truly are."

"You are smart, Jannet," Joe said grinning. "When people hear me speak less than fluent English, they see only what they expect. I do this to make sure I am not deceived into showing the Talisman to the wrong people."

"Why didn't you just tell us when you saw us?" I asked.

"I did not know if you were the fulfillment of the vision or decoys. My vision showed there is more than one force in the world. I wanted to be sure before telling you who I was."

"And, who are you?" I asked expectantly.

Joe got to his feet and took a noble pose. "I am Ntrikana Zakia Azima Athumani, son of the village head elder, called to defend the Chosen as she protects the Talisman. You call it Watcher. I accept the call." He paused. "But, only if you call me Joe."

"That was far more eloquent than my reply," Jannet said dryly.

Jannet stood. Joe was several inches taller than she was. He extended his arm to Jannet. She reached to shake his hand; he reached further up and embraced her wrist. "Jannet, you are my partner in this."

He let go of Jannet's arm and then turned to Wizard. Wizard began wagging his tail as Joe bent down and held Wizard's head in his hands. "I look forward to having you by our side, one-like-a-wolf." Wizard rewarded the compliment with a full-face lick. Joe laughed and wiped his face.

Then Joe turned to me, "Chosen, will you accept my skills to protect the Talisman?"

"I will. But, you should probably call me Nadia in public. 'Chosen' might raise a few eyebrows."

I looked at the tile of silver in my hand. It was about the size of a pink eraser bought by school children and never used. "How am I going to carry this? I don't want to put it in a pocket and I don't see a way to put a string on it."

Joe reached into one of the pockets of his cargo shorts. He pulled out what looked like a silver bracelet with a dent on one side. "The one who carried the Talisman before had this. I do not know if it was made here or if it was given to us by the one who gave us the Talisman." He held out his other hand.

I reluctantly gave the Talisman to Joe. I had to trust he wasn't going to make off with it. He took it and placed the silver tile next to the indent. A metallic click sounded. He then handed the ensemble back to me.

"Silver isn't magnetic. Why does the bracelet hold the Talisman?" I asked.

Joe shrugged. "I hoped you could tell me."

I took the band from him. "It's too big for my wrist. I would be afraid it would slide off."

Joe chuckled, "It is not a bracelet. It is for your arm." He pointed to his upper arm.

Embarrassed, I took the band and began pushing it up my left arm. After sliding it up to my bicep, the circlet contracted to a comfortable size. I could tell it was there, much like the bracelet. However, I hardly felt it.

Joe was intrigued. "It has never done changed shape before."

"It might have something to do with this," I said pointing at the bracelet on my wrist.

Joe said something in reply; I didn't hear it because my consciousness was flooded with Mahrah.

"You have found another Watcher and the Conceal Talisman," she said jubilantly.

"I have recovered the Talisman with the help of the Watcher." I replied proudly. "His name is Joe."

"We do not have long to speak. I must show you how to use the Talisman."

"Why don't we have long? Are you still dealing with a situation in your world?"

"The matter is resolved at the moment. The reason our time is short is because those who oppose you are not far."

To say I was unhappy was an extreme understatement. I had questions about how they found us but knew that it would be useless to ask. Mahrah taught me the command by sending me an image. I was to think about that image and push energy into the Talisman at the same time.

It must have worked because I heard alarmed gasps around me. I opened my eyes and saw surprised looks on Jannet and Joe's faces. Wizard had begun to sniff near my feet. I found I could still see myself. I ceased putting energy into the Talisman. I was confused when I started talking to the others and they couldn't hear me.

"The Talisman stays active until you command it to stop. It was created so the bearer could focus on the trouble."

Mahrah then sent me the image I needed to deactivate the Talisman. When I used it, the Watchers all looked relieved.

"I know how to Conceal myself. What about the Watchers? Shouldn't they get some protection from our opponents?"

"For the Conceal Talisman to work on those without a band, they will need to be in physical contact with you. Once the Watchers activate their bands, you will be able to Conceal them as long as there are two or more who are using the protection energy. Be careful. The energy use is great when you are Concealing more than yourself, if it is not a Watcher."

"Are you telling me I should not practice now because I may need to save my strength?"

"Precisely. I will let you concentrate on moving to a safe place. Contact me once you have done so."

When I turned my attention to the clearing, I noticed the shadows were deepening. It wouldn't be long before it would be night. "We are to skedaddle. Mahrah didn't say explicitly but someone looking for us is not far."

"Which part did she not say explicitly?" Jannet asked while putting stuff back into her pack.

"The part of who exactly is not far."

"My guess is it is the Devlin Duo," Janet offered a nickname for Kelly and her brother. Joe looked a little confused so Jannet caught him up with a brief synopsis of the key players while I put the things back in my bag.

We went back to the thicket door. Before walking through it, I took a good look around. It would be an amazing site to study. I sighed realizing I would not be able to divulge this secret any more than the others I was keeping. I couldn't help asking a question though, "Joe, how long ago was this clearing created?"

"Three generations before the Maasai came to this area, my people decided to enclose the hiding place of the Talisman. It is said the keeper of the knowledge foresaw the invasion of the land by other tribes."

We walked back down the trail in silence, Joe leading. Jannet had her collapsed staff in one hand. Wizard and I brought up the rear. My thoughts were more on the potential loss of the stories that clearing held. Maybe it would be discovered by another. There would be no risk of the Talisman being discovered and the story would seem like nothing but myth. I was thinking about how to tease information about the dragons from other ancient stories when Joe spun around and waved us all off the trail. At least, I think he was waving. The sun had set and the light was murky at best.

We stopped about ten yards off the trail behind a small group of trees. Jannet, Joe and I put our heads close together. I put my hand on Wizard as he stiffened and began a rumble. He stopped his vocalization but stared back at the direction of the trail.

"I saw lights on the trail ahead," Joe breathed.

"Is there another way down?" I asked quietly.

"We can go any number of ways but we would make noise in the forest and bushes. If they have a tracker, they would know it was us."

"We should wait then?" Jannet asked.

I felt more than saw Joe's nod. We waited for ten minutes. Finally, I asked, "Nobody has passed. What do you think is going on?"

"I am not sure. I do know many are afraid to be in this area at night. There is fear a panther will come here looking for easy food. Maybe they returned to their car." There was a shrug in his voice.

"Or, maybe they are waiting for us," Jannet quipped.

"I think it is time to test the Talisman. I am going to go take a look."

"Do you know if you can move with it?" Jannet asked.

I realized I had no idea. We decided to test it. If I moved slowly, Jannet and Joe reported they didn't see much. Then again, there wasn't much light.

I decided to go to the trail without concealment and walk as far as I thought I could before using the Talisman. The others would try to quietly work their way through the brush parallel to the trail.

I, too, tried to be quiet. I thought I was being noiseless when I heard a voice, "Are you sure they came up this trail?"

It was about five feet in front of me. The foot I was placing came down harder than I anticipated due to being startled. I quickly activated the Conceal Talisman. A moment later, a light came on and shone directly in my face.

Then, it panned to my right.

"Why did you turn on the flashlight?" Kelly snarled.

"I heard something." Bryce said. He turned off the light.

"Don't bother," Kelly said. "If they were close, they now know we are here."

The light came back on as a lantern instead of a flashlight. I could see three people. Kelly had a pistol in a holster and Bryce was carrying a rifle. I didn't know much about firearms but I did know these were not air guns. I recognized the third man as the driver of the hotel minibus.

Kelly began a conversation by flourishing her hand, "Since we lost the element of surprise, we might as well go back to the car."

Bryce looked at Kelly and then the driver. He grabbed her elbow, "Come here, I want you to see something." When the driver moved to go with him, Bryce told him to stay put. They walked directly toward me. I slowly moved a few steps to get out of their path. They missed me by a foot as they walked by me and stopped a few paces later.

"I say we skip trying to find them here and go to the village," Bryce said almost too quietly for me to hear. I edged closer along the side of the trail.

"What makes you sure they are there?" Kelly countered.

A bird sounded and Bryce looked searchingly into the forest. My heart began pounding. Shortly, his gaze returned to Kelly. "Look, if they were here, they found another way down. We don't know if the other car was even theirs. What we do know is they were invited to the village. They are probably there now."

"We should have stopped them from leaving Nairobi," Kelly said ruefully. "If we had been able to catch them by surprise at night, we would have been able to kidnap them. I think once we find that miserable pair, it will be easy to persuade them to come with us," she said patting her revolver.

"I actually think we should find a way to keep anyone from talking about this," Bryce said hefting his rifle meaningfully.

"I don't know if we can get away with making an entire village disappear. Being one of many white people in Nairobi was easy. There aren't so many whites out here. Our haste means we didn't do a good job of being discreet. I don't think we can get out of the country without being detained and maybe caught."

"Let's at least make sure the driver doesn't say anything," Bryce offered.

"Deal," Kelly said unsnapping the retention strap of her holster.

They turned to go back down the path to the driver and exclaimed. The driver was no longer there.

Chapter 15

The chorus of early evening insects was supplemented by many expletives as the siblings rushed to the spot where they had left the driver. Bryce aimed his rifle down the trail.

"Wait," Kelly said grabbing him by the shoulder. "Don't be stupid. First, we can't see more than five yards. Second, maybe he went down to wait for us."

"If he left us to spend the night out here, I will make him pay for it," Bryce said fiercely.

"There is another car. He can't drive both of them. Let's go to the trailhead and find out."

"How are we going to find the village if he left? He was going to take us there."

"He told us the head elder's name. We will ask at the hotel or in one of the other villages. People always love helping a ditzy woman," she finished with a hint of a practiced Southern accent.

Bryce snorted, "Are they more likely to help you when you have a gun or less?"

Kelly cackled in reply. They picked up the lantern and hiked back to the trailhead.

I knew I shouldn't follow them. With the Talisman actively draining my energy, I was already beginning to feel like I did after running a few miles on a hot day. When their light dimmed, I turned off the Talisman and began to slowly make my way down the trail. I thought of panthers and hoped there were none looking to get fat off an American.

After a couple of hundred yards, I heard a bird among the trees. I smiled.

Reclaim

It was exactly the same bird call as before from exactly the same distance off the trail. I stepped into the forest. Within two strides, the forms of the Watchers and the other driver materialized out of the dark undergrowth. Wizard sniffed me up and down to make sure I had come to no harm.

"He was stressed when you disappeared. I think he would have followed you if he knew where to find you," Jannet said quietly.

I scratched him under the chin and addressed the group, "Those two are going to take one of the vehicles and try to find Joe's village. I don't think they are going to be very friendly."

Joe looked alarmed at this. "We will need to get to the village first. Good thing I know a short cut."

The other driver groaned at this and said, "His short cuts are always bumpy." He patted the top of his head for emphasis.

"I hope they don't try to disable our car," Jannet said. Then she asked, "Do they have the keys to either vehicle?"

"We leave keys in the ignition. Then, we do not lose them and someone can move the vehicle if needed," Joe explained.

Not wanting to run into the Devlins, we cautiously moved down the trail. We heard a vehicle start and drive away when we were only a short distance from the trailhead. This meant the Devlin Duo had waited at the vehicles after getting to them. Maybe they thought the driver would arrive. Maybe they were waiting for us.

Once we reached the trailhead, we piled into the four-wheeler. There was a quick exchange between the two men in the front seat.

"They have taken the keys," Joe said over his shoulder. "It is not a problem. I can fix it," he said as he reached under the dash, pulled a couple of wires and made a connection. The engine turned over and Joe began to drive, a different direction than we had come.

The other man wasn't kidding about the turbulence of Joe's route. Jannet and I tried to hang on to Wizard and the roll bars as everything in the vehicle was constantly tossed into the air and fell with a thud. I hoped the suspension would hold through this back-country journey.

After forty-five minutes, we bounced onto a much smoother dirt track. Joe took the leveling as an opportunity to increase speed. He alternately hit the brakes for a known dip and the accelerator for flat sections. We saw the fence around the village only moments before we pulled through it.

Joe pulled the parking brake, jumped out of the vehicle, and ran into the hut across the enclosure, leaving the engine running. Jannet and I looked at each other and then at the other driver. He shrugged and climbed out. There was nothing to do but follow. I think Wizard wanted to kiss the ground. I know I did.

The enclosure was lit by a couple of fires in front of the huts and the headlights of the four-wheeler. A group of people began gathering around us. Before we could greet them, five men and Joe came out of the hut yelling directives. The village was instantly a tumult of action. Joe came over to tell us what was happening.

"The village will pack and move tonight. It will take the other white people some time to find this place and it will be empty when they do."

"Are we going with them?" I asked.

"No, we begin our own journey. I have only to grab my belongings." With this, Joe turned and went into one of the huts. He came out with a daypack and a blanket.

"We need to go get the rest of our things," Jannet said to him when he neared.

Joe smiled with a bit of chagrin, "I apologize for making plans for you. Your things are also here."

He signaled to another man and continued, "When I came back to my village this morning to tell them you were coming to visit, news of white people asking about you had reached my father. Because of my vision, we took this as an omen. It was decided that you would be asked to go to the mountain today instead of tomorrow. If you were the ones from the vision, you would find the Talisman. If not, then we would be the cordial but simple natives."

"How did you get the hotel to give you our stuff?" I asked a little irked by the impropriety of the hotel.

"My father went to the hotel and spoke with the manager. The manager is from our village and knows the stories of our people."

An older man approached us through the commotion, walking with a staff. No one cut him off or got in his way. He was an older version of Joe and spoke to his son in a language I did not know. Joe answered and pointed at me.

"My father wonders if you would do him the honor of showing the Talisman to him," Joe said.

I pulled up my sleeve to reveal the armband and talisman. Joe's father reached out and touched the little silver tablet solemnly. Again, he spoke.

"My father says he thought this day would never come. He is sad to see the gift of the god go, but happy that such a worthy person will protect it. He is proud I have been called to help the Chosen protect the gift."

I was a bit overcome by the sentiment. I bowed my head and thanked Joe's father in Swahili. He smiled, looked me in the eyes, and grasped my hands in his. I knew this was a very unusual gesture for his culture and felt truly honored. He disappeared into the melee of people and cattle around us.

Joe led us to the back of the four-wheeler and said, "Here are your bags. Please check and see all your possessions are present." We assured him we didn't need to; he insisted. Jannet and I opened our bags and did a quick inventory.

"Oh, bother," I said.

"What is missing?" Joe asked with great concern.

"My toothbrush," I answered and smiled.

We left the village about the same time the cattle were being driven from the enclosure. It would be risky to have the livestock out at night. It would be riskier for the village to be there when Kelly and Bryce showed up.

We had been driving about twenty minutes when Jannet asked Joe to stop. Actually, she bellowed at him to stop. "We need to come up with a diversion plan for ourselves," she announced when the vehicle noise had decreased enough to allow a conversation to happen.

"What do you suggest?" I asked.

"If you were our unhappy friends, what would you expect once you found an empty village?"

"I would think the people I was chasing were going to get out of the country as fast as possible."

"Exactly. So, let's make them jump on the assumption. How about we book tickets to leave tomorrow?"

"It is an expensive diversion. Are you sure?"

Jannet knew I hated spending money frivolously. "We need to get some breathing room. I'll book two tickets from Kilimanjaro International to South Africa and a hotel in Johannesburg." Jannet had picked an airport about fifty miles away and a city at the bottom of the continent.

"How are you going to get tickets in the middle of the night?" Joe asked a little incredulously.

I smiled, "It's the middle of the night here, but it is the middle of the afternoon where Jannet's travel agent is." Joe nodded, understanding.

I addressed him, "Are we in a safe enough place to make a phone call?" Joe responded by driving about fifty feet off the dirt road. He turned off the lights and killed the engine. Then, he then got out of the car, pulled a large knife from somewhere on his person and stood a little way between us and the road.

We pulled out the satellite phone and called the chipper agent half a world away. Jannet made sure to have the charges placed on her card immediately. She also told the agent Ben would probably call to make reservations for three people in a couple of days. Jannet indicated the connection would seem like we had not gone to South Africa, but to go ahead with his request.

After she hung up, she asked Joe, "Where are we going now?"

Joe explained we were headed to the village of his mother's cousin's aunt. It was a village rarely visited and most of the people there either worked in the village or herded cattle. We would be able to stay off the radar until we were ready to gather the last Watcher. I looked forward to getting more information from Mahrah as soon as I could. I thought about contacting her immediately but was already drained from all I had done and the cross-country travel.

We arrived at the village shortly after midnight. In the light of the crescent moon, I could tell the settlement had a few permanent structures in addition to the waddle-sided huts, those mirroring the construction in Joe's village. I was exhausted and could tell Wizard was too. Jannet looked like I felt. "You look horrible," she announced. I returned the compliment.

We were led to one of the houses with brick walls. They fed us leftovers from their dinner and then we fell into bed. The last thing of which I was aware was a young woman tucking the mosquito netting in around the bed.

I awoke midday thirsty and hungry. When I put my feet on the floor, I felt something wet pass over them. It took me a moment to realize it was Wizard. He was taking liberties with his kisses.

I heard a murmur of voices through the door, which opened to a common living area. There was a table on the left side of the room with a door to the kitchen. The living room furniture was on the right side of the room. Jannet, Joe and a few others were at the table. After introductions, I found out the others were the woman who owned the house, the chief elder of the village, and Joe's extended family member.

I rubbed the sleep from my eyes as I sat down. A bottle of water and cup of chai were placed in front of me. I could smell fresh pineapple and warm bread. A stack of flatbread, called chapati, was on a chipped plate next to a bowl of pineapple. The matron of the house offered me both foodstuffs. I accepted heartily.

"Our hostess apologizes that there is no other food ready with the chapati," Joe said.

The warm chapati was a cross between naan and tortillas. It tasted amazing. "This is wonderful. I am happy to eat it without anything else," I said after I had swallowed a big mouthful. After some time, the village citizens excused themselves, and Joe went with them.

Jannet spoke after she was sure there was no one nearby. "I have told Joe our story. And, I have successfully fulfilled my diplomatic duties. I would say it has been a very productive day."

"And it isn't even dinner yet. Bravo."

Jannet did a chair curtsey and then said, "What do you think about talking with Mahrah? It is going to be hard to book tickets if we don't know where we are going."

"My thought exactly."

I wandered outside and found a nice spot in the shade of one of the large banyan trees. Mahrah was waiting for me.

"All is well?"

"As well as can be. We avoided being seen by the two following us. I think Joe's village is safe from them and we are in another village far away. Also, we sent them on a trip to the other side of the continent."

"They are far enough to let you finish gathering the Watchers?"

"That depends. If we have to go south, we put them exactly where we need to go," I felt a flare of frustration. "Where do we need to go? It isn't exactly easy to get from one part of the world to another. If we need visas, it could take a month before we can get into a country."

"I can now speak freely about the location of the last Watcher. The one who opposes me here has been neutralized."

"You killed him?" I asked with some apprehension.

Mahrah answered emphatically and with a bit of a roar. *"No. It is unforgivable for one of my kind to kill another."* She continued in a more even tone. *"He has been placed in a living situation where he is comfortable and cannot communicate with your kind."*

"Do you know which of my kind he has contacted or what he said?"

"He," here she sent an image of the black dragon, *"will not give information. I can only tell you what I suspect."*

"Will you tell me everything or just part of it?" I asked a bit peevishly.

"I will tell you all I suspect. Again, the lack of information was to keep you safe and not meant to cause harm."

I sensed she was hurt that I had not let this go. I guessed dragons forgave each other on the first apology.

"I believe what happened was the Talisman and some information about it was found, perhaps in a document or ancient story. There were enough details to bring the Kinetic Talisman out of dormancy but not fully activate it. The black dragon noticed this before any other of my kind and traced the energy trail back to the Bearer. That is when the conversation between them began."

"The black dragon told this person how to use the Kinetic Talisman? Do you think he gave information about the Watchers or anything else?"

"I do know he did not reveal the secrets of Watchers, but he did reveal the idea of them."

"How do you know he didn't give all the information?"

"Because only two dragons alive know how to create the protective Watchers. He is not one of them."

That was a bit of good news. "I believe the Kinetic Talisman was used a couple days ago to cause an accident. Many people were hurt and some died."

Remorse radiated from Mahrah. I felt a keen loss in my own being. I could not tell if it was from her, me, or both.

"I knew the Talisman had been used; just not to what end. It was a greater use of energy than before. I feel responsible for the loss of life of some of your kind."

"How about the three Watchers and I go find this person and get the Talisman?" I reasoned we had could easily trace the Devlin Duo.

"It is an impatient plan. The protection from the four Watchers will be more capable. If you activate the bands now, the fourth will never be able to join. The fourth Watcher brings talents that none of the other three have."

"Which brings me back to the problem of needing to know our next destination."

"The last Watcher is waiting where it all began; at the place where we returned to your world."

I thought back over Mahrah's memory of the gateway. During the time Mahrah searched for the Amulet Bearer, she had also been busy there. Mahrah wanted to create a way to sustain the energy needed for the gateway. After convincing the settlements near there she meant them peace, she worked with them to shape a monument. I slapped my hand to my head. The suddenness of it startled Wizard. He jumped to his feet and looked around.

"Stonehenge," I cried out. "You helped put the stones up in the circle to stabilize the gateway." I sent an image of the monument.

"Truth. There are more stones there now. Your kind and I had only put one circle of large stones."

"If I remember, there are a lot of burials in the area. Was that because of you?"

"They had already begun to create places for their dead near the gateway. We believed there were some of your kind who sensed the connection between the two worlds. They considered the place sacred. My kind appearing as if from nowhere convinced them it was magical."

"Did they treat you as magical?"

"At first, yes. When we lived longer than they did, it strengthened their

belief. We grew careless after a while and they saw we ate as they did, so they began to question. We left before they realized we were mortal."

Another question came to mind. "You said you measure time differently than humans do. Does that mean your life spans are very different from ours?

"How many trips does your world make around its sun for most humans?"

"The average is about seventy-five; some people will live for one hundred years."

"One hundred years," Mahrah repeated slowly. *"From the day we hatch to our last breath, most of us would make ten thousand trips around the sun on your planet."*

"Which gives 'living a full life' an entirely new meaning. I can't imagine the retirement plan." I regretted making a joke when I sensed Mahrah's confusion tinged with frustration.

"I will give Jannet the information so we can figure out how to get the four of us to England," I said.

"I hope you are able to travel quickly. Let me know when you are able to leave."

We used the satellite phone to call Ben's office. Jannet's face lit up when she heard his voice. She missed him. Another wave of regret swept over me as I realized the impact her decision was having on her and Ben. I cared about them both.

After arrangements had been made, the Watchers and I walked back out under the banyan tree. In the fields, insects chirped, animals bellowed, and birds sang. It was a hot day. The intermittent breeze brought scents of cooking fires, cattle, and the hanging wash. We sat on a few rough wood chairs, placed in the shade under the tree.

"Jannet," Joe began, "Since we are to protect and fight together, we should know each other's skills."

"What would you like to know?" Jannet asked. Anybody who didn't know her would have thought her reply to be blasé. But, I saw her hands grip the water bottle she held a little tighter.

"I do not mean to disrespect the decisions of the Chosen. I just am not sure what you can do if someone tries to take the Talisman from us."

Jannet shot me a glance. I hid a smirk by reaching down and picking some dog hair off my pants. I had an inkling of what was coming.

"What do you propose we do to find out?" she asked in the same even tone she had before.

"Let us test each other a bit. I believe it is called sparring," Joe replied.

Jannet stood, kicked off her sandals, and put her hair quickly in a ponytail. She and Joe faced each other. Joe was tall, dark, and lean. Any casual observer would have thought Jannet had made the wrong decision.

"I will attack, but I will be careful not to hurt you," he said. It was exactly the wrong thing to say to Jannet.

"We don't have sparring equipment so how about you try to hit me and I will show you that you can't." Jannet's voice contained the same challenge her words did.

Joe's eyes narrowed. He gave Jannet an assessing look.

Joe's feet shifted ever so slightly. He swung with one fist. At the last moment, he switched and swung with his other fist. By the time his fist reached where Jannet was, she wasn't there anymore. Joe then tried a combination of fist and foot. Jannet defended both easily.

I could tell the moment Joe decided to put more into his efforts by the set in his jaw. Jannet either dodged or blocked every move he had. A few of the children gathered around to watch. Joe's attempts came faster and with more force. He finally charged Jannet and found himself sprawled out in the dirt for his efforts.

Joe got up, dusted himself off, and said something to the children. They all left hurriedly. Most scattered to homes in the village; one went into the house in which we were staying. A few moments later, he came back with a spear. This was getting serious and I was going to say something; Jannet stopped me with a look.

"You are good at hand-to-hand fighting, Jannet," Joe said tossing the spear from hand to hand. "Can you defend yourself against weapons?"

"I noticed you didn't have a spear brought out for me, which is hardly fair," Jannet said coolly.

Joe looked grim, "Fights are rarely fair. We can stop now if you wish."

"I am fine on my own. I just wanted to make sure you would be okay if our sparring created a bruise or two. I don't feel like dodging the end of a weapon all day just to show you I can."

Joe nodded agreement and took a stance to use the spear. Jannet changed her foot position once she noted Joe's position. Joe attacked. Jannet dodged the blade and grabbed the shaft. Instead of pulling, she pushed. Joe hadn't expected the motion and stumbled. A maneuver later, Jannet had the tip of the spear pointed at Joe's chest. He smiled his gapped-tooth smile and clapped his hands. In reply, Jannet gave the spear back to Joe and began to bow.

I was horrified as I watched Joe once again move to use the spear offensively. I wanted to call out a warning; the only thing that came out was a strangled 'ah'. I didn't see exactly what happened because the next moves stirred up quite a bit of dust. When it settled some, Joe was on his back.

Jannet was seated on top of him pinning his arms and the spear across his throat. Joe had a shocked look. Jannet's blue eyes had gone cold with fury.

"Don't you ever try that again," she said icily. Then, she hurled the spear to the side, got up, slid her sandals on, and stalked off toward the edge of the village. She didn't look at me once. Joe began to go after her.

"I wouldn't," I said. "She is quite angry. It is better to let her cool off."

"What did I do wrong? We were testing each other."

"When she bowed, she was telling you she was finished and she respected your skills."

"What if she does so when we are attacked by others?"

"Joe, she won't. She knows the difference between sparring and fighting."

Joe went and picked up the discarded spear. He stood in front of me and leaned on it. "I have learned she is very skilled," he said with awe.

"I hope you have learned something else," I said. When he looked at me inquiringly I added, "Never mess with a diplomat's daughter."

Chapter 16

I had never seen Jannet so angry. Part of me wanted to go and help her calm down. Most of me knew it would only create more difficulties. I thought about calling to her through the ring; I realized doing so would just be another form of going after her. It would not help her fury dissolve.

With Jannet away cooling off and Joe announcing he suddenly needed to attend to some village matter, I unexpectedly found myself alone with some time on my hands. Where Jannet had extra amenities in her luggage, I had a few books. I retrieved one which had information of Late Bronze Age settlements in Asia Minor. I had pinpointed the part of the world in which my ancestor, the warrior woman, had lived. I scoured the reports and footnotes for any mention of dragons in the artifacts of settlements from between the Black Sea and the Caspian Sea. There wasn't a single mention of large scaly beasts, winged or not.

I tried a different tactic. I focused on graves of women who were also buried with weapons, now there was too much information. In the last several decades, archaeologists discovered burials of women with extensive funerary goods. Among the goods were swords, bows, axes, and knives. Though interesting, it didn't help much.

The report which drew my attention was one of three women's tombs. Their graves were distinct but close to each other. Where almost all the other tombs had many gold-plated or gold items, these three had virtually nothing more than weapons like the ones I had seen in Mahrah's memory. I conjectured the lack of wealth meant a hasty burial for them, and wondered why.

The summary of the excavation report indicated the site had been discovered in the 1940s. As I was near the end of the report, I felt a mental nudge. When I paid attention to it, I found it was Jannet instead of Mahrah. She wanted me to join her.

She stood with her back to me and her arms wrapped around her as I approached. I could tell when she knew I was close because she stiffened a little. Never having to navigate this particular emotional journey in our friendship, I was unsure what to do. I chose to stand next to her and look at the cattle grazing in the distance.

"I lost my composure," she said with self-recrimination. "I haven't since I was a girl and I am so embarrassed."

"Joe knows he blew it. He won't do it again. I believe he really didn't know how offensive his actions were."

"That helps a little bit. Still, I am frustrated I lost it. My parents would be so disappointed."

"Jannet, he attacked you when you were bowing. This isn't about speaking a harsh word to someone who spills a drink on you at a party. Besides, I would rather you lose your composure like that if we have a group of thugs intent on taking us out, even if your parents wouldn't approve."

Jannet smiled wanly and wiped her eyes. She took a steadying breath and then turned to me. "And, when will you embrace your inner warrior?"

I was taken aback. "I don't think I have one."

Jannet smirked. "You haven't seen yourself when you feel a wrong has been done to others. There is a reason I stand behind you when someone makes rude comments. You get fire in your eyes."

"I could ask Mahrah if it could be transferred to a stream of fire."

We laughed and hugged at the same time. Jannet's good humor fully returned as we walked back through the village.

Joe was uncomfortable around Jannet at dinner. Finally, they stepped outside to talk. When they returned, Joe had rebounded and was his jovial self. I envied and admired Jannet her ability to smooth things over with people.

After dinner, Joe asked if we wanted to go for a walk. We talked about life in this part of the world until we were sure we were out of earshot. We had agreed we would tell his village we were American tourists who had a conflict with other tourists. It was a story which would hold until we had left.

"Jannet tells me you are an archaeologist," Joe began, steering the topic of conversation. "I am," I admitted not knowing if that was a strike for or against me in Joe's eyes.

"Do you take the things you dig up?"

"No, I don't. I believe anything I find belongs to the people of that country. I try to work with the nationals of every country I go to when looking for sites and artifacts."

"I see." He took a few steps before continuing. "What if the country is unstable?"

I noticed Jannet had dropped back a step or two to let us talk. Wizard was nearby, poking around in the brush. "If it is unstable, it is best to leave the past where it is until it can be appreciated by its people."

Joe nodded satisfactorily at my answer. "The Talisman is important to my people. You were allowed to take it only because you were foretold and possessed the power to call the Talisman from where it was hidden."

"I am honored your people have trusted me with the responsibility of it."

"What do you plan to do with it?"

I could tell my answer to this was going to make our break my trust with him. I weighed my options of what to say as we walked a bit. I realized the only option was to be honest.

"Joe, I don't exactly know. Mahrah wants me to collect the Talismans. Her goal is to make sure they are not used to harm or destroy. I think she gave up on humans using them for good. I would like to show her they can be used to accomplish the purposes for which they designed. But, I don't know if it will happen. It is up to her. Sadly, I also think it means your people have given up their Talisman."

"In our stories, we tell of how the Talisman came to us. We have a song of how it was to help our warriors hunt without being killed by the lion, cheetah, and boar. There is another story that is only told among the holy people. It tells how the Talisman was used for evil and how the one who gave it to us asked us to cast it into the earth. I think it is good that it is away from my people."

The sky was dark enough for a few stars to be seen. Joe had led us in a large circle, and the village was now in front of us. "I wondered why you, a white woman who does not know my people, was picked. I wanted the vision to be wrong. I believed it should have been a man." His words indicated he was wrestling with his expectations and tradition. "I think I have much to learn about you and what makes you the best protector. I will abide by the dragon's decision."

"It is a privilege to have you join as a Watcher," I replied. "I hope I do not disappoint you as the protector of your people's gift."

***

Where Kenya's weather was like a warm, but overwhelming hug, the air in England had a cool detachment. I welcomed the change. However, Joe lamented on the chilly climate. Even though he had brought a blanket with him, he bought a coat before we left London.

Instead of staying in the town closest to Stonehenge, we picked a small town about ten miles away from the monument and not far from a forest.

It was with some trepidation Jannet and I let Joe drive the rental car, but he had experience driving British style. Jannet and I agreed his reactions to an emergency would keep us safer than our own.

The sun lit the light-colored stones of Stonehenge, contrasting it against the green fields. Clouds lined the horizon; it looked as if rain was at least several hours away. Joe was still somewhat sullen at the temperature, but became more animated when he saw the monolithic stones.

The rings of stone rising from the surrounding flat landscape were captivating. The upright stones jutted up over two stories. No one had come up with a universally satisfactory answer to how the stones got from their origin in Wales to a place seemingly in the middle of nowhere. I wondered if my explanation of dragon power would be any more acceptable.

We followed the public walkway around the outside of the stones. At the path's closest point, we were twenty feet away from the titanic markers. I wanted to ask Mahrah about why lintels had been placed between the uprights, but thought I should focus more on the people around me.

Joe, who spent most of his time looking up, wondered aloud about why there were so many stones. I told about the archaeological sites in the area: Stonehenge, the great earth works kilometers long, and the burials. As I began to speak about Woodhenge to the northeast, I stopped mid-sentence.

"What's wrong?" Jannet asked, following my gaze northeast.

"I just made a connection. Mahrah said the dragons went to the northeast to discuss after they first arrived. I wonder if it is why Woodhenge was built."

"It is as good as a theory as any, given what you are saying about the mystery around these structures," she replied.

We finished our circuit around the circle of stones that marked the gateway to another world. The others looked at me for direction. I had not seen even the slightest inclination that anyone wanted to speak with us beyond expressing their wonder at the construction of something so massive. Everyone else we saw was there to see the ancient stones and came away a little sobered by the fact ancient people were not the simpletons they had been portrayed as.

"Should we wait or come back later?" Joe asked.

"Mahrah said the Watcher was here and waiting." I had connected with her before leaving the hotel that morning. She was practically giddy with relief.

We circled once again with the same result. I thought about contacting Mahrah as we walked back to the carpark. I was climbing into the car when Joe, who had walked to the front, said, "We have been followed."

Jannet, Wizard, and I quickly joined Joe. The lot had a greenway with trees separating the two rows of parked cars. So not to draw attention to myself, I acted like Wizard needed to hang out on the grass. "Who? Where are they?" I asked quietly. Jannet had pulled out her collapsed bo staff.

"Not who, what," Joe replied. He lightly nodded to the tree at the end of the greenway. In one of the lower branches sat a beautiful bird of prey - the body was a mottled gray and white; the legs, beak, and eyes were an intense yellow; its throat and breast were beige; and the head was gray with the color coming down in streaks on either side its face past its eyes. It stared at us intensely, then called 'kak-kak'.

I remembered the bird type after a few seconds. "The Peregrine Falcon is following us?"

"It was in these trees when we arrived and then flew to the tops of some of the stones inside the circle. Did you not see it?" Joe asked.

"I was busy looking for a person. Do you think. . .?" I trailed off.

"Let's get in the car," Jannet said briskly.

We looked at her a bit stupefied.

"If the bird is following us, it will follow the car. I want to get away from here just in case," she stopped and looked around, "our diversion didn't work as well as we thought and there are people here looking for us."

Joe began to drive down the road, slowly. His speed was much slower than the traffic.

"What are you doing?" I asked.

"I want to make sure the bird can follow us."

"Joe, it's a Peregrine Falcon. It easily flies over fifty miles per hour." Joe looked at me blankly. I did a quick calculation, "Eighty kilometers per hour."

Joe made an 'oh' noise, looked at the speedometer, and accelerated to the speed limit. Jannet's commentary came from the back seat. "Its following us. Hold on, it's gone. It's back. The bird is swinging back and forth across the road."

"Probably because we are going so slow," I opined. "Did you know those birds can dive at up to two hundred miles per hour?"

Joe whistled. "They are faster than cheetahs," he exclaimed.

"They are faster than anything," I added.

There was a small town a few miles from Stonehenge. We pulled in and found a spot we believed a bit out of the way. Except, it was hard to find an out-of-the-way spot in a small town. People came into their front yards to watch the odd-looking and crazy tourists look at a bird in the tree.

Finally, I pulled out the map the agent at the rental car agency had given us. I could have used a phone, but we had decided to use our phones as little as possible in case financial transactions were not the only thing the Devlin Duo could trace.

"I think we need to go to the woods outside of Wilton. It seems the only place we can get a little privacy."

Chapter 17

On the twenty-minute drive to the woods, Jannet kept us up to date on the bird's movements. At one point, it flew alongside us and looked in the passenger window. I admired its ability to maneuver while observing us and its surroundings.

Once we reached a town north of Wilton, we turned off the main road. A smaller road took us across the river, through a field of heather, and into the woods. Joe found a wide spot in the road and pulled over.

While we were traveling, I talked to Mahrah. After our greetings, I got to the point. "Our last Watcher is a bird?" I asked almost accusingly.

"You have found her."

"A bird?" I asked incredulously. "I was expecting another human."

"She is a queen among birds. She has abilities that no other has," Mahrah said with some pride.

I agreed with her assessment and had objections. "She will be difficult to travel with. The planes are not meant for animals. And, I am not sure I can even get permission to take her out of the country. Humans are picky about other beings with them in small places."

"I have been pondering the possibility since you showed me the tubes in which you travel. I have a solution to the problem of planes. We can discuss the matter later."

"What about communication? Does she understand language?"

"You will speak in images. She and I have been able to connect since she often sits on the stones of the gateway. She is willing to become a Watcher."

I was a little jealous the falcon also communicated with Mahrah. It made me feel less special. In my mind, the word 'chosen' had taken on the meaning of unique. The fact that a bird was also connected to the dragon made me feel more like a pawn.

There was no more time to discuss the matter. Joe turned off the car and we all piled out. The falcon came out of the tree and perched on a nearby post. Joe and Jannet looked at the bird and then looked at me. I walked over to her. She spread her wings, but she did not take flight. I noticed she was standing on one leg. When I looked closer, I saw that she had something bright grasped in the other talon. It was a familiar shape, smaller than the others. I had no idea how she came to have it. Without thinking, I reached toward the clenched talon and the falcon let a silver band with a dragon signet fall into my hand. I turned and showed the ring to Joe and Jannet.

"Now what?" Jannet asked, as they both joined me next to the falcon.

"Let me find out," I replied. Then, I addressed Mahrah, "She has a ring like the others. The Watchers are assembled. What do we do next?"

"The Watchers must put on their bands at the same time." Her tone had that underlying edge you get from people when they think you are being stupid.

"That seems easy enough for the humans. What about Wizard and the bird?"

"What is her name?" Mahrah asked unexpectedly.

"Sorry? What was that?"

"What name should she have? All your other Watchers have names." Now Mahrah was becoming a stickler about names.

"Usually names are chosen by the individual. I am not sure I should choose her name," I replied.

"She does not know words. I think a name which reflects the exalted bird she is would be appropriate."

I dug into my memory of things I had read about birds. A word came to mind.

"Iolani," I announced. "It captures her wildness and her distinction among those that fly."

"Iolani's band must be put on her leg at the same time the others put on theirs."

With my outside voice I said, "Mahrah wants you to get ready to put on the bands."

Internally, I asked, "How will Wizard wear his?"

"It will slip over one of his fangs and then adjust so it will not come off."

"How can I put both the animals' on them at the same time?"

"You may need assistance from one of the other humans." She added, *"Joe or Jannet."*

For sentimental reasons, I wanted to put Wizard's on him. Jannet wasn't about to get close to Iolani's talons so Joe volunteered. We decided to count to three. There was a discussion about whether that meant the bands were donned on the number three or right after the number three; I was reminded of a comedy sketch.

When all four bands went on, I heard the same low hum I had heard with the Talisman. Accompanying this was the sense of walking into a room with a party. Only, this room was in my head. There were combinations of images, words, and feelings that jumbled over each other. I could tell something similar was happening to Joe and Jannet because of the uncertain look in their eyes. Wizard was cocking his head to one side and then the other. Iolani also cocked her head and adjusted her wings.

The initial confusing thoughts started to become chaotic. A familiar alto voice intervened, *"Calm."*

All our thoughts settled. Mahrah introduced herself to each Watcher either by word or images. Wizard and Iolani had already interacted with Mahrah so it wasn't a shock. Joe and Jannet were awestruck. It was one thing to know I communicated with Mahrah, but an entirely different thing to have her communicating with them.

Mahrah went through the formalities of having them accept being a Watcher. Then, she began to train them on creating a connection among themselves. As near as I could tell, their connection was creating some sort of field of energy. I was about to ask about it when Mahrah announced the four Watchers needed to move to a larger open space to continue working. She gave them a task.

Iolani took wing and came back within two minutes. She projected the image of a nearby clearing. Joe was able to take the visual clues she offered to direct us where to go. At least, I thought it was going to be us. Mahrah stopped me as I began to walk.

"Chosen, you will stay here."

I took affront, "I can't be without Wizard." What also stung was the perception of being left out.

"I will watch over you."

My bruised ego recovered a little. "I don't think you can get me the help I need if anything were to happen."

"The chances are small, and I can call the Watchers."

I conceded and found a place on the grass to sit. I still felt the sting of rejection when the four Watchers went down the lane and then turned into the forest. It helped that Wizard kept looking over his shoulder at me.

This endeavor was going to be quite a transition for Wizard and I. We had been in the world as partners for years. He was devoted to me, and I loved him deeply. I wondered what would happen to that connection when he began to interact more with the other Watchers. Since Joe was more upbeat, would Wizard start to prefer his company? Some of this thinking must have slipped out to Mahrah.

"I sense Wizard will always look to you first. Your bond is strong. It will stand. The bond among the Watchers is needed for the protection of you and the Talismans."

"Is that why you sent them away?"

"My intent was two-fold. First, it is safer for you to be away until they can manage the energy. Second, they need to begin to learn to trust each other's strengths and learn each other's weaknesses."

I blurted a mental question, "Do you trust me?"

"I do."

"But, you do not know me."

Mahrah rumbled in cogitation. *"Truth. There are things I know about you but am unacquainted with your whole being."*

"Aren't you curious?"

"I would like to know more about you."

"Then, why haven't you asked?"

Mahrah radiated indignation. *"It is extremely rude to ask another about their life. One must be invited."*

I could hardly believe my mistake, forgetting one of the basic tenets of dealing with other cultures. I had spent time pumping Mahrah for information that would satisfy my curiosity without considering if it was an acceptable form of interaction. Thinking over our conversations, I could not remember a time she had asked a question. I chastised myself for not noticing.

"I am sorry," I said with embarrassment. "I should know better than to have made assumptions about your culture. I have been diverted by all the events so I jumped to conclusions. It seems I have a lot to learn."

"We both have a lot to learn," Mahrah said in a conciliatory manner.

A silence fell between us.

"Would you really like to know more about me?" I asked hesitantly.

"I would. I know only facts about your heritage, a few about your past, and your energy make-up. I would like to know more about the being you are."

The former feelings of being a pawn turned into a flicker of paranoia, crowding out the delight of making a connection, "Why do you want to know?"

"Why do any beings get to know other beings beyond necessity? I would like to know more about you because I am intrigued and," she paused for a moment, *"I like you."*

I could tell Mahrah was being vulnerable and wondered how unusual this was for dragons. To me, the conversation felt like the first time someone asked me to be their friend in school. Only, now I was more mature and knew I had a choice to embrace the vulnerability or to turn from it; I chose to embrace it.

"I am so glad. I too am intrigued and like you." I hoped this was an appropriate reply.

Mahrah radiated a deep happiness.

"My kind often begins with an introduction that includes our name. I believe it is a way to say we are unique from all other beings that look like us."

"I am learning names are as important to your kind as images of self are to mine."

"Let me introduce myself, I am Nadia Kokinidis."

Mahrah was a little confused. *"Chosen, I know your name."*

"Yet, you don't use it."

"There are many Nadias. There is only one Chosen. It is the name of a unique being."

I realized that Mahrah called me what she did because she saw me as unique. I sat a little taller.

"What would you like to know about me?"

"What is it like to be human? You have only two legs and no wings. You are much smaller in size. How does your shape feel as you move through the world?"

"Didn't you ask the one before me, the first person you chose for the Amulet?"

"We did not speak of such things. I wish we had."

I portrayed what it felt like to take a run, to hike, to swim. I sent images of standing before insurmountable cliffs and of climbing into small places between rocks. I shared memories of climbing trees as a child and hiding in cardboard boxes. After I shared, I waited. Humans are used to judgment from others. Did dragons do the same thing?

"It is a very different way to be in the world," Mahrah said thoughtfully. *"The world is more formidable to you than it is to my kind. The world is also more detailed for you. I wish I could climb into tiny spaces and observe the small things around me."*

"Can't you see those things? I thought your vision allowed you a wider range of light than mine does." After I spoke, I wasn't sure how I had come to that conclusion. Maybe it was something from the memories Mahrah sent or just an intuitive conclusion.

"Yes, small places can be seen. What is different is you can experience them physically where I cannot. I have not been your size since the very first of my life." She paused. *"May I ask another question of your experience?"*

"Mahrah, in my culture it is perfectly okay to ask about a person. I hope it will not be an affront for me to give you permission to ask questions." I realized I had better include the caveat, "But, we also reserve the right to not answer a question."

"For my kind, if a question is asked, it must be answered," Marah said with understanding. She continued, *"What is it like to have a covering that is so easily damaged by the world around you?"*

"My skin?" Mahrah confirmed. I looked down at my arms and thought for a few moments. "I guess it has its good points and its drawbacks. You are right, I can be injured easily. But, I wouldn't go without the sense of touch."

I delved into my memories. As I called them up, I shared them with Mahrah. There was the time I sat close to the fire and warmed my chilled hands. I recalled waking up in the morning and feeling the warmth and weight of the blankets. There were lots of memories of petting Wizard and the wind in my hair. I threw in feeling different fabrics as I walked through stores. I was focused on revealing as many different tactile experiences as I could. I pushed out the memory of being held by a lover before I knew what I was doing. I discontinued it as soon as I realized what I had done.

"Sorry," I murmured with disquiet and sadness.

"It is part of being human. I found it appropriate. I do not understand why you are feeling the things you are as a result of sharing. Have I offended?"

"Not really. I mean, no." I was being brought up against my upbringing and something I had not thought about for a while. I took a deep breath. What was it I had said at the beginning of this venture? I didn't want to reveal all to a dragon. Now, I was going to and I was glad for the opportunity.

"First, there are many of my kind who are not comfortable with our reproductive lives." I sensed confusion from Mahrah. "I know. It doesn't make sense. It is part of many of the cultures in this world. It is not rational, yet we persist in being ill at ease."

"We can speak of other things if you find it uncomfortable. I would be considered ill-mannered if I were to expect you to continue when you are uneasy."

"My culture is not where my hesitancy comes from. It brings up memories of when I had a person in my life with whom I wanted to be intimate." I wasn't sure how to explain the next part to Mahrah. She beat me to it.

"However, you were not compatible for reproduction. The type of bond you mention is not confined to your kind. I do not judge a relationship based on whether it will be successful for the survival of the species."

I was still embarrassed. Additionally, I had opened a memory I had tried to ignore for a couple of years. I could feel tears welling up. My emotions started to churn.

"Chosen," Mahrah said with gentleness. The one word calmed me. I took a deeper breath. The hurt from the broken relationship was still present but recalling it with Mahrah changed something. I had lived the last two years feeling like I was unfit for an intimate relationship. Sharing it with a being not of my kind in a world not of my own paradoxically helped me begin to realize how much I had to offer someone.

"Thank you," I said sincerely.

I shared enough of my thoughts and feelings so Mahrah knew why I had thanked her.

"Your kind normally says, 'You are welcome' at this juncture. I hope it is an appropriate response here."

I chuckled, "It is."

"Thank you for allowing me to begin to know the being that you are."

"It is an honor," I said sincerely. Then I added, "May I ask a question?"

"I think you and I will start a new culture. Questions are allowed without being rude."

I smiled. "I want to make sure to honor what both of us bring to this culture. Otherwise, you are just adapting and we are not creating anything. How about including we must answer any question asked?"

A rumble of agreement. *"What is your question?"*

"What is it like to be you?"

"I have given you memories of dragons so you know what it feels like to move through the world on wing and foot."

"I appreciate all you have shared. However, those came from other dragons. I would like to know what you have liked and disliked about your own life."

Mahrah was contemplating when we both received some insistent nudges.

"The Watchers are returning. I will answer your question another time."

Jannet, Joe and Wizard stepped back on to the pathway. Wizard started trotting toward me. The two humans were grinning and waving. Iolani alit in the tree next to me. I was happy to see them, but also sad for my conversation with Mahrah to end.

Chapter 18

We ate dinner at a pub on Silver Street, a name I smiled at as I thought of the Talismans. The clouds which had been around the horizon in the morning had come overhead and let the rain fall. We sat inside to stay out of the wet. Iolani, once realizing we were going to leave her outside, fluffed her feathers and then went in search of her own meal. The establishment was packed so Joe, Jannet, and I crowded around a small table meant for two. Wizard found a way to squeeze in to the corner behind the table.

We all ordered ale. For dinner, Joe ordered fish and chips, Jannet chose lamb with potatoes, and I had a steak pie. I imagined each of us were probably reflecting on the events of the day, even though I could not hear the others' thoughts. Mahrah had told us she thought it better to turn the connection off when we were around other people until we learned the nuances of communicating and using the energy between the rings and the bracelet.

The food came and we told the server we were fine for the rest of the meal.

"What do you think we will be doing over the next several days?" Jannet asked after sampling her dish.

"If it is like the work I had to do, she will have a set of exercises which will help you hone your ability to use the energy field. Do you know exactly what the energy field does?"

"I believe it will keep the powers of the Talismans from hurting us or being used against us," Joe theorized. "Jannet said there is an Amulet created to combine the powers and the person had Watchers to protect her. I think we have the same ability."

"But, I don't have the Amulet," I replied.

"Maybe the Amulet isn't what protects the Watchers from the Talismans. Maybe it is the Chosen," Jannet said giving me a studied look.

Joe changed the subject slightly, "Why were you not with us when we worked this afternoon?"

"Mahrah said it would be safer for you to practice away from me until you learned how to manipulate the power of the bands."

"Maybe we will accidentally knock you on your butt?" Joe replied and laughed at the visual. Then, he sobered at the thought of impropriety, "I apologize."

"No worries," I replied laughing. "I will be doing more of my own exercises until I know I am safe from a power surge. Also, I believe Mahrah thinks the other Talismans are buried."

Jannet reached out and put her hand on my forearm, "Why don't you make sure you are a safe distance but not out of sight. I worry when you expend all that energy; Wizard does too."

I looked over my shoulder at him. His eyes were bright because I had been feeding him pieces of steak out of my pie. I reached my hand down and he nuzzled it. I wasn't deceived; he thought I had more steak. "How do you know?"

"Part of what we did today was to connect our thoughts. I could sense his reticence to leave you behind. He was also a bit distracted during the exercise Mahrah gave us."

Joe perked up, "Maybe that is why Iolani pecked him?"

"It was a light peck," Jannet said hurriedly when she saw my shocked response.

"I am all for the bird being part of the pack. But, if she hurts him, there will be words," I said protectively.

"Chosen, um, Nadia, I am not sure she understands words," Joe said.

I shook my head in resignation. I knew I was going to have to explain idioms to Mahrah. It seemed I needed to explain them to Joe also. Joe disabused me of that notion immediately with his large gap-toothed smile, indicating he was joking.

There was a small commotion at the doorway. Two drunk patrons were remarking about the falcon in the tree. I heard one bellow he wanted it as a trophy. The other decided they could knock the bird out with a rock. I had no doubt which bird they were talking about. I was torn between a desire to keep a low profile and a desire to keep the men from hurting her.

I hoped I could open a connection to Iolani without the influx of all the minds. I focused on her and found I was able to zero in on her mental processes.

Before I could warn her, she mentally conveyed to me how agitated she was. She wanted to be out of the rain also. Ignoring her complaint, I let her know about the plans of the two men at the door. One had just picked up a sizable stone from the pathway. I watched with my mind's eye as Iolani took off, circled around the tree, came up behind the man with the stone, and dropped a dollop on his shoulder. She banked out of view before I heard his vulgar response coming back through the door.

Joe and Jannet heard the expletive and looked at me quizzically. "She took care of it," I said a little abashed, "I think one of her abilities is to be raw." It was the only word I could come up with which fit. Jannet looked at the door with understanding and chuckled. When Joe figured it out, he slapped the table with laughter. Other people in the pub turned to look at us. So much for the low profile. Then again, I should have known better. It is hard for two white women, one tall black man, and a large dog to go unnoticed in a small countryside English town.

We walked back to our inn through the drizzle. Joe and Jannet chatted about places they had both visited in England. The feelings of being a third-wheel were beginning to surface again and I unintentionally slowed. I was thinking about the responsibility I had taken on when I felt an arm slip into my own on either side. When I looked from one person to the next, I could tell I had been asked a question and hadn't responded.

"I think that is a definite 'yes'," Jannet said.

I was wary. "Yes, to what?"

"Joe was saying he wasn't very tired and maybe we could all grab a drink of choice and spend an hour or two relaxing."

"I think we need a little privacy and the rooms are a bit small for all of us," I replied.

"I bet I could arrange that," Jannet said. "The inn has a sitting room I think we could occupy for the evening."

"What about Iolani?"

"The room has a large window and no screen. As long as she kept her voice down and behaved herself," here Jannet eyed the falcon who was hopping from tree to tree, "we would be able to have her in the room with us."

"There is a chair with a narrow back. I can put my coat on it for her to grip," Joe added helpfully.

I looked back and forth between them. "When did you have time to tour the inn?"

"While you were busy trying to figure out the building sequence from the foundation," Jannet replied. "You were at it for about fifteen minutes."

"I just had a quick look around," I said defensively. Then, I cracked a smile. Fifteen minutes was on the low end of the amount of time I could take poking around.

Jannet arranged for the exclusive use of the sitting room with the Front Desk. At the same time, Joe and I went into the room down the hall which served as the pub and restaurant. Joe ordered a pint of the local stout. I bought a bottle of French Syrah for Jannet and I to share.

We entered the sitting room and shut the door. The preponderance of furniture made the room feel somewhere between cozy and claustrophobic. In addition to three chairs with curved backs, called corner chairs, there were three brown leather loveseats. Two of them sat on either side of the small door. A diminutive desk had its own chair. Next to it was a large brown leather chair and matching ottoman. Another leather chair occupied the last corner of the room. A quick look around revealed two more ottomans which could be used for low chairs. This truly was a sitting room.

Joe took off his coat and threw it over the desk chair while I opened the window behind one of the loveseats. Pulling back the curtain, I checked to see if anybody was around. It was clear so I imitated Iolani's call as best I could. She glided in and alit on her prepared perch.

Jannet had seen to filling our wine glasses and had them sitting on the round table in the middle of the room. It was with some horror I saw the five-point deer antler displayed in the center of the table. I hoped the animal had not suffered and our two animal Watchers were not offended.

There was warmth coming through the fireplace cover. Wizard laid down about four feet from it on the ornate, red and white, Persian rug. I made a mental note to check for fur before we left.

Jannet, Joe and I ambled around the room as best we could before settling down. In addition to all the other items, there were two suits of armor about four feet high. I mused about the existence of elves in response to seeing them. An antique record player from the early twentieth-century stood on top of yet another piece of furniture in the room. A nearby cabinet held vinyl records and board games.

I noticed all the drawings on the walls were of buildings whereas the drawings in the rest of the inn were all of people. It was a bit hard to see the details with the chandelier and small lamps providing the light. From what I could tell, most of the pictures were of manor houses. There were a couple of sketches of cathedrals in the area. Surprisingly, one was of the great library in Wales.

I chose the loveseat by the window and closest to Iolani. Jannet settled into the loveseat on the other side of the door. Joe sank into the third across the room from Jannet and facing the door. He kicked off his shoes and sank his toes into the rug.

"Much better," he said with a sigh. "I am not fond of wearing shoes but understand it when in such a cold place." It was then I noticed he sat closest to the fireplace.

We all looked at each other for a moment. Three humans, a dog, and a Peregrine Falcon had been brought together to complete a task given to us by another race of beings. Mahrah was right, I believed the unbelievable. When we all took a sip of our drinks without a toast, it brought home how little we knew of each other. The rapidity of events which brought us together gave us little time to get to know each other. I found I wanted to know more about the other beings who had been recruited into this undertaking.

"How were you able to connect to just Iolani earlier tonight?" Jannet asked. Joe nodded, he had the same question.

"I focused intently on her and just on communicating. I had done something like it before when I called you, Jannet. I wonder if it is something we can all do."

Joe took a long sip of his beer and then put the pint down on the low table in front of him. "Should we all try at once or one at a time?"

"How about you try to reach out to me," I replied.

Joe looked at me. A moment later, I heard his voice mentally. I sat up a little startled. The voice ceased.

"The look on your face was funny," Joe proclaimed.

Joe, Jannet and I took turns connecting individually and collectively. After we could reliably connect with each other, we included Iolani and Wizard. Iolani was a little perturbed because she wanted to nap. Wizard was intrigued but agreed with Iolani.

I examined the falcon. She was more stunning up close. Her face had two streaks of gray on either side with beige under her beak, melting into a gray and white mottling on her chest. I saw the others were also admiring her. She preened a bit under the attention. Iolani knew she was a gorgeous bird.

The animals were content to sleep while the humans talked. They were not sure what all the noise coming out of our mouths was about and preferred a good sniff, in Wizard's case, or eyeing, in Iolani's case, to find out about others. The three humans agreed to use conventional modes of communication and let the Connection drop.

"Joe, where did you study in England?" Jannet asked.

"Manchester. I picked it for its football team." He grinned a bit sheepishly. "My father thought I picked it for the studies. I think I played more than I studied, but I still earned a degree."

"How did you get to England in the first place?" I asked.

"It begins with the fact I am the third born of my father. In my tribe, the first born is to become the head chief when he is of age. The second born is to become our holy person. It does not matter if it is a woman or man. The third born is to help the tribe continue to prosper. I knew from my youth I would not be allowed to follow my heart's desire."

"You wanted to become a warrior," I said.

"I did. I admired the skill, bravery, and camaraderie they had. As the person who was destined to help the tribe, I was often alone. My job was to tell the tribe what to do with its cattle and such. The elders agree it is important, but the person is not well liked. I did not want the job; it was my destiny.

"To deal with my disappointment, I ran. I told my father I was scouting the area for good grazing places for our cattle and to find possible places for a new village. We move our village if the rains do not come or predators take too many of our animals.

"I had hidden a bow and set of arrows and a spear many miles from the village. On days I did not go to school, I would watch the warriors practice in our village and then run to my weapons. When my age group were allowed the machete, I practiced it also."

"Who did you practice against?" Jannet asked.

Joe smiled broadly. "I am afraid there is a tree which has been greatly harmed. I give thanks to it for allowing me to use it as a target."

Joe finished his pint, put the glass on the table and settled back. He ran his svelte ebony hand along the top of the white wainscot. I marveled at the grace and strength his hand showed.

"One day, a small bunch of cattle became lost. I persuaded the elders to let me go look for them. I argued it was my responsibility because it was about feeding the village, and was surprised when they consented to let me go. But, they said, I was to take another with me. I chose one of the boys from my age group who was the closest thing I had to a friend.

"We found the cattle with three people from another tribe. They had stolen them from us. Instead of going back to tell the village, I confronted the three men. My friend was not happy about it, but he stood with me. I demanded our cattle back. The three men surrounded us. I knew then that they meant to kill us.

"My friend pulled his machete out but I did not have one. One of the cattle stealers saw I was unarmed and swung his at me. I dodged the swing, grabbed his wrist, and slammed it into my knee. He dropped his machete and I picked it up. My friend looked at me nervously because he did not think I knew how to use it. I began to swing it back and forth like I did when I attacked the tree. The man in front of me fled.

"Now, there were two of them and two of us. The next man in front of me was the leader of the group. He had been a warrior for some time and attacked fiercely with his machete. I dodged many of the swings and blocked a few. After a few minutes, I noticed he would take a step before swinging hard. On his next hard swing, I ducked under it, came up behind him and kicked him in the knees. My machete was across his throat before he knew where I was. 'Tell the other man to stop.' I told him. He did so.

"I said to him, "'You have stolen my people's cattle and tried to kill us when we came to claim them. You have acted dishonorably.' The man agreed. It was my place to take his life. He did not want to die but did not object."

I found myself holding my breath. I could tell Jannet had also been pulled into the story. "I could not do it," Joe said with resignation. "It was my place to protect my tribe from cattle stealers and I did not follow through. I realized I was not fit to be called a warrior as much as I wanted to be one. The cattle stealer said as much when I let him go."

"What about your friend? Did he kill anyone?" I asked.

"He did not; he let him go. We agreed to not tell the village about the men, but to say we found the cattle roaming."

"You do not need to kill to be a warrior," I said solemnly. "And, I am not saying that just because I am an American. There are other cultures with the belief warriors can be peaceful. You defended the interest of your tribe. You acted honorably."

"I have told myself so; I still have doubt. In my village, a boy becomes a man once he kills either a large predator or an enemy. That day, my actions declared to all I would never be a man nor fully a warrior."

It took everything in me not to start a litany of reasons why Joe was a man. His beliefs were handed down through centuries. It was heart-breaking he was caught between them and his merciful nature.

"When did you get the ring?" Jannet asked as she refilled her glass, tactfully changing the subject.

Joe shook himself as if from a dream. "It came in the post while I was in Manchester. A note said to keep it safe and show no one until I was with others who had the same sign. It also said I was not to wear it until I was with three others who had the same ring."

"You saw my bracelet immediately?" I asked even though I was pretty sure I knew the answer.

"After I saw Wizard," Joe pointed at the sleeping dog with his foot.

Wizard thumped his tail against the floor. Maybe he wasn't sleeping after all.

"Is that why you didn't leave us on the side of the road?" Jannet asked jokingly.

Joe looked serious despite her tone. "That man was thinking only of the money in his pocket. It is more important to think of creating good in the world. It is worth much more than the coins you can get."

"Agreed," Jannet and I said in unison.

There was a light knock on the door. I quickly stood and stepped in front of the desk chair to block anyone from seeing Iolani. Joe sat on the edge of the love seat ready to spring. One of the barmaids poked her head in and asked if there was anything else we wanted. Jannet swept up the glasses, snagged the bottle, and went with the barmaid. When Jannet returned, she had three glasses of port and a package printed with the word 'biscuits'.

We clinked glasses and opened the package. The cookies had raspberries and dark-chocolate. They were a good way to end the day.

"Chosen, I mean, Nadia, how are you able to travel so freely?" Joe had changed his address when he saw my brow rise.

"I am between contract jobs to look for archaeological sites," I explained. "Also, I planned to take a couple of months off and travel. I wasn't sure if I was going to go to South America or another continent. Mahrah's contact helped me decide. It is a good thing I had saved for an international trip."

Joe gave Jannet a thoughtful look. I decided to explain for her since I knew she didn't like to talk about money. "Jannet's husband, Ben, used to own the company he now works for. The owners paid him well for the company and give him a generous salary." I decided not to add Jannet and Ben often took trips on their own.

"And how did you end up with such a beautiful animal you are allowed to take anywhere?" Joe asked me.

"You are probably used to seeing service animals with people who have more apparent needs."

"I have seen them with those who do not see well or who are unable to manage without a wheelchair," he answered.

"I have epilepsy. Nobody knows exactly why. I have had episodes, seizures, on and off since I was twelve."

"I have only heard the word. I do not know what it means," Joe admitted honestly.

"It means the signals in my brain get confused and begin to do their own thing. My parents first noticed it when I would blank out and smack my lips. When they asked me what I was doing, I wouldn't answer initially. They thought I was being cheeky when I finally said I didn't know and grounded me. After a few episodes, they realized what was happening."

"They must have felt bad when they found out the truth," Joe supposed.

"They did. We saw some doctors and thought we took care of it. I had a grand-mal seizure when I was fifteen. It was the most embarrassing thing which ever happened to me. One minute I was talking to a really cute girl and the next thing I knew, I woke up on the floor with a soaked shirt and pants. I had lost control of all bodily functions. Everybody looked at me awkwardly. I never wanted to go back." My cheeks burned at the memory.

"You never told me this," Jannet said with interest.

"Like I said, it was the most embarrassing moment of my whole life." I took a sip of the port to ease the sting of those memories. "I told my parents before we left the hospital I wanted to be home-schooled. They did the parent thing and told me I may change my mind."

"What happened?" Joe asked.

"I was dead set on my choice even as I left the hospital. When we pulled on to my street, I thought the neighbors were having a party. Then, I realized the party was for me. The students at my school had organized it.

"After then, there was a group of students who watched out for me. If I looked gray or started to look like I was losing awareness, they made sure I either made it to the Nurse's Office or called someone to come and take care of me. It really helped as I was dealing with the doctor's visits and medication."

"Your story is very different from what I hear about American teenagers," Joe said.

I continued, "Not everyone was accepting. For one, my brother became very distant after my episode. Also, some of my closest friends at the time wouldn't hang out with me anymore. I didn't realize it then, but they weren't true friends. I had chosen them to be accepted. The ones who helped me were really my friends."

"Was it the end of your big seizures?" Joe asked with concern.

"I never had one quite like it. The most severe one I've had since then was the day Jannet found me in the library. I had broken up with my girlfriend the day before. We had been together for two years and I thought it would last forever. I hadn't slept or eaten. Jannet found me twitching and babbling. She got me to the emergency room and stuck around long enough to meet my parents.

"It was decided I needed to have a service animal. Wizard came into my life six months later. He has helped nip some minor episodes in the bud. He lets me know to take my medicine. I would be much more limited in my activities without him."

"And what about me?" Jannet asked with faked affront. "Am I chopped liver?"

"Let's hope not or you will be Wizard's breakfast," I replied chuckling.

Chapter 19

"Jannet, what was your most embarrassing moment?" I asked reaching for another biscuit.

Jannet chuckled. "I am not sure which of my many missteps in the countries I have been in would be worthy of such a title."

"You?" Joe asked incredulously. "You have so much poise. I cannot see you be anything but tactful."

"I have had lots of practice at being awkward and brash," Jannet replied, taking another biscuit, and sliding the package across the table to Joe.

"My most embarrassing moment?" She paused and chewed her bite slowly before beginning. "One time my parents and I had just entered a new country. Usually, my parents were very good about letting me know about the customs and such before we went to any events. This particular time, they were called away early in the morning after we arrived. Later, another member of the staff told me my parents would be bringing a dignitary back to the embassy and I needed to dress for a formal dinner.

"I had just bought a beautiful, emerald green, satin dress with a brocaded bodice before we left the previous country. The skirt was floor length so I thought it would be perfect. I was running late so I slipped into the receiving line without anybody noticing.

"My mother saw me before my father and a look of horror came over her face. I checked my skirt and bodice to make sure I hadn't ripped it or spilt anything on it. I was about to step away when the dignitary also spotted me. To his credit, he did not change his expression, but I could tell something was wrong by the look in his eyes."

"What was the matter?" Joe couldn't determine anything which would cause such a reaction.

"There were actually two things. First, the color of the dress was exactly the same color of the flag oppositional forces in his country used. I had unintentionally insulted him by wearing his enemy's call to arms.

"Second, I had been in such a hurry, I had forgotten to grab my shawl. I remembered it as I was coming into the foyer, but thought I was dressed appropriately because my legs were covered. However, in this country, it was taboo for women to reveal their upper arms and my gown did.

"By the time the dignitary got to me, I could feel the tension in the air because everyone else had noticed my attire. I was ready to bolt; instead, I curtsied. My mom said my face was bright red. The man bowed, took my hand in his, and asked, 'How old are you, Little Miss?' I told him I was twelve. His eyes softened a bit. 'I too have a twelve-year old daughter. She loves brilliant colors as you do. Thank you for honoring me with such a beautiful gown.'

The whole entourage relaxed. He moved on to greet my sister and someone slipped a shawl over my shoulders and arms.

"When my parents told me later, I was mortified. I didn't want to go to another event. I even became sick before a couple of functions that were held over the next week. I think it was the stress at being scorned."

"His reaction could have been serious because parents are often judged by their children. How did it turn out for your folks?" I asked.

"It was one of those times when humans show how amazing they can be. The dignitary told my father he had beautiful daughters. When my father tried to apologize, the man indicated there was nothing to apologize for and he was probably more at fault for insisting on a meeting so soon after our arrival. He often asked if I would be at events, and he always treated me kindly when I went. One time I asked him why."

Here she paused. "He said that he knew I did not mean to offend and he would not be a great man if he took offense. He was a great man. He went on to reconcile with the armed opposition in his country and helped promote peace."

We finished off the last of the biscuits at about ten thirty. Iolani wanted to stay out of the rain; I looked and let her know it was no longer raining. She gave a mental chuff and flew out the window in search of a dry perch.

The next morning, Wizard and I were in the restaurant area early. I had coffee and a bap, a type of biscuit with sausage. It was tasty, and I wondered how many I could have and not look like a glutton. Jannet came down the stairs which were right outside the breakfast room, nodded curtly, and headed straight for the espresso machine. Joe came down, stopped next to the bottom of the stairs, and turned to look back up the staircase.

I was intrigued so I went and stood next to him. Looking up, I didn't see anything out of the ordinary. Joe began, "Adults spend much of their life looking down at their feet. Children look up. There is so much more world above one's head than at one's feet. Maybe children have something to teach us, yes?" Then, he ambled into the restaurant. I followed with thoughts of the incongruity of the depth of his statement about life and the shallowness of mine about breakfast.

We picked up the makings for lunch at a bakery on the way out of town and went back into the wood. Mahrah was pleased we had figured out how to connect with each other without also triggering the protection energy. Jannet compared it to power settings on the microwave. When we tried to communicate the idea to the animals, they indicated they knew there were different types of energy in the signal.

"Why didn't you tell us?" I asked clumsily with images.

"We thought you knew," they both replied.

Our task for the day was to create a type of fence with the stronger energy, was much like a force field. I was surprised when Mahrah directed me to stand in the middle of a circle made by the four Watchers. She arranged us so the two humans were to my sides and the animals were in front and behind me. They started an arm's length away and began activating their rings. Slowly, they increased the diameter of the circle. The difficulty was to keep the field in the same configuration between the four rings while the Watchers moved. Iolani had the hardest time since her movements happened in uneven hops. It took the better part of an hour to become consistent.

Next, the three earth-bound Watchers made a triangle around me and Iolani joined from time to time as she flew above us. She alternated flying tight circles with resting on a nearby branch. The goal was to change the shape of the defensive field into a pyramid of protection. The intent of the configuration was to keep us safe from any attacks which came from above. This was important in the time of archers, but I did not think it would be useful to us. Since Mahrah seemed to be in a no-nonsense mood, I didn't point this out to her.

By the end of the next morning, we were tired and cranky. When we decided to break for lunch, Iolani took off into the forest. Joe, Jannet and I sat on Joe's blanket looking blankly at the woods around us. Iolani came back after ten minutes with a now dead bird which she proceeded to strip of its feathers. At least she was kind enough to do it downwind from us.

The small flame of doubt I had been harboring about this enterprise grew. "Do you think we can pull this off?"

Reclaim

"It is much tougher to control the higher level of energy than I thought," Jannet muttered. The efforts of the morning had created a burnt spot in the middle of the meadow and a large broken limb off a tree.

"Maybe we fight without the rings. We are all warriors on our own." Joe speculated.

"I think Mahrah would have skipped the rings if our own abilities were sufficient," I said. "There must be a reason for them. Maybe you can't just take a Talisman from someone."

"Let me try," Joe said with a sudden burst of energy. He got up and motioned for me to join him a few feet away. I reluctantly climbed to my feet.

"What do you want me to do?" I asked standing in front of him.

"I will try to take the arm band. You may resist, but I do not think you will hurt me."

Joe reached for my arm. I knocked his hand away with a move I had seen Jannet do during her kata that morning. He shook out his hand and looked startled; his eyes narrowed a bit. In a flash, he had one hand around my left bicep and the other around my left wrist. A moment later, he was flying backward. He landed five feet away. Upset about how this turned out and feeling guilty, I took two quick strides to make sure he was okay.

"Are you hurt? I am so sorry."

"You knocked me on my butt," he called from the grass, laughing heartily as he sat up. He looked fine so I left him there.

"Stop. What are you doing?" Mahrah let her displeasure be felt. *"The power you have is dangerous. You can hurt one another with it."*

"If Joe can't get the Talisman from me, how will we be able to get the other one?" I asked turning the emotional force of my embarrassment and guilt on her.

"Your instruments are made to keep you from taking them from each other." When Joe's ring had touched my bracelet, he went careening. Mahrah had built a safety feature into the system. Was she worried one of the Watchers would desert?

"You could have told us that when we activated the rings." I said what the humans were thinking. The animals gave an image of innocence. After all, they had not participated.

Mahrah rumbled.

"You will be able to get the Talisman from the human who has it. If it is not active, it is merely a matter of taking it."

"And if it is active?" Joe asked. This meant Mahrah had included all of us in this conversation.

"Your kind is creative and you will find a way to get the Bearer to deactivate it."

"Won't the Bearer's Watchers make a fence and keep us from it?" Jannet asked.

"If the other has protectors, they do not have bands. The Bearer does not have the power the Chosen has. When you are trained, you will be able to collect the other Talisman."

Mahrah then directed us to our afternoon tasks. We grudgingly began. Since the broken tree branch was a result of the pyramid formation, as I called it, Mahrah wanted the Watchers to practice it on their own. She indicated it may not have been such a good idea for me to be in the middle while they practiced that morning. I whole-heartedly agreed.

My task was to once again work on retrieving the Talisman by pulling it with energy. Instead of pulling it across a surface, I was to bury it. I pulled a trowel from my messenger bag and buried it about six inches down. The task was tedious and intriguing. Tedious because I spent the better part of the afternoon thinking 'Pull'; intriguing because I was in wonder that an object actually moved as I envisioned a rope of energy. The scientific part of my brain kept trying to develop a theory around how this was even possible. There was an occasion or two that Mahrah called me back to task when my brain had wandered off to think about electromagnetism and photons. It was a reversal from the problem most teachers had with their pupils. I was being schooled to think about my surroundings instead of my previous studies.

We took a break in the late afternoon. I told the group I was going to stretch my legs. They were ready to kick back on the blanket and watch a few clouds sail by. After a half-hearted warning to 'not go far' from Jannet, I headed down the lane with Wizard trotting at my side.

"I have an answer to your question." Mahrah started before I realized she was connected enough to communicate. I wondered which question and realized she was referencing our conversation the day before. She was addressing what it was like to be her.

"To be me has many layers. I am regaled as the ruler of my kind. Many gifts have been bestowed on me – the learning of our forbearers, the opportunity to travel to your world, the ability to create changes to help the plight of others, and power none other of my kind have.

"You have seen the splendor of flight. I realized what a gift it was after coming to your world. I also understood the privileges my size and abilities give me. Even though I hardly employed it, I enjoy the strength of my being and the ability to generate fire and energy."

"You do breathe fire! I have wondered all this time if your kind kept the ability, but haven't asked."

Mahrah chuckled. *"Yes, the fire organ is as important to our systems as our stomachs. We do not make a habit of expelling flames but can if we need or want. Are there any stories among your kind of our ability to do that?"*

"Definitely. Many stories feature a fire-breathing dragon who singes anybody who opposes it." I felt Mahrah wince at that statement.

"It is unfortunate our fire generating ability is portrayed negatively. We used it to help start your kind's campfires." She seemed lost in a memory. *"Unfortunate."*

I did not want to interrupt her thinking, but was curious about what some of the other layers were. She began after a few more moments.

"But, there is something which comes with all my gifts. Even though my days are spent around my kind, I find I am not known well. I am free to converse with the others who know of the depths of our knowledge of existing in this world and traveling between the two worlds. I may converse with anyone I choose on any matter. Yet, it is not enough.

"If I have found the right word, I am lonely. Dragons, like humans, are social creatures. We may not have the linguistic capabilities of your kind, but we do communicate. I feel I am not able to communicate deeply about myself with those of my kind because of who I am among them."

"Even with your Watchers?"

"They know me best among my kind. Yet, I find myself unable to convey to them all that I feel. I must make a confession. You have experienced more of my emotions than they have."

"What about a mate? Do you have those like we do?"

"I had a mate." Here she breathed a deep and loss-laden sigh. *"He has ceased his existence."*

"When was that?"

"Long before your time but after I returned from your world. We had our brood and they had begun to learn the skills of flying, hunting, and maneuvering the unseen forces. He became ill and we could not find a cure. He passed long before the time of most dragons. He was well-respected among dragons - was kind, wise, and light-hearted. I try to emulate him to bring honor to his memory, but do not believe I succeed."

Her voice was so full of sadness. I wiped my eyes before I realized I was crying. "It is a great loss and I am sorry you experienced it. It sounds like your mate was someone you connected with in many ways."

I heard a sound which seemed to be expressing a very deep emotional wound. It was a cross between a sudden intake of breath and a wail. I wished I could hug Mahrah or provide some element of comfort. I didn't even know if or how dragons hugged. I would have embraced her if we had been in the same world.

I felt a wave of gratitude. I wasn't surprised Mahrah had felt my wishes. *"Thank you. Your thoughts do provide comfort. I did not mean to burden you with my history. We tend to reveal those depths to only a few. I am honored you have listened and held my thoughts as your own."*

I wished I could help. "Mahrah, are there any of your Watchers you think would communicate deeply with you?" I tried to remember the wording she had given.

"It is a question I ask myself. I wonder if I am the one keeping a connection from happening or if my solitude is because of my standing among my kind. It is something to ponder."

"You know, if you can't find anyone to connect with you there, maybe you could start talking to one of our world leaders. They may be able to sympathize with you."

"Ah, you are jesting. It is one of the things I like about our interactions."

"Really? You mean I make you smile?"

"Sometimes," she rumbled with mirth.

A mental nudge by Jannet and Joe interrupted us. They wanted to make sure everything was okay. Wizard answered. His image told them unequivocally that he was taking good care of me.

Mahrah indicated she wanted to check our progress from the day. I had been fairly aware of my surroundings while chatting with Mahrah and knew it would take some time to walk back to the clearing where the others were. So, I jogged.

On my way back, I took a wrong turn. Wizard herded me before I went very far down a side path. It also helped Iolani decided to escort us back to the small meadow. I wondered how she perceived our pace as she flew circles around us. I didn't think I would like her answer so I didn't ask her.

When I reached the clearing, Jannet and Joe were sparring. Joe had his large knife, and Jannet was showing him some ways to defend against attacks. I didn't know Joe had brought it with him. I felt uneasy as I realized the number of weapons we had, all in the name of establishing peace.

We started showing Mahrah our progress by repeating our tasks from the morning. It was now straightforward to maintain communication and add the layer of defensive energy. Mahrah reported the defensive field stayed intact, even while the four Watchers moved. She indicated she could sense the layers through feel and sound. Wizard chimed in that he too could hear the different types of energy.

Because of the broken branch from the morning, I was uncertain about staying in the circle of three watchers and having Iolani stretch her node as she whirled above us. She climbed above the trees so she had more room to maneuver as she circled, the energy field weakened. It was as if the field were a net and Iolani's distance stretched it out.

"You can help strengthen the defense. Your abilities allow you to amplify this energy. Move in close to the fence. Think about manipulating the energy like you do when retrieving the Talisman only broaden it to cover an area rather than to create a Pull."

I did as I was instructed. As I approached the space between Wizard and Joe, I felt the energy flowing between them. I expected a big glob of energy; it felt more like a plane. I marveled; it really was a fence. Slowly, I began to edge my hand between Wizard and Joe. I was going with the dip-your-toes-in-the-water approach when Iolani indicated that she was tired of flying in that particular circle. I think she added something rude about humans, but I wasn't well-versed in falcon imagery. My suspicions were confirmed when Mahrah chuckled.

I plunged my hand into the field and felt it jar me to my core. Then, I reached up with my other hand and pointed to Iolani. I could tell she felt a difference because her trajectory changed and she let out a couple of alarming 'kaks'. I felt slightly smug at the payback.

The boost in the signal allowed Iolani to change her path. She experimented with flying further up and then with flying wider circles. The pyramid of protection held strong. When all the humans were breaking a sweat, we deactivated the force.

Joe was, of course, grinning. Jannet walked over to her bag and pulled out a hand towel and water bottle. I should have expected she would come prepared for a workout. Her expression was one of satisfaction of the accomplishment. Iolani landed in the grass and bobbed her delight. Wizard was wagging his tail. We were all happy with ourselves and ready to call it a day.

Mahrah had other plans.

Chapter 20

We all groaned like school children told to complete their studies when Mahrah ordered the Watchers into a circle with me in the middle. "She is a task master," Jannet whispered under her breath. I hoped Mahrah didn't hear and, if she did, didn't understand the comment.

Instead of the full force from the rings, the Watchers were to only the energy to connect. We stood there for a minute. All of us could hear a low hum.

"Chosen, activate the Conceal Talisman." I did so and could tell I blinked out of sight by the responses of the others.

"Now, extend the effect to the Watchers. I will be able to tell if you have extended it to all."

The first attempt caused only Jannet to be Concealed. I backed the energy up and tried again. This time, three of the Watchers disappeared. Iolani was behind me and still not Concealed. On the next try, though, I accomplished enveloping all Watchers with the Conceal Talisman's energy. Before Mahrah confirmed I had, I was certain because I had a sense of each of the Watchers.

"Third time is a charm," I said after deactivating the Talisman.

"It is good." Mahrah wasn't effusive but seemed pleased. She directed us to practice a few more times.

Our day of exhausting ourselves and our energy was finally over. I wasn't sure we would be able to do many days like this one. Frankly, I was hoping for a day to rest up and think about our next steps. I wondered if we could figure out where our adversaries had gone after their futile search for us in Johannesburg, assuming they had taken the bait.

We ate at a different pub that evening. It was agreed we had been a little too conspicuous with Iolani's display. She was irritated when she learned we blamed her, but she found a less prominent spot in a nearby tree as we dined. With good food, good drink, and a day of labor behind us, we were all ready for bed as we walked back to the inn. Before we got there, Jannet's phone rang. It was Ben.

The smile she had upon answering quickly turned to a frown. At the same time, Mahrah spoke, *"The Kinetic Talisman has been used again. I need to investigate."* Her words were said with sadness and then she closed our connection.

The event with the Kinetic Talisman took place in London in front of the US Embassy. The ambassador and his wife were returning from pre-dinner drinks. The newsfeed video Ben forwarded showed a hooded man stepping in front of the ambassador's car. Instead of the man being hurt by the car, the car bounced as if it had hit a brick wall. Two armed guards shot at the man. People walking down the street were hit by ricocheting bullets and fell to the ground as the man ran. He turned before going around the corner and the lamppost lit his features enough for me to tell who it was. It wasn't Bryce as I had originally thought. It was Reginald.

"How many people were hurt?" I choked out the question. Jannet repeated it to Ben.

She relayed his reply a few seconds later. "Six. Two of the people who took a bullet are in serious condition. No one is dead."

My emotions stormed. I expressed the desire for Reginald to promptly go to Hades, Tartarus, and some other hot underworld. Impulsively, I swung to slap the pole of a sign. I yelped in astonishment, not pain, when the pole dented enough to make the sign sag even though I had not made physical contact with it. I stopped in my tracks and looked at my hand. It was a meaningless thing to do, but I was too shocked to do anything else. Joe gave a low whistle and looked wary.

"It has something to do with the bracelet," Jannet said to him. He nodded, not entirely convinced.

I wanted to speed to London to find the Kinetic Talisman, logic held sway. Rationally, I knew we couldn't wield the tools we were given effectively enough to stop Reginald. Everything went well in practice, but I doubted our foes would stop to let us stand in one place and create force fields. Still, I was sick to my stomach with the thought people were getting hurt.

I cursed myself because I had let Reginald slip my mind. After finding only the Devlin Duo in Kenya, I thought he was not important to their mission. Now, it seemed he was an integral part of the activation of the Kinetic Talisman. But, who was he to Kelly and Bryce?

We continued to walk back to our hotel, Jannet finishing her call with Ben. When she pocketed her phone, her face held the same grimness I felt.

She got to the point. "Ben thinks the attack on the embassy was a direct statement to us. He thinks our adversaries are telling us they know who we are and where we are."

"They attacked the embassy to say they know you have diplomatic connections and London because they know we are in England," I said gravely.

Jannet nodded. "Ben has a plan to keep us off the radar. He happens to be in Paris and his company told him he could take a few days off. A friend of a colleague can book a summer house anywhere on the island. He just wants to know where."

"Aberystwyth," I said without hesitation.

Every one of the four Watchers looked at me. You would have thought I suggested a magical kingdom. "Where and what is that?" Jannet asked.

"The town where the National Library of Wales is located." I said as if it were common knowledge.

"Is it far enough away?" Jannet asked.

"If a mouse is quiet enough, it is very hard to find him," Joe responded.

"Is that a proverb of your people?" I asked.

"No," he responded, "I made it up just now."

"Then, let's go to Wales and be very quiet," I said chuckling.

"We should probably tell Mahrah we are relocating tomorrow," Jannet said.

I tried to connect with Mahrah but could not find her. I even stopped and sat on a low stone wall to boost the signal. She still did not respond. I was troubled by her absence.

"She is the ruler of her kind. I think she will be able to take care of herself," Joe said.

"She has a set of Watchers. They are experts at the abilities we are only practicing, Mahrah will be safe," Jannet added.

Wizard sensed my anxiety and nuzzled my hand. For her part, Iolani flew to the lowest branch of a nearby tree and sent a message of concern.

We discussed the wisdom of staying at the inn for another night. Since we had paid with cash, we felt it would be harder to find us. Besides, we probably couldn't arrive much before noon at whatever house was booked. Joe also mentioned that we were going to need some food for the next day and almost all stores had closed for the evening.

Even though the risk of being discovered was low, Joe said he was going to stay up all night to make sure we weren't accosted in our sleep. Jannet and I pointed out he was driving the next day and we wanted to get to our destination in one piece. After a short discussion, we reached a compromise. Joe would watch until about midnight and then Iolani would watch until morning. Joe looked at the bird with uncertainty. He respected her but didn't entirely trust her to stay awake. She assured him she would.

Jannet called Ben as we climbed the stairs, relaying our destination to him.

"How much do you think Iolani understands?" Joe asked before we entered our rooms.

"I think Mahrah made sure she knew everything," I answered.

"How much do you think she cares?" Jannet asked.

"Hard to say. Not knowing much about bird culture, I would say she cares enough to stick around and fulfill any promise she made to Mahrah. Beyond that, I get the sense she feels the rest of the world is beneath her."

Joe laughed. "You are very funny, Nadia. Of course, the world is beneath her."

Jannet and I went into our room and tried to get as much sleep as we could. I was still upset by the injury and destruction being done with the Kinetic Talisman and shaken by the event with the pole. Eventually, I slowed my breathing and fell asleep.

As we packed to leave the next morning, Jannet received a call from Ben. A house near Aberystwyth had been rented. He gave her the information and indicated when he would arrive. Jannet smiled broadly at his announcement.

It was a standing agreement Jannet would handle checkout while I took bags to the car when we traveled together. Joe was in the parking lot looking up at the trees which lined it. They had struck me as odd when we pulled up the first day of our stay. Without all their leaves, they looked like live versions of menorahs. Instead of wondering what was wrong, I walked up and joined him.

"We should get some supplies for Iolani," he announced.

"What type of supplies?" I asked.

He turned to me. "She and I spoke last night. I mean, we communicated. She is okay with trees but would like to be closer to us at times. She wonders why you do not have a special glove-perch."

It took me a moment to determine what he meant. "A long, leather glove that they use in falconry, a gauntlet?" I paused. "The good news is we are in the right vicinity to find falconry supplies easily. The practice has a long history here."

"It is what she wants. She also wants a perch for when we are using our rings on the ground. She cannot see much when she is in the grass."

I began to wonder how long this shopping list was going to be. "Anything else?"

"That is all for now. She is honored to be part of the ones who will protect the Talismans and hopes it will help protect her kind from all that humans have done."

"I cannot guarantee we can fulfill her hope. I want to at least keep the Talismans from those who want to use them for their own purposes."

The drive through the countryside was exquisite. I loved my home, but nothing could beat the greenery of the area. It was both cultivated and wild. There was something almost hypnotic watching the patchwork fields interrupted by copses and villages.

We were just turning north when Jannet received a text from Ben. She had forwarded Iolani's request to Ben and asked about a falconry store somewhere along our route.

"We are in luck. There is a place in the town up the road."

"What is it called?" Joe asked.

"Abergavenny."

Joe nodded. "I hope it is spelled much like that. It can be hard when there are many more letters than sounds in the words." I knew exactly what he was talking about. It was my greatest challenge with French.

Like many small towns, Abergavenny was a hamlet which had become a village and then grown even more from there. The streets wound along landscape features rather than following the structure of an orthogonal system of roads. After reaching several dead-ends, we parked the car and walked. The market area was quiet and quaint. I wished we weren't in such a rush.

The first person we asked gave us directions and walked to the first turn with us. In my travels, I was overwhelmingly impressed with the kindness people showered on travelers.

The shop was very small but well-stocked. Some of the equipment looked quite uncomfortable for birds. Before entering, we had agreed Jannet would be our point person because she was most fluid in unknown situations. She regaled the shop keeper with a tale about her cousin having a decade birthday. We had decided to take a drive today, she continued her story. On our drive, we received a text from her mother who just found out the cousin was going to start falconry. It was such a lucky thing we happened upon the shop. I almost believed Jannet myself. She tossed in false locations in case anyone asked about our strange group.

The shop keeper knew his products and threw in a few stories of his own falconry adventures. We were able to scrape enough cash together among the three of us to buy a low-end long glove and a perch which looked like an oversized golf tee. When the gentleman insisted on giving us a hood to designed keep captive birds quiet, Jannet accepted with aplomb. We departed with haste.

Iolani buzzed us almost as soon as we were out of the store. I figured she would have done more than just an idle fly by if she knew what we had in the bag. Still, two of the items were things for which she had asked.

The hills rose up to the north of the town. Our route took us to the tops of them and through a more forested area. I was idly marveling at how much lusher it looked here when I became aware of Mahrah's presence.

"How long have you been there?"

"For a small space of time. I was enjoying the scenery and the calm you were experiencing. You are okay I observed?" she asked, suddenly wondering if she had offended me.

"I am glad you are also enjoying the view."

Then, I remembered I had not been able to reach her. "Is everything okay? I could not get in touch with you."

"I was among some I did not wish to know about my interactions with your world. I thought it best to not engage."

I wondered where she had been, but didn't ask. Instead, I told her our plans. "We decided it was best to change locations. We think our foes know we are in this country."

"It is a wise choice. It is the same thought I had when I learned the Kinetic Talisman was used near your location. I am not surprised to find you have journeyed."

"You can tell where the Talisman is?"

"Only when it is active. Then it draws on some of the energy in this world. We can determine its general location. You and the Talisman were close."

"We will be in a place which should be a good hideaway for a couple of days." I didn't say it also had a tremendous library I intended to use for research.

"I will leave you to enjoy your travels. Contact me when you are rested."

"You don't have to go. If you are able, you can continue to watch."

Mahrah's reply was to stay a few more minutes. I then felt her absent herself. I wondered about how she had slipped into my consciousness without me knowing and wondered what it meant about our connection.

The rest of the trip was just as delightful and uneventful. We arrived at the guest house a little after noon. The house keeper was happy to see us. He and his wife were waiting for our arrival and could now go on about their busy day. We were happy to let them do so.

Iolani wanted to rest after the flight. Though we had not exhausted ourselves while traveling, the rest of us decided to join her. I stretched out on a wicker couch in the sun room attached to the back of the house. Wizard splayed out on the cool tile floor. I must have fallen asleep because the sun was in a much different place when I opened my eyes.

Wizard stood at attention right before I heard tires on the gravel driveway. Iolani gave me a mental inquiry about what to do. The image was of a dark car and a man inside of it. I was relieved when the man had light-colored hair. I reassured Iolani it was a friend, Ben.

Wizard and I went around the outside of the house and came up on Ben as he was stretching from his long drive. He had turned his back to the front of the house. Joe was walking down the driveway and also gave me a mental query. Wizard surprised Ben by brushing up against his leg. At the same time, Jannet came out the front door. She quickly crossed the small front yard. Ben turned just as she reached him; they embraced and kissed. Then, they embraced some more. It was both endearing and difficult to watch. Seeing other people in love was often a bittersweet experience for me. So, I left them to continue their reunion and went back into the house. Joe gave them wide berth and followed me.

"It is a very nice neighborhood. I think we will know if anyone is coming because we are on a road that does not connect to another," Joe said.

"Out doing some reconnaissance?" I asked as I dropped onto the living room couch.

"Making sure I understand how we are in relationship to the country around us. By the way, have you told Mahrah about Ben?" He gave me a pointed look.

I thought back over the last week. "No, I don't think I have," I said uncomfortably.

"Chosen, you may want to do so. Soon."

Jannet and Ben came in holding hands. Joe was introduced, and we went into the kitchen to discuss our journeys. I was always perplexed why people, with perfectly good living rooms and dens, stood around in kitchens.

It became apparent to Joe and me the couple wanted some time alone. It was only late afternoon so I announced, "Joe, let's go to the library so I can apply for a reader's card."

"Should we go with you?" Jannet asked. I could tell she was hoping for a negative answer.

"I think you two should have some time alone. Though, I think Iolani will probably want to continue to rest outside. We will leave her here."

Joe snagged the rental car keys from the counter, I grabbed my messenger bag, and we left. When we climbed into the vehicle, Joe said, "You are very considerate, Chosen."

"I think it is what I would have wanted if I had been traveling without the person I most wanted to share my life with." I tried not to sound jealous.

When we arrived in town earlier, we had seen the large library building on a hill so Joe was sure he knew how to get there. As he drove, he asked, "Do you think I can get a reader's card also?"

"What would you like to research?"

"I am wondering about how the dragons' instruments work."

"Joe, I am not sure you will be able to figure that out in the amount of time we have here."

"I agree, but I would like to start."

The library sat on the hill like a crown. It was an imposing monument made of Cornish granite and Portland stone. Since it held manuscripts from the beginning of the written history of the Welsh people, it was a well-known building to people who studied the past of the area. The original gray building had been supplemented with several other less prominent buildings over the better part of the last century. If one was a bibliophile, the National Library of Wales was a sanctuary. It even boasted a reading room with the dimensions of a cathedral, including a vaulted ceiling.

It took us a half hour to get reader's cards. We wandered around the main area of the library for another half hour. Wanting to give Jannet and Ben as much time as we could, the two Watchers and I decided to wander the grounds around the library.

We found the track and field area for the nearby university. Joe and I looked at each other with understanding. He kicked off his shoes and I dropped my messenger bag. By the time I had finished four laps, he had finished five. It was a short work out, but we both enjoyed the sensation of running.

We then wandered over to a green space with trees around its perimeter just to the north of the library. Joe indicated I may as well tell Mahrah about Ben and then began wandering down the tree line. He was looking up into them as he strolled.

Mahrah was happy I had contacted her, until I started talking.

"There is something I need to tell you."

"Have you been found?" She was instantly tense.

"We are safe and there is no sight of our foes. This matter is about who we need to help us perform the task of getting the Kinetic Talisman."

"You are finding a way to get assistance without revealing information." It was a statement; not a question.

"For the most part, we are." I was really at a loss at how to handle disappointing or angering another with any grace. Jannet would know what to do and it would be the right thing. I went for the direct approach.

"Jannet's mate, Ben, has been very helpful to us. He has kept the Bearer of the Kinetic Talisman and his group from finding us. He is also helping us travel without being discovered easily. The only reason we have not been ambushed is because of him. But, we have told him much of what is happening and why."

Mahrah's emotions churned. I was waiting for her to reprimand me. I put an arm over Wizard and shut my eyes. Instead of being harsh, Mahrah responded evenly.

"It is not optimal. We found long ago that it was better to have fewer humans with the knowledge of the Talismans. I wish you had discussed this with me first.

"It is good Jannet's mate, Ben, is helpful. When we found out she had coupled, we wondered about his involvement. I will trust your judgment on revealing information to him."

"I am sorry I did not tell you earlier. In my kind, it is unusual for couples who have strong relationships to keep things from each other."

"It is the way of my kind also." Her tone had sadness in it. I thought back to our conversation the day before.

"I will consult you before revealing information to any other," I promised. It was a promise I sincerely wanted to keep.

"I wish there was more I could do to help you. You have taken on a great task and I am anxious I have not prepared you well for it."

"You have given us incredible abilities which allow us to do many things. We will find a place to practice for the next couple of days and then go get the Talisman and end the harm the Bearer is inflicting.

"Chosen, the loss of life is much, but it could be so much more. I am grateful it was the Kinetic Talisman which was found. If the Torch or Weir Talisman had been found, it could have been used with devastating effects."

"Well, let's cross that bridge when we come to it."

I was showing and explaining the meaning of the phrase to her when Joe sauntered up.

"I am hungry," he declared.

Chapter 21

The smell of basil, lime and coconut greeted us when we walked in the front door. Jannet was sitting at the table in the nook which adjoined the small kitchen. She looked more relaxed than she had the previous few days. An open bottle of white wine stood on the counter. Ben had brought the ingredients for a red curry he liked to make, one Jannet enjoyed.

"You found red curry paste in England?" I asked skeptically taking the glass of German wine Jannet poured for me.

"Actually, I picked it up in Paris," Ben replied.

"We made plans to meet here late last night. Were the stores still open in Paris?"

Ben turned back to the curry and stirred it unnecessarily. He wasn't quick enough and I caught his smirk. I remembered the car he drove had French license plates, which meant he had taken the ferry over the channel. He could not have driven from Paris in a morning.

"You were going to surprise us in Wilton."

"I knew it wouldn't take you very long to figure it out, Rascal." He came over and put a hand on Jannet's shoulder. She looked up at him and squeezed his hand.

"You are a man who honors his wife," Joe pronounced after taking a sip of his wine.

"I try to do so. She deserves it for putting up with me." Then, to his credit, he changed the subject. "Jannet has been telling me about the things you can accomplish now the rings have been activated. It is intriguing."

We spent dinner discussing the possible scientific and engineering explanations for the bracelet, rings, and Talismans. My theory was the bracelet acted as some sort of relay for a signal which traveled between Mahrah's world and ours. Her initial signal was widespread because she wasn't sure about the geographic location. Later, she concentrated the signal to a smaller area once she knew my energy signature.

Ben agreed with the hypothesis and added he thought the rings were transmitters. There was some debate among us as to if they were also receivers. We decided there was a receiver function since they created a two-way communication link.

How the Talismans worked was more perplexing. They seemed to need energy to activate, but they then changed it to accomplish a specific task. I added Mahrah said the Bearer needed to add energy to help it. Jannet thought both ideas were true of the rings also. We were stumped as to how the devices were pulling energy from us and changing it into some other electromagnetic signal. Ben threw the idea of dark energy into the conversation. The rest of us had only just heard of the concept so there was not much discussion about it.

Each of us had begun to yawn when Joe said, "And we do not know how Nadia bent the pole without touching it."

"What?" Ben asked with raised eyebrows. Jannet clearly had not told him about the incident. She suddenly became interested in her wine glass. I guessed she had said nothing about the propelled rocks either.

Joe took the hint and clammed up.

Ben looked between Jannet and me. "Would one of you lovely ladies like to explain?"

I opted to be the storyteller of the very short story. "It happened last night. I was really upset after hearing about the people getting injured in London. I was even more upset when I saw it was the guy who had been tailing me in the States. Not thinking about my hand, I swung hard to slap a pole. Somehow, the pole bent before I touched it. We looked this morning on the way out of town. It looks like a car hit it but much higher."

Ben took off his glasses and began using the bottom of his shirt to clean them. Jannet and I had tried to break him of the habit years ago. He started thinking out loud, "The bracelet had enough power to bend a metal pole? I may have to rethink my receiver hypothesis. Perhaps there is something in our psyche which supercharges it. How would the bracelet know the difference between a mere wish and an emotional command?"

I instantly noticed he focused on the bracelet and said nothing about the dragon drop I had swallowed which had caused me a bit of distress. I looked at Jannet. She looked down and to her right, then picked at something on her sleeve. We had developed the signal to help me understand when I shouldn't say something in conversation at a party.

Hoping neither Ben or Joe figured out what was just communicated, I followed Jannet's lead by saying, "I don't know. I think we are going to have to see what else happens. Though, I hope I don't often have such strong emotions." I was definitely going to talk to Jannet about this later.

The next morning was gray. There were food items for breakfast left in a basket on the porch by the care takers. It wasn't bacon and eggs or even baps, but it was enough to hold us over until lunch. Joe went out with the gauntlet after he ate. Making sure he could not be observed by anybody but us, he called Iolani. She perched on his arm. He fed her some cold cuts from breakfast. After receiving permission, he stroked her chin. I was three shades of jealous.

"Nadia," he began while continuing to stroke the striking bird, "Why don't you hold her?"

"She seems perfectly content to let you take care of her," I said a bit peevishly.

"She has not approached you because she believes you do not approve of her."

I decided to amend that mistake by reaching out to her and letting her know how amazing I thought she was. When she landed on my arm a few minutes later, I could feel the strength in her talons through the thick gauntlet. She was surprisingly heavy. The brown and beige mottling of her chest and legs was almost comical up close. However, the blue-gray feathers on her wings were exquisite; they looked like a sophisticated tiling.

She craned her neck and pulled her wings back in pride when I communicated how pleased I was she had accepted being a Watcher.

Mahrah nudged us all with the message it was time to work.

Ben decided to stay and work on a computer program while we went to practice. It took us a half hour to find a place which would allow us to work without being noticed. Most of the morning was spent working on continuity with the defense energy while all the Watchers moved as if defending themselves. Joe pulled out his knife and went through the moves he had developed for himself. Jannet practiced with and without her bo staff.

Wizard spun circles. When we asked him why, he indicated he was practicing evasive maneuvers. He was happy with himself until Iolani snickered at him.

For some reason, Mahrah had me spend most of the time in the middle of all this action, sitting. I worked on drawing the Talisman through the dirt. There was progress. I could bury it deeper and use the Pull to retrieve it without stopping.

Right before lunch, it started pouring rain. Iolani ducked in under the branches of an evergreen and the rest of us fled to the car. Not wanting to get asphyxiated by the smell of wet dog, wet humans, and sweaty clothes, we decided to head back to the house. We reckoned it would stop raining by the time we finished lunch.

It was still raining after we ate and Iolani was insistent she was not going to get her feathers wet. Mahrah knew we were tired and indicated we could spend the afternoon resting and working on the communication links. She wanted us to be able to target only one or two others at a time to communicate. She said it would help us understand the nuances of manipulating all the energy levels.

I took her direction to mean we could go to the library.

Instead of going to the cathedral-like reading room on the south side, I headed to the north side of the building. The sign above the door indicated, in Welsh and English, that it was "The Print and Maps Room". Now, it was the place to go to see copies of some of the oldest writings in Wales.

After presenting my archaeological credentials, I was allowed to see a manuscript from the Middle Ages. Because of the age of the book, I had to go into a climate controlled room. Wizard was not allowed in but could stay right outside the door. Jannet volunteered to wait with him. Joe reported mentally he was in the library looking around.

The manuscript the librarian brought was a tome. Written on vellum and bound in red leather, it was ten inches thick. It smelled of cellars, ink, and animal. The librarian gently set the book on the table. I could tell it was a manuscript she knew and loved. I wasn't allowed to touch it but could ask her to turn the pages for me.

It was simply titled, "The Red Book". Jannet and I had read a Welsh story from Ben's dragon book about a story of two kings who opposed each other. There were also two dragons in the story — one red and one white. The dragons were responsible for plagues inflicted on humans. In a battle analogous to the war between the kings, the red dragon vanquished the white dragon. I wondered if there was something more in the original tale which would let me know how old the story really was.

"Do you read Welsh?" the librarian asked.

"I am not able to do so. I have read a translation of the *Tale of Two Kings*. Would it be possible to see it?"

"The myth is one of my favorite stories."

"Because the Welsh flag has a dragon on it?" I asked her with a smile.

She smiled back and said, "Yes, I like it because it is the origin of the red dragon on our flag, but there are other reasons. The story is thought to come from the Dark Ages or even before. I believe there is more to this story than people think." She found the beginning of the story as she spoke.

Unlike many Medieval texts, the book was not lavishly illustrated. Some of the paragraphs started with larger letters written in red. Letters at the top of the page trailed into the margin. Notes in another hand filled the margins, annotations made hundreds of years earlier. I noticed faint handwriting underneath running up and down, indicating the page had been used before.

"This is a palimpsest?" I queried. The librarian nodded enthusiastically. "What was found in the underlying text?" I asked.

"The text is much the same text as you see here. There were a couple of illustrations but not anything the scholars found noteworthy."

I sensed disagreement in her tone.

"What do you think?" I asked.

"There are a few illustrations I find give additional context to these stories. This story was also previously written on another page." She found a page much further back in the book. She turned the book ninety degrees. I could make out some faint lines.

"I have something which will help you read this." She walked to the other side of the room and pulled what looked like a desk lamp out of the drawer. Along with the on switch, it had a dial.

"This light goes through the color spectrum from red to blue. If we turn out the overhead lights and use the right frequency, we should see the underlying text and illustrations more clearly." She turned the lamp on and then turned off the florescent lights.

When the light reached closer to the orange part of the spectrum, it was as if a ghost text appeared. I saw rows of writing in a script tighter than the one clearly visible moments before. The librarian handed me a magnifying glass and pointed to a small illustration. It would have been at the top of the page of the older writing. It was composed of the outline of two dragons facing each other. Both were depicted standing erect. Their wings trailed behind them and fire came out of their mouth. I noted, with some amusement, they had horns.

Something was below them. Initially, I thought it was a castle. I took a closer look and then gasped.

"Stonehenge," I breathed, "without the later construction."

The librarian's eyes were shining. "I think so too, which means this tale is much older than the kings it is thought to represent."

I thanked the librarian profusely. My mind was whirling with what I had seen. I had suspected something happened when the dragons left all those years ago. The Red Book confirmed my hunches.

Everyone else was ready to leave but I had other research to do. Joe and Jannet decided to test the distance of our connection by walking around outside. I paid them peripheral attention as I went about my investigation.

It took me a little while to find a book I had noted while reading about the possible origins of my ancestor. It led me to a translation of the archaeological report from the site where the three women warriors were found, the ones I had read about. After getting the report and two other articles photocopied, I sent a professional introduction and query to the Director of the repository for archaeological artifacts at the museum nearest the site. Before I left, I took advantage of the relative anonymity of using a library's computer to research one Kelly Devlin and her brother, Bryce. The search gave me some useful tidbits, but nothing solid. I sent an email to my brother to ask him to look for more information in public legal documents.

As I was leaving, my mind went back to the Welsh manuscript. The information meant Mahrah had not told me everything, again. I should have asked Jannet about how to address the matter or waited until Mahrah approached the topic. So, I said nothing to Jannet and asked Mahrah as soon as I could.

"You did not tell me everything which happened when you left this world." I sent her the image of the illustration I saw in "The Red Book".

Mahrah didn't say anything immediately. I sensed her hesitation. There was also regret and sorrow.

"We did not all return to my world."

"Your coloring was redder than it is now. You and the white dragon fought. It died..."

"She died," Mahrah interrupted with some force. Her emphasis was on the word 'she'. *"She was. . .We were close."*

"Did the other dragons stand by while this was happening or were they also involved?"

Mahrah was unable to contain her response at being confronted with this. Her emotions were anger, frustration, and profound grief.

"I vowed to not recall this with anyone."

"Your vow probably included dragons only. I think this is something I need to know about."

"It is not directly related to the Talismans."

I listened for what she didn't say. "It is related to the Amulet."

"Truth," she said dejectedly. *"Very well, I will reveal to you what happened."*

The memory began with the dragons approaching the gateway, as I saw before. As the memory continued, the first four dragons went through the gate. The white dragon and Mahrah were still diving when the white dragon pulled out of the dive and veered to the right. She nearly hit the upright stones.

Mahrah was surprised but followed. She sent an inquiry to the white dragon.

"Return to our world, Mahrah. I wish to stay," the white dragon said curtly and began to climb.

"We were to try and set things right and leave, not to stay. Doing so would cause more interference." Mahrah followed.

The white dragon laughed derisively. *"I do not intend to merely interfere; I intend to rule it. I want this world for my own."*

"No. As the firstborn of the ruler of our world, I forbid it."

"Which means nothing here. Our queen is not here to enforce your whims. You have no power over me here."

By this time, the dragons were circling each other high in the sky. They had roared at each other in frustration. The white dragon dove at Mahrah with the intent of ripping her wing. Mahrah folded her wing and rolled out of the way. She felt a surge of heat from the white dragon's fire. Dragons did not use fire on each other unless they meant to kill. It had not happened in an eon.

"If you leave now, I will not harm you," the white dragon commanded. *"Stay, and you will die. I will not return and be a peon among our kind when life here would be so much richer."*

"I cannot leave you to impact this planet with your whims. Please, come with me. We can discuss your position there. We can change it."

The battle roar of the white dragon was her answer. Before Mahrah could maneuver to face her, the white dragon, who was slightly above Mahrah, dove at her and landed on her back. Mahrah bellowed in pain as the white dragon sank her teeth into Mahrah's shoulder.

Mahrah rolled over to try to shake the white dragon. It didn't work. The white dragon then tore at Mahrah's wing with sharp claws. Somehow, Mahrah used her tail to knock the white dragon off balance. She then twisted until the white dragon lost its grasp and began to fall away. The white dragon spewed fire at Mahrah. Quickly, Mahrah spun to counteract the blast with her own inferno.

Mahrah's wing was hurt and she had trouble staying aloft. The white dragon sought to press her advantage. She again tried to attack Mahrah from above. So sure was the white dragon of her victory, she roared triumphantly as she descended, keeping her from using fire. At the last second, Mahrah rolled over and blasted the white dragon with a conflagration. Having taken the blast to her face, the white dragon pulled up short and bellowed in pain, allowing Mahrah to get some distance. She blew fire in Mahrah's general direction to express her rage.

"Stop this madness. Let's go home. I will forgive you and ask all the others to if you quit now," Mahrah pleaded as she circled away from the other.

The white dragon turned and flew directly at Mahrah. Only one of them would come out of this encounter alive. As they collided, both tried to find purchase on the other's scales with their claws. Mahrah succeeded first and ripped off the scale which protected the heart of the white dragon.

Instinct took over Mahrah's actions. She threw a bolt of energy into the exposed flesh. The white dragon became paralyzed and fell from the sky. She hit the earth with a sickening thud.

Mahrah's injured wings kept her from flying directly. By the time she was able to land, the white dragon's breathing was shallow.

"Lay still. I might be able to heal you." Mahrah began to envision the bodily damage the other dragon had and started to hum to bring together healing energy.

"You won't. I will die as your beloved human will."

Mahrah stopped humming. The energy dissipated. *"What do you mean?"*

"If I was to rule the world, I needed to make sure I was the most powerful. You gave the human too many abilities. I have made sure she will not be alive to use them."

"How?"

"I sent a tribe of humans against your Chosen and the Watchers she has. Since, you told her to bury the Amulet, she will be almost powerless against so many foes. And, they will bring her secret back to me. I know you told her to hide it in her belongings. It is so like you."

Mahrah's thoughts scattered. She wanted to go to the warrior woman to help her. A promise was made to protect her and her people and now the promise would not be realized. Mahrah also wanted to stay, pull her thoughts together and create healing energy for the dragon she had wounded so terribly.

The white dragon read Mahrah's thoughts. *"You are too late. The woman will be dead by the time you reach her. You are too late for me also. Pity you came out of your egg so early and now are too late to save life."*

The white dragon exhaled heavily and died. Her body began to burn. Mahrah retreated to a safe distance and keened. It was a wailing that turned the blood of those who heard it cold.

Chapter 22

I was paralyzed by what I had seen. Not being able to speak, all I could do was send Mahrah emotions of regret, sympathy, and support. I thoroughly regretted my impulsive decision to ask her about the white dragon. We sat linked but not speaking for some time. After a while, I felt her put her grief aside.

It was still some time before she spoke. *"I was put in the judgment circle when I returned. I had done the most abominable deed known to dragons. I had killed another."*

"Surely they understood the circumstances?" I stammered from my shock.

"Some did. They pointed to my injuries and said I had no choice. Others called for my death to redress the wrong even though my memories showed I had tried to avoid the conflict. Some said there should be no exception and I, too, should die."

"They were going to kill you for killing another?"

"No, it is not our way. One who is condemned for taking another's life must take their own."

My training as an archaeologist was the only thing which kept me from vehemently objecting to this ritual. It surprised me that my technical training was taking over in the midst of such emotional upheaval.

"But, they did not convict you. You are still alive."

"I am. My deed is a burden I carry. I have been largely withdrawn from my own kind because of it. I spent much time over the years wondering how I could have avoided the loss of life, both my kind and yours, and regretting coming to your world."

"You have been more careful this time because you do not want me to come to harm like the first Chosen did," I said with a deeper understanding of her actions.

"Truth. I feel I did not protect the first Chosen well enough. I swore I would not let it happen again." She paused. *"Chosen, will you refrain from telling the Watchers and the other, Ben?"*

"I will refrain." A question came to me. "Why didn't you use the healing energy on your mate?"

"To use it, one has to know what is wrong. We could not determine why he was ill."

"It sounds like you blame yourself for his death also."

"I know I did not cause it but wonder if my former deed had impact on his life."

"We all wonder things like that. I think it is time for you to not ruminate on that anymore. We have a saying, 'To err is human, to forgive is divine.' I think you should practice being divine."

"Chosen, you would like me to become one of the gods you curse?" Her tone was no longer sorrowful.

I winced. "You know I curse using the names of different gods?"

Mahrah chuckled.

The evening was perfect for sitting outdoors, so we chose to eat dinner in the backyard of the house. We took turns holding Iolani. Wizard was a little perturbed that he was not the center of attention and let us know by periodically sighing heavily.

"How are you going to travel with her on a plane? I don't think you will be able to have her loose and she doesn't seem like the type who will be caged," Ben queried.

Joe, Jannet and I looked at each other. We realized we had no idea.

After our conversation earlier, Mahrah and I had agreed to stay aware but not fully connected to each other. She noticed the question in my mind and gave our connection more attention. I repeated Ben's question to her.

"As I said before, I have given this thought. Chosen, you can extend Conceal to more than yourself. I think you will also be able to draw it in to Conceal less than your whole."

"Could I Conceal while she is sitting on her perch?"

"Whatever you Conceal smaller than yourself will need to be touching you. Hold Iolani and try to Conceal just her."

Mahrah had spoken just to me, so I relayed the plan to the others. After Iolani was perched on my arm, I activated the Conceal Talisman. Even I could tell I hadn't made a small enough field because Ben started. Jannet put her hand on his arm and told him it was all right.

My second try was a little more successful. The others reported only my arm and Iolani disappeared.

It took almost an hour before I could Conceal Iolani, and only Iolani. After about twenty minutes, the novelty wore off for everybody else. They started chatting. I would ask if I had accomplished the task after activating the Talisman. The humans would glance over and give a quick assessment. Mostly, they told me something else on my body had disappeared or they could see parts of Iolani. Sometimes Wizard chimed in with a mental image of what he saw.

I was just getting the hang of it when Joe said, “Will you be able to carry her on your arm? She is heavy and I think it would be hard to walk through the detectors with her there. People may wonder why you are wearing a large leather glove.”

I swore. “Where else can I carry her? My head?”

Jannet had a reasonable suggestion, “How about on your shoulder? We can say you are unable to turn your head. If we don’t say why, we won’t be lying and most people will assume it is because you pulled something in your neck.”

Joe warmed to the idea, “We can buy you a leather jacket and sunglasses. It would be very cool.”

“Do you think the jacket would show the indents from her talons?” I asked. We decided to test it even though my energy was beginning to flag.

We told Iolani about the change in plans, draped the gauntlet over my shoulder, and tried again. Once I changed the focus of where to direct the Conceal energy, she winked out of sight. No indentations in the glove were visible.

“I think we have a workable plan. There is just one problem,” I said.

“Which is what?” Joe could see nothing wrong with the idea.

“Iolani needs to go on a diet.”

She understood we had just joked at her expense, flew up into a nearby tree and began preening. When I reached out to her, I could tell she was not truly irked; I was relieved.

Ben started a new topic, “I am going to leave in the morning. Today, I worked on a way someone can reach your phone without the signal being tracked. Well, someone will have a dickens of a time tracking it.

“I linked a computer program to a phone line at work. Once someone calls it and types in the access code, the program will ask who the call is for and then route the signal through three randomly chosen nodes before sending the signal to your phone.” He handed out pieces of paper with a phone number and four-digit code. I had forgotten how impeccable his penmanship was.

"How are we going to get this to people who have our current number?" I asked.

"I thought you could email them and let them know about the change. You can use my computer tonight. It is running through a virtual network connection and should be difficult to trace."

Ben then turned to Joe, "I am not sure if your family, friends, or other village members have email or cellphones."

"Cellphones are becoming more common place. But, I think I will need to contact them through a social media app. May I use your computer?"

Ben was happy to lend his computer, and Joe began to text people individually. His message included hopes that all was well. He received a return message before reaching the end of his list. The incoming text said everyone and everything was fine. Joe breathed a sigh of relief and visibly relaxed. He had such a positive demeanor that I didn't realize how much the safety of the village and his people had been on his mind.

More messages pinged his inbox. Joe summarized the information from them. There had been great concern when the Devlin Duo showed up at the hotel without the driver. They demanded to know where Joe's village was, but everyone pretended not to know or understand. Eventually, they coerced someone to tell them how to get there. They, of course, found nothing. The two were last seen driving south into Tanzania.

"Too bad your people couldn't take the vehicle from those two," Ben said.

"It is better to put trouble further from you than closer," Joe countered. "The loss of one vehicle was much less than the trouble they would have brought to my village."

After Ben left the next morning, we went back to the field from the day before. By mid-morning, we could tell we had reached a point where the defense field was balanced and I was able to extend the force of the Conceal Talisman easily and consistently. The low hum when the rings and Talisman operated before became more harmonious. Wizard confirmed dissonant sounds had disappeared. We had finally reached a balance. After deactivating the Talisman and the defense energy of the rings, we decided to take a break.

I opened my messenger bag and yanked the gauntlet out from the bottom. As a result, the bird hood which had been pressed on us at the falcon store fell out. Iolani spotted it immediately. I felt a wave of panic go through her and she took flight. Within seconds, she was beyond the reach of our Connection and kept climbing.

We all looked at each other, alarmed. I called out to Mahrah.

"I too am unable to reach her," she said to all of us after trying to contact

the falcon.

"She is too far for the rings or my bracelet. What are we going to do if she leaves?"

"No harm will come to her or any of you. It would be unfortunate to lose her abilities. You say she is too far for the rings or the bracelet. Is she too far for the rings and the bracelet?"

I caught the distinction. "How can we combine them?"

"Instead of you focusing your energy out among the rings, the Watchers should focus their Connection energy to you. Then, you reach with the same technique you do for Pulling."

"I don't think I can pull her from that distance."

"You do not need to physically move her. You are just trying to contact her."

Joe, Jannet, and Wizard stood around me. Instead of focusing on each other as Mahrah had instructed them to do, they focused on me. I, in turn, focused on the dot wheeling high above us. I felt a brush against the edge of the Connection energy. It was like reaching for something behind the dresser and catching it with the very tips of your fingers. Eventually, the connection caught.

Iolani settled a little bit. She indicated she wasn't going to come back immediately but she would be back. We waited a half hour before she landed. We all noticed it was at the very top of a tree.

Joe expressed the remorse we all had for the hood. He told her how we came to have it and that there had been no plan to use it. Iolani accepted the explanation, but was still rather, well, ruffled.

Jannet asked her why it bothered her so much. The falcon answered with a barrage of images. When we sorted them out, we were appalled.

Iolani had a mate. They had raised a brood and were headed south to winter. One minute, they were darting in and out of trees and enjoying the day. The next minute, her mate was no longer with her. She circled back and found him entangled in a net.

The male Peregrine could have freed himself if he had time, but two men were there almost immediately after Iolani found him. She buzzed the humans, stopping when one pulled another net out. The men put a bird hood on the male Peregrine before putting him in a cage. Iolani called to her mate and he called back. He told her to stay away. One of the men shook the cage savagely and then tossed it into a van.

Iolani followed the van to a large building which had no windows. She perched in a nearby tree. Her mate no longer responded to her calls. She waited. Days went by and she still did not see him. She could not wait much longer because the winds would shift and she would not get to the wintering place. With a heavy heart, she left.

"Poachers," Joe said angrily.

"Who knows why they took the falcon. I wonder if they put it in a zoo or sold it to someone who does falconry," Jannet was trying to make sense of why someone would take birds of prey from the wild.

"One of those would be a better outcome. I hope there is not a market for Peregrine Falcon feathers," I added with a heavy heart.

It was Wizard who finally calmed the bird. We were spectators to the image conversation as he showed how humans could also be very kind and caring. He vouched for us and showed the extremely good care he had received from us. He began overdoing it when he started sharing details of how wonderful belly rubs were for him.

When I glanced at him instead of Iolani, he was on his back, wiggling in the grass with his tongue hanging out of the side of his mouth. I think Iolani saw him at the same time. She glided down to the grass and rubbed her beak along his now upright ear. She was still kept out of reach but was no longer upset.

Mahrah had been watching. She rumbled her satisfaction.

"Chosen, Watchers, I believe you are ready for the task of recovering the Talisman."

We all beamed in our own way.

The challenge, we acknowledged that evening while sitting in the sun room, was to find the location of the Kinetic Talisman. Iolani perched on the back of one of the wicker chairs. Wizard was enjoying the cool tile floor. Joe, Jannet and I sat in the rest of the chairs on the enclosed patio.

I had a plan to use us as a lure. I reasoned it would keep other people from being harmed. Joe was opposed to the idea. He made a good point about our foes.

"We do not know how many there are," he stated plainly.

Jannet agreed, "We know about the three. I would say Kelly, Bryce, and Reginald are key players in this game. Since they have been able to find out who we are and where we go, there are others working for them."

"Or, someone else is directing the whole thing," I mused.

"Since we know Kelly's name for sure and Bryce is her brother, do you think we should try to use our own connections to track them? I am sure Ben can find a way to inquire on their credit cards." Jannet had been upset her privacy had been violated.

"It would give us the most up-to-date information on their whereabouts. I like the idea. I want to get my hands on the Talisman before any more people are harmed by its use," I replied.

"It is illegal to access their financial records. Would doing so mean we are like those who oppose us? How is it said in English?" Joe asked. Jannet's phone binged and she rose to retrieve it from the dining room which was just inside the sunroom door.

He concentrated, "I remember. It doesn't matter how we accomplish our goals as long as it is a good ending. Is this our way?"

It was a thorny question. I didn't have a chance to answer because Jannet called us at the same time Mahrah pushed into my consciousness. Joe got up to see what Jannet wanted and I turned my attention to Mahrah.

"The Kinetic Talisman has been used again. It was not as close to you this time."

"Can you tell me anything else?"

"The draw on energy was not as great this time. We have been paying close attention to the signal so we may tell you each time as quickly as possible."

Joe was at the back door right after Mahrah finished. "Chosen, come see the news. We think the Kinetic Talisman has been used."

I told Mahrah I would continue our conversation later and went into the living room. There was a breaking news report about a jewelry store which had just been robbed in southern Germany. The news program had a security camera photo of a man whose face and head were mostly covered. A guard was pointing a gun at the man. The news reported that the man left the store apparently unharmed even though the guard fired two shots. Another security camera photo showed the man getting into a car. There was someone else in the back seat. The person's hair, most probably a female, was very light.

"It looks suspicious, but how do we know for sure?" I asked. "I don't want to run to a country only to find there is another explanation for the events."

"Same shoes," Jannet said evenly. "The photos show the person's shoes and they are the same one Reginald had on the day he and Bryce tailed us in Denver."

Thinking back to the day in Denver, I said, "You are right. It is amazing the lengths people will go to conceal their identity and forget about their shoes."

We wrestled with the decision to leave right then. We were exhausted from the day of working with the rings, bracelet, and Talisman. Joe wondered if the whole thing was a set up and worried about being attacked. We decided to wait until morning to leave Aberystwyth, called the travel agent, and booked tickets.

It was early morning when my dreams became active and disturbing. The world switched from present to past. One minute, I was looking over a field I knew had been the site of a town in the past. The next, it was as if I had been transported back in time to when those settlements were inhabited. I saw horses and people milling about. A large shadow passed over, but no one noticed.

The scene flipped back to the present and I interpreted the shadow to be an airplane. I stood in the center of a ring of stones which became a ring of men with guns. The sky began to undulate with shades of black and red mahogany. The Watchers flicked into view around me. The men leveled their guns and charged. I woke up screaming.

Mahrah was there. *"Chosen, the black dragon has escaped, which changes things in my world. We now know he has told his human about the Amulet. Do not pursue the Talisman. You must find the Amulet. It must not be claimed by the other."*

The intensity of her communication initially kept me from seeing Jannet at the end of the bed. She was talking, but I did not hear what she said. She came around the edge to sit next to me when Mahrah started again.

"I do not know when next I can contact you without putting you in danger. You need to know about the Amulet. When it is paired with the Talismans it will give its Bearer the power of the dragons. I told your ancestor to leave a message about the location of the Amulet among her things.

"You must find it. If you do not, I fear for your world. I trust you. I believe in you."

I called out Mahrah's name, but she was not there to hear me. Jannet's brows were furrowed. She had a hand on my upper arm and was looking at me with great concern. "What happened?"

"The black dragon escaped and is wreaking havoc in the other world. We need to find the Amulet." Jannet closed her eyes and shook her head. "Let's wake Joe."

We made tea because it was the only thing available in the house. After a hot cup of beverage, I cleared the tendrils of the dream from my mind. Mahrah's words about the Amulet and its potential disturbed the Watchers. We came to consensus Mahrah wasn't acting maliciously by keeping its secrets from us. We, including Mahrah, had all been focused on the Kinetic Talisman.

"Do we have any idea where the Amulet is?" Jannet asked.

"I do. Mahrah told me my ancestor bore the Amulet and she showed me memories of meeting the woman. I was able to use her appearance to determine approximately where she lived."

"How amazing; you are a detective." Joe exclaimed.

I blushed a bit. "It helped some of her clothing was distinct to a certain part of the world. Her sword and mount also narrowed it down."

"It took you knowing a lot about all those things," Jannet said. "You have always impressed me with all the stuff you remember about people, artifacts, and sites."

"She had a mount? Was it an elephant?" Joe asked.

"No, horses. I figured out she was from the area roughly between the eastern edge of Turkey and the Caspian Sea. Long story short, a set of burials south of the Caucasus Mountains is our best lead. If it isn't those burials it is close. We need to go to Georgia." I could tell the details were not of utmost interest to my companions.

"It is not the most stable of countries," Jannet said with unease.

"It will be less stable if Reginald and company, or whoever, gets their hands on the Amulet." I said.

"Do you think the black dragon told his person where the Amulet is?" Joe was starting to put together a plan of attack.

"I have no idea. Mahrah knew its approximate location because she worked with the woman who had it. She never said if all the other dragons knew where the first Chosen lived."

"I think it is wise we make plans either way, we will either be first to the prize or last," Joe said.

Despite the early hour, we began our plans for Operation Amulet.

Chapter 23

By the time dawn came, we had rebooked our flights, checked our email, and packed our bags to go to Tbilisi, Georgia. We were lucky the same airline leaving from Manchester flew to both Germany and Georgia. Hopefully, our adversaries would see only the first booking and not the second.

When I opened my email, I was happy to see a reply from the Director at the museum. However, her news was a mixed bag. She was aware the artifacts from the excavation existed, but wasn't sure exactly where they were. She indicated the museum had gone through an upheaval in organization and storage and they were still relocating all the collections.

I thanked her for her reply. Letting her know my travel plans had changed and I was now due in her country in two days, I asked if I could visit the museum and speak with her about the site and the items found there.

My brother's terse email gave me information about Kelly and her husband. In light of the German robbery, I sent him another couple of questions and hoped I wasn't using up all his goodwill toward me as I hit send.

Jannet said Ben reserved a two-room suite for us at a hotel near the National Museum using the name of a small company he still owned. It would be difficult to trace because the company's paperwork had been filed years ago, physically. He had kept it going just in case he needed it for taxes. Since using it as a front would help keep us off the radar, he was now doubly happy he had kept it active.

Our travel to Manchester was difficult only because of Joe's nostalgic sighs. He regaled us with stories of his football games, dart games, and foot races. I wondered aloud how much time he had spent actually studying. He retorted that he wanted to make sure he was a well-rounded individual. Jannet snorted at the comment.

Iolani was exemplary as we traveled through the airport, boarded, flew, and then reversed the whole process in Georgia. The sustained effort and weight on my shoulder gave me a tremendous headache. When we finally made it out of the airport, I made sure to find a discreet area before turning off the Conceal Talisman and letting her take off.

Because of my pounding head, I was only dimly aware of our arrival at the hotel. Sensing this, Wizard lead me as we followed Jannet to our two-room suite. We breathed a sigh of relief as we closed the door, hoping no trouble found us in the night. Joe, not wanting to just hope, rose every hour. He quietly opened the door to the suite, checked on us as he walked across the room, and checked on Iolani who had made her bed in a tree outside our window. After his fourth time of doing so, I assured him Wizard would sound an alarm if something threatened us.

The next morning, there wasn't much of a dawn due to the cloud cover. After a filling breakfast of a bread which held cooked egg and cheese, we walked to the nearby park. A short stroll took us to the eastern edge of the park, which was across the street from the National Museum. The forbidding three story gray building was the same hue as the sky. I reached out to Iolani who was chasing pigeons. I told her to be cautious by sending an image of a bus with a bird on the windshield. She replied, and I must have had an odd look on my face because Jannet asked what was wrong.

"I think I just got the bird's version of a middle finger," I said.

While I had been concentrating on Iolani during our flight, Jannet had been learning rudimentary Georgian and learning about the country. She told us some of her findings. "The building is in the old-Georgian architectural style and has a collection of gold and silver artifacts from burials that were created about 450 BC."

Wizard's attention was caught by a pack of dogs trotting through the north side of the greenway. "I read that a woman was attacked by a street dog. I hope we don't have any trouble with Wizard getting into the museum," Jannet said in a more subdued tone.

"I think we will be okay. I did let the director know I had a service animal."

"What was her reply?" Jannet asked

"Now that I think about it, she was noncommittal in her response."

"We could Conceal him," Joe offered.

"I would need to stay in contact with him and I am afraid it would take too much of my concentration."

"I can only imagine what people would do if a huge dog suddenly blinked into sight," Jannet said with a smile. "Let's hope the ticket agent for the museum is a dog lover."

Joe was looking odd wearing a heavy jacket on a day I considered warm. He pulled out a pair of large, dark-framed sunglasses with costume gemstones along the arms. It was the most hideous pair of sunglasses I had ever seen and I wondered where he had gotten them. He must have guessed my assessment of the glasses for he donned them with an air of sophistication. He looked to his right and stepped off the curb.

Jannet and I reached forward as one, grabbed him by the shoulder, and pulled him back just as a car passed from the left. The driver looked at us with the internationally recognized glare of 'idiot'.

After reminding Joe about the traffic direction in this country, the four of us crossed the street without incident. Jannet spoke with the ticket agent in a combination of English and Georgian. She was able to get the woman to understand we had set up an appointment with the Director. The woman kept looking over Jannet's shoulder at Wizard. She pointed to him and said something to Jannet.

Jannet turned to look at me. When she turned back she gave the woman her most disarming smile. "Oh, the dog. She needs him. He is a service dog." She put a lot of stress on the word 'needs'.

The woman frowned slightly. Joe was a few feet to our right. He whistled a tune as he looked up and down the building and then up and down the block. I wanted to tell him to quit gawking because I didn't want to attract any more attention. He removed his glasses and caught the ticket agent's eye.

"It is a beautiful building in a beautiful country. You must be very proud," he said to her. "I am glad you let others see the amazing contributions your ancestors have made to the world."

She smiled. Jannet, to her credit, kept her features completely neutral. I turned and coughed with amusement. I was traveling with a Maasai con-man. I should have given Wizard to Joe. He could have convinced someone not only to let the dog in to the museum, but feed him as well.

The ticket agent was now ready to believe our request and phoned the director. Her side of the conversation was in Georgian and too quick for Jannet to translate. There must have been a request for a description of our party because the woman looked at each of us as she spoke. After hanging up, she wrote something on a piece of paper, handed it to Jannet, and waved us to the entrance. The usher looked at the paper and then looked us all over.

He stepped aside. Once in, we made our way to the archaeological exhibition on the first floor. We stopped in front of a case that had some bone points, stone axes, and pottery figurines. The click of high heels came up behind us.

"Ms. Kokinidis?" said the voice pronouncing my last name correctly.

I turned and saw a tall woman, with a flawless olive complexion, and dark hair which flowed over her shoulders. She was dressed in a cream blouse unbuttoned just enough to create a V-neck, a fitted pinstripe skirt, and patent black heels. She had amber eyes, high cheek bones, and full lips. I found her stunning.

I must have been staring because I felt a mental nudge from Jannet and Wizard stepping on my foot. For having four feet and weighing less than I did, he could exert a lot of pressure with just one paw.

"Yes," I replied, "Ms. Apakidze?" She nodded. I hoped I had pronounced *her* name correctly.

I extended my hand and continued, "Nice to meet you in person. I heard you have done a wonderful job with the artifacts which have been uncovered over the last ten years."

"Thank you, I have read that you have found sites unrecognized by many others," she smiled and paused briefly, "You said you wanted to look at a particular set of artifacts from the Late Bronze Age?" Her accented English was lyrical. She walked to a nearby case filled with swords and other objects from the era. The swords were squared at the end and flat. They were more for swinging to take off someone's arm rather than stabbing them in the heart. I followed Ms. Apakidze. Jannet and Joe trailed behind us.

"Yes, there was a grave of three warriors which was found to the north of here. All three were women. I believe one of them was buried in a sitting position," I recounted.

"There were very few funerary goods in the burial compared to the extensive ones in some of the burials on the north side of the Black Sea. I began looking when I received your email and we do hold the artifacts from the excavation of the three women in reserve here." My heart leapt. It was *almost* entirely because of the good news she had just given me.

"Can you tell me what you plan to do with the information?" she continued.

"Some of the burials in this area have similarities to a few now being found in Greece. I thought I would look at the artifacts and the burial of these warriors in more detail to determine if the similarity provides evidence of cultural contact. I would also like to see photographs of the site if you have them." I hoped the reason sounded plausible.

Ms. Apakidze studied me for a minute. Her amber eyes drifted to my messenger bag and then to Wizard who was sitting. She didn't smile which worried me on two levels. I was afraid she was going to kick us out of the museum and, on a personal level, she didn't want to speak with me.

"What can you tell me about these objects?" she asked gesturing to the swords, not taking her eyes off me.

I looked them over. "They are part of the Late Bronze Age to Early Iron Age. The geometric designs on these are typical for the area, but no one knows what they represent. But, those are not my specialty. I can tell you more details about this pot here," I said turning to a large pot on a pedestal next to the display case. I rattled off some details about probable firing temperatures and surface treatments. I walked over to another pot close by and described the type of clay in the area. Her expression relaxed.

"Please, call me Michelle," she said as she nodded. "I am sorry to have tested you. We have had people try to come and steal artifacts." She again looked at my messenger bag.

"I am sorry to hear of such a blatant contempt for your country and its history. I assure you I am here to make observations. These two individuals are part of my team," I said pointing to my companions.

Introductions were made. Surprisingly, she asked to see our passports. I was glad we had decided to use our real names.

"And, this one?" Michelle asked pointing at Wizard.

"His name is Wizard. I have a medical condition which necessitates a service dog. I can show you his certificate and the paperwork if you would like."

"It won't be necessary. Can I pet him?"

I nodded and she squatted down to scratch Wizard under the chin. I sent a message to him to keep his tongue to himself. He ignored me.

"I am so sorry," I said as he caught Michelle's chin.

"It is okay," she said scratching his ears as she stood. "Most people, like the ticket agent you saw, hate dogs because of the wild dog packs in the city. I adore them. It may be the time I spent in Europe."

After hearing this, I knew things were going to be okay. I found people who accepted Wizard, accepted me along with him. After giving his ears one more rub, Michelle led us downstairs to a room with tables and a rolling shelf system. She motioned to a table for us to sit and then spoke to the assistant sitting at a desk on the right side of the room. He checked his computer and then disappeared among the filing shelves, as she went to her office. Within minutes, the clerk delivered three bank boxes. At the same time, Michelle returned from her office and put the original excavation report in front of me. It was in Georgian.

"I am sorry I have no English translation," she said with real apology in her voice. "But, perhaps you know of some details from the German summary?"

"I have gleaned some of the details from reports of this version. The maps and pictures will give me quite a bit of information. I assume the artifacts are in the boxes?"

She nodded. "We try our best to make sure they are kept in conditions to keep them from deteriorating. The room is climate controlled, but we do not have the funds to properly store all the artifacts. I will not be far if you need more information or something translated."

"Thank you very much." I watched Michelle as she walked into her office. Jannet communicated mentally to stop drooling. I glared at her, but she was right. I didn't expect to meet someone to whom I had such a physical attraction. I quickly pushed away fanciful thoughts of asking her to join me to look for sites in her country. I gave myself a mental shake and focused on the task at hand.

Jannet, Joe and I drew up chairs and began. It took over an hour to look through the excavation report. Jannet took notes as I described positions of artifacts and remains. Joe surprised me by truly examining the pictures. I was unsure what he was synthesizing. After finishing the report, I stood to open the first box.

The clerk was there instantly, put his hands on top of the box, and called Michelle. She came out and looked at us crowded around the table. She looked worried. I felt a wave of anger at the thieves who had caused such mistrust.

"Would you be okay with your team moving to the other table?"

They used their Connection to let me know it would be fine. Jannet took my bag with her, Wizard followed her across the room.

Once everyone was situated, the clerk relaxed. He put a cloth on the table, removed each artifact from the first box, and placed it on the table. I could tell by his body language he was to be the only person to handle them. My intuition was it would be impossible to retrieve the message Mahrah told us to find without touching the object which held it. This was a snag in our plan.

It was my turn to call Michelle from her office. "I would like to examine just a few of the artifacts closely. Would it be okay if I picked them up?" Michelle pursed her lips, nodded tightly, and said something to the clerk. I could tell from his expression, he was not pleased.

The objects were phenomenal. Each box had the grave goods of one of the women who had been buried. The summaries I had just read indicated two of them had been mortally wounded. The death of the third was not discoverable by marks on her bones. None of the pottery, beads, or weapons in the first two boxes gave any hints. The few pieces of pottery were fine for their time and the weapons were beautiful Bronze Age pieces much like the ones in the case upstairs.

The third box contained similar objects. There were spherical clay vases with small necks and a fluted opening. Each had a piece missing from one side. They had been decorated by scratches made into the clay. Most of the decorations were vertical lines. I could tell there had been a different decoration on the missing pieces because there were circles which interrupted the lines. Random triangles jutted out of the circles.

There were two golden rings, the only gold among all the artifacts. After nodding to the clerk, I picked them up and looked at them closely. One was a plain band and the other looked like a serpent with its tail in its mouth. I looked at the bracelet on my own wrist. I hoped they had been made by the same person, but the two pieces of jewelry were not similar. I put the rings back; the assistant let out a breath he was holding.

The bronze sword had some geometric etchings on it. There were also deep scratches on the edges. The sword had been well used.

There were only a few objects left and no evidence of a message. From the report, I knew the necklace with the jasp-agate beads I was looking at were found with the sitting warrior. Red and white swirled through the stone beads of the necklace, with hints of yellow and black. I leaned in for a closer look. As I focused on the pendant, my hand brushed the jaw bone of an animal on the table. A scene flashed in my vision. A green field furled out below the viewpoint, rising to a ridge. Beyond the ridge was a massive peak encased in snow. The scene faded and I desperately tried to recall it.

After the vision, I realized I was practically on top of the pendant and the clerk was speaking, loudly. I spent another five seconds pretending I could see the stone which was almost at the end of my nose.

"The crystalline structure is amazing," I said as I straightened up.

Michelle had once again come out of her office. Jannet was sitting and smiling tightly. Her hands were clenched in her lap. I almost jumped when I turned and saw Joe squatting in front of the pots. Wizard, on the other hand, was practically snoring. With a look at him Michelle sighed, said something to the assistant and went back into her office.

I looked again at the jaw bone. "Is this from the horse?" I asked pointing to it.

The clerk looked at me with confusion and quite some hesitancy.

"Horse?" Jannet asked in Georgian. The clerk nodded tightly. After wordlessly asking to pick it up, he gave another tight nod. I turned the jawbone over, but nothing happened. *Great*, I thought, *no repeat performance*. I spent another couple of minutes looking for etchings or marks that may have indicated trauma and then thanked the clerk. Jannet echoed the thanks in Georgian.

The clerk began to put the objects back in the box. Before he could get very far, Joe spoke, "Nadia, please look here again. There is something."

I bent down and took a closer look at the markings around the hole. The circles were interrupted with small triangles in different places. I took those for decorations from the missing piece and part of the geometric design. "What are you seeing?"

From his kneeling position, Joe pointed to the bottom of the circle where there was more than triangles. I saw the design was not geometric but artistic. It was the edges of four scaly feet with claws.

Chapter 24

The other triangles on the top edges no longer looked random. They were the ends of the two wings and the tip of the tail of a dragon, its body in the missing piece. The rounded triangle to one side I had noticed before was the edge of the nose. I looked at Joe and then the clerk. "Do you mind if I take a picture?" I asked and pantomimed at the same time. He nodded his same tight nod. We were finished a few minutes later.

Michelle walked with us back to the museum entrance. As she did so, she said, "I think I remember another analysis done on this site and its artifacts. It would have been published either locally or in Russia. If I find it, would you like me to let you know?"

"I would be interested, thank you," I replied courteously.

"Where can I reach you?"

I fumbled for a moment. "I have a number my team and I are using while we are abroad. Once you enter our group code, you can pick one of us from the menu."

"I have never heard of such a set up for an archaeological team."

"We are testing it for a friend."

I gave Michelle the number We exchanged goodbyes and left. I let Jannet pick our next destination as I had a lot to think about. I was absorbed with what I had seen and with trying to figure out why I was so attracted to a woman I was never going to see again. My thoughts ping-ponged between the two topics.

Jannet led us to a park a block north of the museum and around the corner. I looked around to make sure we could not be heard by anyone before sitting on a bench to discuss the visit. Iolani flew to the tree under which we were sitting. I idly wondered if she had been snacking on pigeons.

"What happened to you in there?" Jannet asked. "First, I have never seen you so smitten with anyone. Second, I thought you were going to eat those beads."

I chose to ignore 'first'. "Mahrah was right. The warrior did push a memory into one of the grave goods. I thought it would be in something she was wearing, but it was in the horse's jawbone."

"She loved her horse much, yes?" Joe asked.

I turned to look at him. "Good catch on the pottery. I thought the triangles were just geometric decoration."

Joe gave a wide smile.

"Did you understand what the clerk said when I almost ate the necklace?" I asked Jannet.

"Oh, he invoked a deity and asked Michelle to call security."

"Good thing Michelle has a cool head. I think she took her lead from Wizard. Maybe she figured if he wasn't upset, nothing was going to happen."

"And, she likes you," she said in a teasing tone.

"What did you see in the memory?" Joe asked.

"It was a mountain. I think it is close to where the Amulet is buried. The problem is, I have no idea where the mountain is. It could be to the south or to the north. For all I know, it could be in the Himalayas."

"It is north." Joe said with confidence.

Jannet and I looked at him incredulously.

"How can you possibly know?" Jannet asked.

"Because, the woman warrior was buried with her face to the north. The other warriors' faces were East. Her face and the broken parts of the jars all pointed north. I saw this in the pictures of the excavation."

"Jannet, get out the tablet." I commanded. It was a good thing she was used to this tone when I was involved in a project.

She did so and I flipped through her notes. I had been focusing on the minutiae of what was in the grave rather than the overall alignment of the site. Along with Joe's findings, there was something else. The silver knife which had been resting on her leg was discovered pointing almost north. The lead archaeologist theorized it had been placed pointing exactly north.

"Joe, would you like to be an archaeologist?" I asked.

"Not so much. It would not be useful while raising cattle," he quipped.

As we began our walk back to the hotel, we passed a church adorning the corner of the park. Jannet caught me staring at it.

"This is one of the churches in the area I was reading about yesterday. It is called Kashveti Church of St. George. It is only one hundred years old, a fairly typical design for an Orthodox church. Let's go for a closer look," she invited.

We approached the front of the church and tried the door, which was unlocked. The church was lavishly decorated. An oversized painting of the Madonna and child was at the front of the church. Underneath it, another painting depicted the twelve apostles. The screen at the front of the church, called an iconostasis, was also quite ornate. I was looking at the pictures on the walls when Joe tugged on my sleeve. He was looking up. Again.

The scene above me in the cupola was of a man on a horse with a spear. "St. George," Jannet breathed into my ear. What drew our attention like flies to peanut butter was St. George's horse dancing on a dragon, a white dragon. I held my breath as I recalled the horror Mahrah had when she realized she had killed the white dragon. The mural confirmed to me some of the events from when the dragons were on the earth were in old stories.

We didn't get much more of a look. One of the priests came over and indicated dogs were not allowed in the church. We said our apologies and left. As I approached the door, I saw some pamphlets on the far side of it. They advertised other Georgian Orthodox churches in the country. Jannet, who was between me and the pamphlets, was about to walk by them when I grabbed her arm to stop her.

"What?" she asked.

"Take one of those pamphlets from the second row," I said quickly. I cast a look over my shoulder. The priest who had asked us to leave was following us to the door, making sure we obeyed.

She looked at me like I had lost my mind but picked up a pamphlet from the holder.

"Why did you want the pamphlet?" she asked.

"The church on the right of the pamphlet. The mountain. It's the one." I babbled, "That's the mountain. It is the one I saw in the memory."

Jannet looked at the pamphlet more carefully. She turned it around to show us. "Gergeti Trinity Church under Mount Kazbek," she pronounced.

"Is it north?" Joe asked.

Jannet flipped through the pamphlet and found a map. It took her a minute to find the church on it. "Not far off," she said grinning.

"Well, now we know in what part of the country to look. How do we know where the Amulet is in relationship to the mountain?" I asked.

"Nadia, figuring out the answer to your question is your job," Jannet replied.

It was early afternoon and we were all hungry, sans Iolani, who actually had been snacking on pigeons. We were going to stop at a market and grab some items for lunch but realized we had very little currency. So, we went back to the hotel and ordered olives, a cheese assortment with flat bread, and salads. Joe was skeptical of the cheese but tried it anyway. He was not used to cultures which built most of their dietary choices around milk products.

Afterwards, we all went to the room Jannet and I shared. Jannet's job was to get in touch with Ben and plan our excursion to Mount Kazbek. We learned it was a very popular climbing mountain and there was a town nearby used by tourists. I hoped it meant there was enough traffic in the area to keep us from being noticed.

By the time Jannet finished her call, I was reading one of the manuscripts I had copied from the National Library in Wales. When my phone rang, Joe, Jannet and I all looked at each other. Jannet picked it up and handed it to me. It was Michelle.

"Ms. Kokinidis, I found the document I told you about today. It provides a more thorough analysis of the artifacts and makes a hypothesis about the origins of the women in the burial you read about today. I thought we could go through it if you and your team would like to come by tomorrow."

"That is a very kind offer. However, we are planning to depart tomorrow for another part of the country. Maybe you can email it to me?"

"It is in Georgian and there is very little in the way of diagrams or drawings." She paused. "Would you happen to be available for dinner this evening?"

Jannet had been eavesdropping and nodded her head emphatically. "Sure," I said while glaring at Jannet. "I don't have a car so it would need to be within walking distance of the hotel or close to a transportation stop. Oh, and Wizard would be with me."

"Wizard is not a problem and I can pick you up. How about 7:00 p.m.?"

"Again, thank you for a very generous offer."

Jannet was now pantomiming. I looked at her for a few moments before realizing what she wanted me to ask Michelle. Realization dawned before the silence with Michelle became awkward. "What should I wear?" I asked.

Michelle chuckled a bit. "I would be overdressed for the restaurant. If you wear what you had on today, you would be a little underdressed. Do you have something a little less casual?"

"I do. It is made with a Kenyan material. Are bright colors acceptable?"

"They are. I will meet you in your lobby at 7:00."

I gave her the hotel name, hung up, and sat there completely flabbergasted. I couldn't decide if I had a date or not.

"You are going on a date!" Jannet exclaimed. "When was the last time you had one?"

I was a little perturbed. I didn't want Joe to think I was a total recluse. "Last year. I went out a few times with a woman who worked at a solar company."

Then, a thought came that soured the whole possibility. I went from elation to dejection with an epithet. "What if she is associated with Kelly and company?"

This brought Jannet up short and earned a quick glance from Joe.

"It is something to consider." Jannet began somberly, "If true, she could be trying to get you away from us. Alone, you would be easier to overpower. Maybe you should call and cancel."

"I do not think canceling is a good idea," Joe said turning a page. He was in a chair with his long legs stretched across the footstool reading a newspaper. "If there is a plan and we cancel, it will tell our enemies we suspect something. If there is not a plan, Nadia misses on dinner with a beautiful woman."

His last remark made me realize I didn't know how he felt about same-sex couples. "Joe, I haven't asked you about your thoughts on same-sex relationships."

"It is fine. I understand there is more to marriage than children. Though, many in my village would be very upset to know for sure."

"What do you mean 'for sure'?" I wondered if his people had some special ability to tell to whom people were attracted.

"We have noticed that when two white women travel together as you did, it is often because they have a passionate relationship."

"So, your people thought Jannet and I were a couple?"

"Yes, until I told them she had a husband."

Joe went back to looking at the newspaper he had picked up from the lobby, which was in Georgian. I figured he wasn't having much success reading it. But, he kept up the pretense by turning a page every few minutes. From behind the paper he said, "I think the Chosen will be safe. She will have Wizard. We can ask Iolani to accompany her. If anything happens, Nadia can use the Conceal Talisman, move to a safe place, and send Iolani to tell us where to meet her."

"Then, I think we should get a car," Jannet announced. "We are going to need one to get to the mountain anyway; let's get it early." She texted Ben. Within a half hour, he had worked out a rental and its delivery before 7:00. Joe and Jannet would be ready if I needed an escape vehicle. I wondered if they would come save me from cold feet.

I was in the lobby five minutes early, but Michelle was already there. She rose from a plush chair as I approached. She looked as stunning to me as she had that morning.

"I apologize for keeping you waiting," I said extending my hand.

"It is no problem. I was early." She took my hand in both of hers and then stepped closer and kissed me on the cheek. It had been some time since I had traveled to a country which practiced this greeting so it took me by surprise. I tried not to read anything into it.

"I am sorry we will be traveling by car even though it is such a short distance. I am afraid of how my feet will feel if I try to walk much further today," she said gesturing at her heels. "I do not usually wear them, but we had an important meeting at the museum."

"I am impressed you can wear them at all. I gave them up some time ago. They were not very helpful when hiking through brush and rock."

She laughed, which I took it as a good sign. As I followed her to the car, I noticed her heels made her only slightly taller than me. The restaurant was less than a mile away. The seating area for the eatery was in a courtyard surrounded by buildings on three sides and a brick fence on the fourth. Iolani glided into a tree on the edge of the courtyard as we entered through the gate. The server greeted Michelle warmly.

"The owners and chef are friends of the family," she explained. "They are honored I have brought a foreign guest to their restaurant."

I let Michelle order, which she did in Georgian. I listened to the flow of the language during her conversation with the waiter. There was a combination of lyrical and guttural sounds, highlighting the many influences on her culture.

During appetizers and salad, we discussed archaeology in general and how we decided to enter the field. Michelle's family had a history of archaeologists who had worked for over a century to discover and preserve the heritage of their people. She was proud to carry on the tradition. My tale was shorter. I decided to become an archaeologist because I didn't want to be bored. We both laughed because one thing most people complain about when it comes to excavating is boredom. Lucky for me, I had a knack for finding archaeological sites and could spend much of my time doing search and rescue work for past habitations.

She stated she wished for someone with my skills in her country. Very few ancient villages had been found in Georgia. The graves were easy to spot because of mounds, which made them a target for tomb raiders. Michelle very much wanted to find out more about the people who were her ancestors and felt finding more settlements would help the most.

The main course was actually a cornucopia. There was a yogurt soup, two meat dishes, eggplant stuffed with a walnut filling, several more vegetable dishes, and cheese bread. The aromas of tarragon, coriander, dill, and garlic wafted from the prepared food. My eyes must have shown the surprise I was feeling at a table overflowing with food.

Michelle laughed and raised her glass of white wine. I followed her lead. "To remembering who we were and becoming all we can be," she toasted.

After our initial sampling of the dishes, Michelle asked me about my role in finding and excavating a site in Peru. It was unique because it had no evidence of human sacrifice, whereas most of the cities in the area did. The archaeologists in the country knew there had been some habitation in the area but could not find the city. By the end of the season, we were all amazed at the size of the ancient sprawling metropolis.

We then discussed the report Michelle had found. Some analysis of the teeth of the skeletons indicated the women had spent time to the east of where the burial was. The theory was they were native to the area just southwest of the Caspian Sea, but had come into the countries of Armenia and Georgia while they were still young. The horse had been born and raised in the shadow of the Caucasus Mountains.

I admitted to Michelle I didn't know a lot about the people in the area during the Late Bronze Age. She gave me a short exposition on what archaeologists had determined about the lives of her ancestors. They were egalitarian and not very sedentary. Women went to war as often as men. Men took care of domestic duties as often as women. I pumped her with questions about political organizations in the tribes and among them, oral traditions of the area, and possible religious beliefs of the people. Her answers showed she was extremely knowledgeable about the history of her people. I hardly noticed it had grown quite dark outside.

Michelle took another sip of wine, put down the glass, and leaned forward, "You have not once mentioned Greece this evening. What are you really doing here, Nadia?"

I didn't sense any coolness in the question; it was direct. Even after hours of conversation, I still could not determine if this was a trap or a tryst. I was taking my cues from Wizard and Iolani who had given no signal anything was amiss. With their senses, I was confident they would catch any trouble in the vicinity. Still, I decided to play my cards very conservatively.

"I am trying to keep history from repeating itself."

She sat back and studied me a moment. "Which part of history?"

"The part which reveals the ugliness of humanity," I replied vaguely.

"I understand about ugliness. My people have experienced that ugliness throughout most of their existence. Since we are along the trade routes between Europe, Asia, and the North, we have been overrun and subjugated time and again. Even now, we are being used as pawns by those around us." She sighed. "Yet, we are still our own people and we still welcome those from outside our borders."

The server came and picked up some of our dishes. There was a quick exchange between them. She turned and smiled.

"I hope you do not mind an after-dinner coffee. It is a habit I picked up when studying abroad and the staff is willing to serve us some," she said.

I was glad we were not going to open another bottle of wine because I thought having any more would keep me from being alert. Even though I thought I couldn't eat or drink anything else I replied, "Sounds wonderful."

After the server finished clearing the table, he brought two cups of thick coffee and a plate of dried fruit. We were then left alone.

Michelle busied herself with the coffee and fruit for a moment. "I think you and I have also experienced the ugliness of others. Intentional or not, I think men often show an ugliness to women. I take small comfort to know it was not always so and hope it will not always be so." I was not sure if she was addressing sexism in general or something more specific.

She sighed and seemed to be debating with herself. After tucking her hair behind her ear and taking a sip of the coffee, I could tell she had made her decision.

"There is a very old story said to have happened when our people roamed the land freely. The story tells of a group of warriors who were out on a hunt with the tribe's leader. They encountered a red bird so large it filled the sky. The leader of the tribe, a woman, kept her warriors from running away by showing she was not afraid. When the bird landed, she rode to meet it to see if it meant her people any harm."

My mind started to spin. Michelle had even more of my attention, if possible.

"The bird was taller than a standing mounted warrior and larger than a house. When the woman warrior approached the bird, it spoke to her and told her she had been picked to defend her people and people of other tribes. The woman accepted the appointment only if her people would be safe for all time. The bird agreed."

"What happened?"

Michelle looked at me with the amber eyes which had captured my attention earlier. I made a mental note they were more brown than gold at the moment.

She held my gaze and continued, "The bird protected the tribe as it taught the warrior how to fight in battle with an invisible shield and sword. The other tribes were afraid of her power and no longer attacked her tribe. She did not use their fear against them and try to make them her slaves. As a result, the tribes in the area coexisted peacefully.

"After some years, the bird left for a short time and then brought a gift to its apprentice, the warrior woman. It was a silver necklace, an amulet really, which had the bird's likeness on it. She was to use it in her quest to defend."

Since keeping your hands on the table was part of the etiquette in this country, I had kept them there as had Michelle. I didn't remember her reaching across the table to take my hand in hers. She now traced her thumb along my bracelet. "The story which comes to us uses the word for bird, but there is another word used to describe the bird. In English, it means 'without feathers'.

I was silent for multiple reasons. "You can see my bracelet?" I finally managed to stammer.

"Yes, I can. Somehow, I know not everyone can. I do not know how I know; it is as true to me as knowing you are here to help fulfill the warrior woman's mission."

"The one the red dragon gave her," I said quietly.

Our eyes locked. Michelle nodded ever so slightly. My heart was in my throat. My head wasn't exactly sure why. I noticed neither of us had pulled our hand away.

The server sent to tell us the restaurant was closing found us that way. Michelle looked at her watch, made a small exclamation and paid the bill. I wanted to object to the expense she took on but did not want to offend her.

When we climbed into the car, the clock on the dash indicated it was after eleven. We drove back to the hotel in silence. The streets were deserted.

Michelle got out of the car and walked around it as I wrangled Wizard out of the backseat, through the small car door. "I am sorry to have kept you out so late," I said.

"It is not a problem. After meeting you today, I do not think I would have slept well tonight."

We hugged. I went to kiss her on the cheek. She pulled back a little, reached up, and turned my chin gently until our noses practically touched each other. When I didn't object, she leaned in and kissed me.

After a few moments of being awash in the glorious feeling of her soft lips, she pulled back. Her hand rested against the side of my face. My entire being pulsed with the beating of my heart.

"And, I do not think you will sleep very well tonight either. Safety and success on your quest. I hope to see you again Nadia Kokinidis."

Chapter 25

My cheek tingled from where Michelle's hand had been moments before. Even though my body was not responding willingly to my commands to move, I walked to the door of the hotel. I began to cross the small lobby when Wizard pulled to the left. Gazing in the direction of his movement, I saw Jannet and Joe sitting in the lobby chairs. They both appeared to be reading.

"Waiting up for me?" I asked. My voice was unsteady and there was still a pulse in my ears.

"We were concerned for your safety," Jannet said trying not to smile.

"Yes, we wanted to make sure all was well with your, um, meeting," Joe added. He was less successful at hiding his impish grin.

"I see. You probably read much while waiting," I said. Jannet nodded.

"Jannet, your book is upside down."

"So, it is," she said snapping it shut and rising with a grace I wish I had. "Let's go upstairs and discuss the evening in more detail." She and Joe were now grinning unabashedly.

Once we reached the room, they admitted they had seen the car pull up and watched while Michelle kissed me. I was both elated and mortified.

"I have never seen you like this," Jannet said. "Maybe this is the start of something for you."

"I am not so sure. I don't think I will ever see her again," I said.

"Why not? Couldn't you do some archaeological work here?" Jannet queried.

I remembered Michelle's mention of wanting to find more sites of her ancestors. "If I did, it would be in a year or two. Applying for permits and getting funds takes time."

Joe turned serious, "Do we know she will not work against us?"

It was a question I had pondered most of the evening. "She saw my bracelet. Kelly was never able to see it. Somehow Mahrah hid it from her. My guess is the effect would extend to anyone who was like Kelly."

"The idea seems a little fantastical. Then again, I am not sure I understand fully how all these things work," Jannet said with a sweeping gesture which included all the devices.

"Let us take it as a good sign for now," Joe said. "Did you learn anything else which might help us find the Amulet?"

I thought through Michelle's description of her ancestors. "The people were not mountain climbers. I think it isn't any further up the mountain than how far a horse can easily be ridden."

We turned in with plans to leave about 9:00 a.m. After twenty minutes, Jannet's breathing indicated she had fallen asleep. Wizard's snores indicated he too was out. I tried hard to fall into a slumber. Michelle was right, I did not get much sleep.

The next morning came too quickly for me. We had just packed our belongings and were getting ready to leave the room when Wizard tensed. His nose sniffed the air coming in through the open window.

I connected with him and he relayed his concern. The smell of our opponents was in the air. After establishing a link with all the Watchers, I asked Iolani to go on a surveillance mission. We saw buildings and birds fluttering out of her path. Iolani turned her attention to the humans beneath her. We were dismayed to see three figures, two men and one strawberry blonde woman, walking about two blocks away. We made a hasty departure from the city.

The drive through the rugged countryside revealed how hard farming and living could be in this country. Though it was rugged, it was also green. I could see why the tables in this country had so much fresh produce and locally made wine. We reached Stepanstminda at noon. Our hotel, blessedly, let us check in early. It was a small bed and breakfast with a view of Mount Kazbek from the balcony. The peak loomed over the whole valley with a commanding air. Gergeti Trinity Church sat on the top of a steep hill between the town and the mountain.

It was too late in the day to search for the Amulet. So, we drove up to the church to see the country around it. The car strained as it climbed and Joe made a remark about the bumpiness of Jannet's driving, a comment which fell on deaf ears. After parking and stepping out into the brisk alpine breeze, I envied Joe his heavy coat.

To the northeast was Mount Shani; Mount Kazbek to the northwest. The space in between looked like a wall of rock. Somehow there was a road that went over the wall. It was known as the Scythian Gate in ancient times. The ruggedness and beauty matched what I had seen of the Himalayas or Alps.

The church was a stout brick structure with a cross-cupola, built six hundred years earlier. The church's bell tower was a separate block building with a round tower poking out of the top. The rough-hewn blocks were an extension of the country around them. I wondered if there was something which drew early Christians to this spot besides the beauty.

After wandering for a few minutes, I stood at the point directly between the church and the bell tower and looked at Mount Kazbek. It was the scene from the memory I saw the day before. "It is somewhere between here and there," I said pointing to the summit.

Jannet looked at the terrain we would be bushwhacking through the next day. "You are going to owe me a weekend at the spa when this is over."

We looked around the inside of the ornate church before climbing back into the car. On the drive back down, my phone rang. It was Michelle.

"Nadia, there were three people here asking about relics from the Late Bronze Age. Specifically, they were looking for a silver necklace."

I swore internally about gods placed in underworlds. "Can you tell me who they were?"

"They refused to tell me or show me any identification. One of them had a Western European accent. I would say somewhere around north Switzerland. The other two were American. They spoke to my assistant before I was able to meet them. Unfortunately, he told them which excavation artifacts you viewed yesterday. He was trying to be helpful."

I repeated my swear verbally. "I apologize for my language," I said hastily. On the other end of the line, Michelle laughed.

"I think I have heard a few oaths in my time," she replied reassuringly. "Though, not with those particular deities."

"Do you have any idea where they are going next?"

"Maybe they will go to the excavation site of the graves. It is not far from here and the remains have been reinterred there. They were very displeased when I would tell them nothing more of your visit."

"Thank you for phoning, you didn't need to do so."

"It seemed important for you to know. Also, it was an excuse to talk to you again," she paused and then continued in a quieter voice, "I meant what I said last night."

My cheeks burned as I realized which comment she was referencing. I remembered I had said nothing in return. "I would like to see you again also."

We said our goodbyes. Jannet was trying to focus on the road and the conversation at the same time. Wizard and Joe were in the back seat protesting her divided attention.

"They are already in the country?" she asked.

"Yes, all three of them. They are quick. Either they had an idea of where to go from the black dragon or they have their pulse on airline tickets."

"Do they know we are at this church?" Joe asked between jostles.

"I would put money on the fact they know we have a car. But, I hope they don't know we are in Stepanstminda. I hope finding a small hotel with little internet connection will keep them from finding us. I am glad the hotel didn't ask for a credit card when we checked in today," I replied.

We spent the afternoon getting what we needed for the hunt the next day. I found myself constantly checking my surroundings. I think all the others felt the same way because I noticed each Watcher sweeping glances more frequently than usual.

We took breakfast early the next morning and drove to the parking area of the trail which headed into the mountainous area below the church and along the sight line between the church and the summit. I believed there was little chance the Amulet had been hidden in the small space between where we stood and the church.

Joe exclaimed at the cold and wrapped his blanket around himself. Jannet and I had bought light coats which weren't doing much to slow down the morning cold from chilling us. Wizard snuffled around as if he were on a recreational outing.

We began hiking. Because of undergrowth and rock faces, we had to divert from the sight line to the summit from time to time. I breathed a little easier once we were over the first crest and out of sight of the road and church.

I hoped for the same prickling sensation I received from the Conceal Talisman. I became worried when hours went by and we still hadn't found anything. Our nerves were fraying from the vigilance and uncertainty. As we stopped for lunch, I hardly tasted our packed food. We did not linger over the meal. When we approached the top of another ridge, my left arm began to prickle. I could tell the others sensed something because they all started.

I sat on the rock I had just climbed over and surveyed the small flat top of the hill. I looked carefully at the rocks, the lay of the land, and the vegetation. Ten minutes went by. We had to be close but I could not pinpoint where the Amulet was.

Iolani wheeled in and reported a group of people were following our trail.

The group included two of the three humans from the morning before. We were running out of time. I started to panic when there was nothing I could see which stood out on this knoll.

"What do you think we should do next?" Joe asked sitting on a rock about six feet from me. Jannet was watching Iolani in the sky. Her posture indicated she had heard Joe and was waiting for my answer. Iolani dropped in pursuit of a bird. As she dropped below the height of the knoll, Jannet stepped onto a rock to continue to watch. I looked around. Something about this hilltop was not natural. Looking again at where Jannet and Joe were and then at where I was sitting, the irregularity became apparent.

I took three steps forward. "This is it!"

Joe and Jannet looked at me quizzically. "How can you be sure?" Jannet asked.

"All of the stones." I pointed at our pedestals. "The grains are all turned in the same direction and perpendicular to the rest of the rocks here. There should be a fourth rock with the same orientation."

The fourth was easily found under some alpine grass. The line which connected the church to the summit ran right between two of the stones. This confirmed to me they had been placed there intentionally. I pulled out a small trowel and dug a hole directly in the center about six inches deep. When I place my hand in the hole, my fingers tingled.

"Well?" Jannet asked apprehensively. Joe stood off her shoulder. Wizard was lying in the grass, resting, and enjoying a sun bath. The sudden barrage of feathers on the wind indicated Iolani was back with lunch. Both Joe and Jannet batted at them with exclamations about Iolani's rudeness.

I grinned triumphantly. "It is here. There is a strong connection."

When I reached out with energy, I determined it was about six feet below the surface. I began to Pull. It was harder than anything I had done since learning to work with energy. It felt like I was pulling a rope with a pile of bricks on the other end of it.

After a few minutes, I noticed I was breathing as hard as I did when sprinting. Jannet shot a look at me and then asked, "You okay?"

I grunted.

She followed up with, "Try not to take it out at light speed."

"Can we help?" Joe asked. "Let us give you some energy."

Iolani left her meal regretfully and joined the effort. The Watchers each took a position on one of the rocks. I could tell when they had completed their connection. There was a small jolt as they directed their energy back to me. My arm felt better and my breathing slowed down. Still, this was going to take longer than I expected or wanted.

I don't know how long we worked. It seemed like an age when Iolani suddenly launched herself skyward. The other Watcher's shifted the energy out to the pyramid of protection. I knew Joe and Jannet were talking, but I only heard muffled sounds.

I could sense the Amulet was close. I would be able to stop and dig for it. However, I knew intuitively it was important not to do so, just a little bit longer was all I needed.

A silver slab reached my palm a few minutes later. As I closed my fingers around it, a bitter taste formed on my tongue. "No," I wheezed. Wizard barked twice and then gave me two pokes. It was the signal I was about to lapse into an episode. Wizard had been focused on the threat coming; he did not catch me in time.

My whole body went limp and I fell over to the side. I was briefly aware of someone catching my head. My last thought as my awareness began to flee was to use the Conceal Talisman which would help in the midst of being so vulnerable. Then, there was nothing.

I came out of the seizure a short time later. Noticing I was lying down and covered, my hazy thoughts reasoned I was safe.

When I woke, I ached all over. I slowly realized I was lying on my side and covered with a blanket smelling of fields and campfires. I gingerly moved my leaden arm to lift the blanket. Stars blazed above me. The air was cool and crisp. I struggled to remember. Why I was here.

A small panic arose when I sensed I was alone. Where was Wizard? Slowly, I pushed into a sitting position. A pain flared up behind my temples. My tongue seemed stuck to my teeth. The realization dawned, a seizure. I almost cried at the thought. But, why had I slept so long after this one? And, where was my dog?

The afternoon began coming back to me. The memory started slowly but then blasted into my consciousness. I looked around cautiously. There truly was no one here now. Feeling tired to my core, I tried to reach out with Connection energy I could extend only a short distance but still became afraid when I found no one. Questions about where they were and their safety tumbled through my still fogged brain.

I sensed a pull on my body. It was a slow flow, a flow of energy. I remembered the feeling; it was when I had used the Talisman on Mount Kilimanjaro. I created the command to deactivate the Talisman.

I then looked at my still clenched hand. My fingers opened slowly to reveal a necklace with an arced plate of silver and two stone beads. The sharp edges of the amulet had cut my hand during my episode. I was lucky I hadn't let go of it.

Reclaim

Realizing I needed food and drink, I looked around and then felt something slide off my shoulder. Wizard's backpack had been placed on top of me but under the blanket. I pulled out the necessities. As I ate, the fact of his absence burned itself in my consciousness. I had not been alone for years and felt almost queasy at the emptiness. When I reached into the other pocket for water, my hands found his little stuffed pig. I laughed and cried at the same time. Now, I needed to drink water and blow my nose, which were hard to do at the same time.

Gingerly, I stood and stretched. The almost full moon was cresting the eastern edge of the mountains. The terrain was bathed with its odd light. It made the way back to the church look like an impossibly difficult journey. My vision dimmed with the effort of staying upright. I plopped back down.

I knew I should go find the others. My mind was screaming at me to do something. My body was adamant about its inability to do anything without rest. I felt helpless.

I looked at the Amulet in the moonlight. It was a band of silver a little more than two inches high. A dragon had been sculpted on the front side. The back was smooth. When I tapped it, there was a hollow sound. Curious, I looked for a reason. It did not take long to find out how to dislodge the back. There were five sets of brackets.

Wondering, I took the Conceal Talisman out of the arm band. The silver tile slid neatly into one of the brackets. I reattached the back and slipped the necklace over my head. It nestled inside my jacket and laid reassuringly against my chest, just below my collarbone. The little bit of movement exhausted me.

I touched the Amulet and wished for Mahrah.

"I am here, Chosen."

I almost cried with relief. Questions tumbled out, "Are you okay? What happened? Where have you been? Do you know where everyone is?"

"Calm." With it came the familiar sense of peace. I was still bone tired, but I was no longer alone.

"We will speak of what happened when there is time. I sense your Watchers are not with you. However, they are close."

"They are okay?" I was relieved.

"They are all alive." I wondered at her choice of words.

"You have found the Amulet. My eternal thanks to you. The actions of my kind have had unintended consequences. We are relieved you have the Amulet.

"Your energy is quite low. I fear for your well-being. Can you rest against one of the rocks?"

I knew what was coming next, but I didn't care. I was having a hard time staying awake and didn't know how much longer I would be able to fight the urge to sleep. I moved slowly and painfully back to the nearest rock and let it prop me up. Thinking it would help, I shrugged out of my jacket.

Just as I started to lose consciousness from shear exhaustion, I felt a warm sensation between my shoulder blades. The blackness which threatened to overtake me was held at bay. The warmth began to spread through my core. My thinking began to clear about the same time I felt the warmth reach my extremities. The warmth continued to flow; it did not become unbearable, like the jolt before. Soon, a hum resonated through my whole body. The bracelet appeared to glow. The Amulet was also activated. It felt like a cat who had nestled under my chin and started purring.

All my exhaustion, aches and pain dissipated. The warmth between my shoulder blades faded slowly. Instead of warmth, I felt intense self-satisfaction and weariness from Mahrah.

"I too have been working with energy and have learned something. I thought I knew all about forces and how they could be handled. You have taught me something, young one."

"You exhausted yourself." I said with concern.

"I am able to rest. Go, find the Watchers."

I packed up the remains of my midnight snack and folded the blanket into a small bundle. I had just decided the best course of action was to return to the church when my consciousness pricked with Connection.

Iolani seemed to materialize out of thin air on top of a large boulder, startling me even though knew she was close. She called with alarm. She radiated her distress through the Connection.

I put the blanket over my right forearm and she jumped on to the temporary roost. I touched my bracelet to her band hoping it would transfer some of the calm I had. The band and bracelet were drawn to each other. Her memories began to flow into my awareness. Seeing them increased the dread I was already feeling about those who had watched over me.

Chapter 26

I watched through Iolani's eyes as Wizard was first to sense the arrival of the group pursuing us. Their odors carried on the wind. He alerted Iolani and she took flight. From the air, she saw six people coming up the side of the rise. She called and buzzed the incoming group. A shot was fired. As she climbed and circled around, she saw Joe, Jannet, and Wizard gathering closer to me. I looked like a lump on the ground.

The group was still a few minutes away and Iolani desperately felt like she needed to do something. A flock of partridges had been roused by the commotion so she herded them back to the invading group. The people hit the deck as the partridges darted among them followed by Iolani, raking her talons across one of the pursuer's scalp. She flew away erratically, another gunshot sounded. After the two close calls, Iolani climbed high enough to be a poor target, yet close enough to watch.

As she peered down, she saw Joe throw his blanket over me and then the mound which was me disappear. The three Watchers began running uphill towards Mount Kazbek's summit. They were out of sight around some boulders when the pursuing group arrived at the hill top.

Iolani was poised for a high-power dive. The group of pursuers walked along the southern edge of the knoll and came dangerously close to stepping on me. Iolani warned Wizard. He bounded out from behind an uphill boulder and barked. The six people began running up hill towards them. I watched with a sinking heart as the distance between the Watchers and their pursuers grew smaller.

Beside Kelly and Bryce, there were four men in black. Each had a rifle and one of them leveled it at the backs of the two fleeing humans. Kelly knocked it to the side as the man pulled the trigger. Joe and Jannet stopped running, turned around, and put their hands up. Wizard wasn't as cordial. With raised hackles, he barked ferociously. One of the men pointed his rifle at Wizard. Iolani began to dive.

Jannet, Joe, or both must have gotten through to Wizard because he backed down. One of the other men threw an object at Jannet's feet. Joe looked up, noticed Iolani, and told her to stay back. She pulled out of her dive.

By the time the falcon had circled back around, Jannet had placed something on Wizard's nose, a muzzle. The whole group turned downhill, walking back to the church. When Bryce got close enough to Jannet, he reached out and shoved her. She kept her feet but he fell. In his rage, he pulled out a pistol and pointed it at Jannet's chest. Kelly grabbed his wrist and pulled the gun out of it. She yelled at her brother before handing his gun back to him.

As they came close to the knoll, Jannet began to take the easier route down around the edge of the hill. She was leading them away from me. Kelly stopped, looked at the knoll, then followed Jannet.

Iolani made it look like she was flying away. She soared so high she was a speck in the sky to anyone who cared to look. She circled as the group hiked all the way back to the church. The sun had set when they arrived. The four men walked to an SUV and drove away. Kelly and Bryce took the three Watchers into the bell tower. Iolani flew back and roosted as close as she could to the buildings until the light of moon would allow her to see well enough to fly back.

I now knew where everyone was. I went through a dozen plans as I scampered back over our trail. I paid for my haste by missing a step a couple of times and losing my footing, gaining scrapes and bruises. The energy Mahrah had given me kept me from feeling any pain or fatigue.

Once we were less than a mile from the church, Iolani flew ahead. The approach to the church was completely exposed so I used the Conceal Talisman once I emerged from the forest near the car. The falcon reported the four humans and the fuzzy four-footed animal were still in the bell tower. She wanted to fly in and take out an eye. I told her it would not help our friends.

Cresting the hill on which the church was built, I saw a man lying on his side. Alarmed, I went over to him. The caretaker had been hit in the head but was still breathing. While I was kneeling beside him, voices caught my attention.

I edged closer to the bell tower, the conversation was heated.

"I told you to wait until they came back to the church," Kelly said. "But, no. You had to take your posse and go look for them. Now, we have no idea where she went."

"She must still be out there. The manuscripts never mention the power of being able to transport yourself," Bryce retorted hotly. "You should have let me search the area more."

I wanted to reach out and connect with the rest of the Watchers, but I didn't know if it would tip off the Devlin Duo.

"She probably took off when you pulled the gun on her friend here. What is it with you and the brute we hired? We want to find out what they know, not just get rid of them." Kelly was referencing somebody else.

"What about the dog? I bet nobody would be upset or even notice a dead dog." Bryce's tone was ugly.

"What are you thinking?" Kelly asked unsure.

"Just a little revenge for all the trouble they have caused us."

"No, don't," came Jannet's voice.

"Get out of my way." Bryce sounded dangerous. Some scrabbling followed. Wizard began a vicious bark.

My concern overrode my caution. I reached out and spoke to all of them. "I am here. Outside. Calm." I was starting to sound like Mahrah.

Wizard's vocalizations stopped a fraction of a moment later.

"She is here," Bryce said in the sudden silence. "The dog wouldn't have stopped otherwise. She can't be far away."

"Let's go out and greet her," Kelly said with malice. I began edging across the small courtyard between the buildings.

"What about them?" Bryce asked.

"We'll take the people. The animal isn't going to be able to break the bars on the cage."

Joe came out first. Bryce was behind with a pistol pointed at Joe's back. Jannet was next. Kelly came out behind her, also with a pistol. They took a right from the doorway and began to walk across the open space. Slowly, they came around the corner of the church. When they didn't see anything, Kelly stopped them.

"Where is she?" Kelly asked Jannet quietly. Jannet shrugged her shoulders.

Kelly's swear insulted Jannet's parents. Kelly followed with, "Tell her she better show herself quickly or you are going to have an accident with a gun."

"Nadia," Jannet said loudly but evenly, "If you are here, these people would like to speak with you." She placed great emphasis on the word 'if'.

Bryce snickered.

"Shut up," Kelly demanded. "The lighting is tricky. I don't want that trouble maker to pull another stunt on us. Keep your eyes peeled."

While they were talking, Jannet, Joe, and I were mentally debating with each other about what to do. That conversation stopped abruptly when I heard Kelly's gun cock. I froze.

"Time's up, dragon girl," Kelly announced.

I stepped away from the side door of the church. Three feet in front of Kelly and Jannet, I deactivated the Talisman. Bryce exclaimed when I winked into view. Jannet's face fell. Joe, who was to my left also looked crestfallen. Kelly smiled wickedly.

"Finally," she said with relish. She looked at me like I was her next trophy, "Nadia, you have given us quite a run for our money. You will pay for the inconvenience you have been. Though, you did make it entertaining."

"I think you should let my friends go."

"I think you are in no position to make any requests. We are supposed to bring you all back alive but I am sure it will be understood if one or two of you don't make it. The Talisman is the most important thing."

I wanted to find out what they knew and wondered how long I could keep Kelly talking. She looked smug. I hoped she would let something slip in the middle of her patting herself on the back.

"This Talisman is not very impressive. It only lets one person do something with it."

"Perhaps for you. If you were actually skilled, you might figure out how to extend its effects," Bryce blurted, earning him a glare from his sister.

"What are you planning on doing with it?" I asked.

"Let's just say we think the world has gotten off on the wrong track. With these Talismans, we can help change things. I think we need fewer people in charge and a redistribution of wealth." Bryce's laugh at Kelly's statement was ugly.

"Let me guess who you think should have all the wealth and power," I said.

"We don't need all of it; just enough to make our lives and the lives of those around us a little easier," Kelly said.

"And, if someone gets hurt in the process, like the people in Kenya?" I asked.

"Oh, you are upset a few people got killed," Kelly said mockingly. "That was your fault. If you had just stayed in the States, we wouldn't have had to pull the stunts in Nairobi and London we did to get your attention."

My jaw and fists clenched. A mental poke from Jannet pulled my next remark up short.

Kelly went on, "What I can't figure is how you found the Talisman so quickly. We were sure you hadn't started looking for it. Bryce is alerted when people access the pertinent manuscripts."

I received an image from one of the Watchers. "I just have really good intuition. And, I am a lot smarter than you are."

With the gun still aimed at Jannet, Kelly stepped forward and slapped me hard across the face. I stepped back, my cheek stung and my eyes watered. I had never been slapped so hard before. I hoped it would never happen again. Joe tensed, ready to act.

"Give me a reason, boy," Bryce said maliciously to him.

"Enough bantering." Kelly said. "Hand over the Talisman." She took another step toward me.

"I don't have it."

"Of course you do, you just used it."

"It takes a while for the effect to wear off," I hoped Kelly couldn't tell I was lying. "I hid the Talisman in the forest. You are going to have to get it on your own."

Kelly glanced over my shoulder to the mountain top gleaming in the moonlight. At the same moment, Wizard blasted us with the command to get down. Joe, Jannet, and I hit the deck as Wizard and Iolani came in from the left and right. Iolani punched Kelly's wrist with one talon and wrapped the other around the gun. It was enough to rip it from her grasp. Wizard launched and locked his jaws around Bryce's wrist causing him to drop the pistol.

The two human Watchers quickly followed up on the animals' attack. Jannet swept Kelly's legs, then leapt over her and picked up the gun. Joe came up from his crouch and hit Bryce square in the chest. The upward momentum knocked Bryce off his feet. Joe pulled his knife from a sheath inside his trousers and held it menacingly over Bryce. Wizard picked up Joe's gun and brought it to me.

"Give me a reason, boy," Joe said with steely coldness to Bryce when he tried to move.

Kelly trembled with anger. She called Jannet many unsavory names.

"By the way," Jannet said to Kelly with mock sweetness, "You are going to want to stay out of the US for a while. The government gets very touchy about people who point guns at their diplomats."

"Don't mess with a diplomat's daughter," Joe crowed. Jannet gave him a smile.

We decided to lock the Devlin Duo in the church since all the doors bolted from the outside. While Joe and Wizard corralled them into the small sanctum, Jannet checked on the caretaker. He was just stirring.

"He probably has a concussion," she said with concern. "I think he will need to have his head checked just to make sure he doesn't have a hairline fracture. They hit him pretty hard."

Joe was bringing water from the bell tower when Wizard indicated vehicles were coming. Shortly after, we heard the laboring engines. Our car was about a half mile down the road at the trailhead. The short grass was not going to give us any cover.

The only way we were going to leave without being noticed was to use the Conceal Talisman. I wasn't sure how much energy I had for the Talisman, so we changed tactics. Instead of the Watchers creating a circle, we decided to create a chain. With one hand, I held Wizard by the collar. Jannet held my hand and Joe's. Iolani, who told us she wouldn't be noticed, flew.

The Watchers activated their rings and I activated the Talisman. The melodious hum let us know we were all Concealed. I didn't feel like I was pouring energy out to each person.

Police cars went by us as quickly as they could on the rutted road. We reached our rental car shortly after the last vehicle passed. The next part was tricky and I hoped I could sustain the effort to do it. Once everyone was in, I switched the field to Conceal the car. We drove back to town without being noticed.

We knew we had to leave town immediately. I went in to our hotel a couple of times Concealed and picked up our stuff. Jannet hated to leave the hotel without paying. I assured her we would get someone to call and pay the bill plus extra for the trouble they were probably going to have once Kelly and Bryce tried to drag us into the trouble they were in.

We pulled off the road once we felt we were a safe distance away. Jannet once again used the satellite phone to book tickets for our departure. The earliest flight we could get to England was the next evening. We discussed our options and decided how we could successfully get out of the country without anyone getting hurt.

Right after the sun came up, we entered the western edge of Tbilisi National Park. After hiking up a trail for a bit, we cut into the forest and found a small clearing. We all ate what was left from the day before and then Jannet and I slept. After a few hours, Iolani and Wizard took over guard from Joe. I woke at about noon. It was earlier than planned, but I knew I needed to get a little bit more information. Mahrah and I spoke until Jannet and Joe awoke.

By mid-afternoon, we were back in the car and headed to our next destination, the grave of my ancestor.

The Zema Avchala Cemetery was large and had been used for centuries. A sign indicated the mound which was the burial of the three warriors was about a ten-minute walk from the parking lot.

The mound was grassy with a plaque marking the site, which we read. I stepped a little bit beyond it, leaned down, and put my hand on the ground. I expected a jolt. Instead, there was the lightest of hums. It could have been a sense of well-being from my ancestor. Then again, it could have been the bees as they went about their business.

We started back along the path back to the parking lot, Joe on my left and Jannet on my right. Wizard was off leash so he could pick his own path, and Iolani was circling above. There were several people visiting other graves. A couple of groundskeepers passed us with a cart full of tools to tend the flowers.

Wizard gave the signal for which we were waiting. We came around a bend where the path widened a bit. A man stepped out from behind one of the large trees. It was the dark-haired man, the one we had called Reginald. A moment after I saw him, Iolani landed on the path behind me and the Watchers activated the field.

"Hello, Nadia," the man said.

"Hello, Aidan," I answered. The man was unsuccessful in concealing his surprise. He recovered quickly.

"Bravo. You figured out I am Kelly's husband." He clapped a couple of times in mock applause. "Good investigation. But, quite amateur. You see, I know much more about you, Mrs. Goodwin, and the Maasai man who has several names."

"Yes, Mr. Steele, I did. What I don't know is why you robbed your uncle's store."

He stopped smiling and his expression grew dark, "I took what was mine. I worked in that store for twenty years and he threw me out because I took a small silver tile he thought was worthless."

"Before or after you came into possession of the ring?"

"It doesn't matter. But, I notice you don't have one. Before I put you out of commission, I would love to know how you are communicating with that unctuous dragon who styles herself ruler."

His comment raised *my* hackles. I hoped I still seemed calm.

Aidan continued, "Did you ever question the truth of her statements? She probably told you that you were on some honorable quest. The truth is she wants to keep both worlds suffering." My surprise must have shown on my face.

"You are such a simpleton. You believed whatever she said because it was magical and you felt like you were doing some good. You've acted like a child," he said, looking down.

The combination of words and action triggered the memory of Joe at the inn in Wilton. Instead of following Aidan's gaze, I looked up. There were two men in the trees above us. They were getting ready to jump. I pushed the image to Iolani. She was between them and the ground with one wing beat.

The men jumped and bounced off the Watcher's protection with curses and exclamations of pain. Iolani made two tight circles and then pulled above the canopy. I didn't have time to watch her because men came at us from several directions. Those who tried to run between us suffered the same fate as the two who tried to ambush us from above.

"Idiots," Aidan hissed, "There is a protective field between them. Attack the dog and the people."

One man grabbed a hoe from the groundkeeper's cart and swung it at Jannet. She blocked it with her bo staff, seemingly appearing out of nowhere. With a smooth motion, she clocked him on the side of the head, hit his hands, and then seized the hoe, which she tossed behind her. The man who was coming in behind her adversary took a blow on the side of his arm before backing up. A third man stepped into his place and began to attack with a series of martial arts maneuvers. She parried and got in a hit or two.

A battle cry drew my attention to the other side. Joe had two men at bay with his wickedly swinging knife. One tried to advance only to receive a gash along his forearm. A third man pulled a large knife of his own. Joe parried it and used a long thick stick to keep the other two from advancing.

Wizard was angrier than I had ever seen him. His ears were flat and his hackles stood up all along his back. His teeth were bared and the sound he made was a blood-chilling guttural growl. Two men were trying to hit him with shovels. I gasped as one swung for his head. He ducked and then latched his teeth on the man's forearm. Wizard then let go and spun to meet the attack of the other man. "Evasive maneuvers," I remembered Wizard telling us.

Aidan called for his men to retreat and made a motion with his hand. Two men stepped out onto the path behind us. They had semi-automatic guns.

Aidan's black eyes glinted. "You have all been a pleasant diversion, but you have become too costly. So, I will take the Amulet and the Talisman and be on my way."

"I agree this adventure has been too costly." I said. "It has cost some people their lives and many great pain. It stops now." The moment I finished my last sentence, we all disappeared. The Watchers moved from where they had been standing. We hoped the energy field would repel bullets.

Aidan was unhappy, but unfazed, by our disappearance. "You know,

Nadia, we could always make the stakes a little higher. There are a few people wandering around here which could be part of the collateral damage of the game."

I looked over my shoulder. The men were aiming at some of the other people in the cemetery. My stomach dropped.

"Stop using the Talisman and I will reconsider," he added.

I asked the Watchers what we should do. We were all in agreement the cost of others' lives was too high. I deactivated the Conceal Talisman; the Watchers turned off their protection. Aidan's look of triumph when we all reappeared stirred my seething to fury.

"Tell them to drop their weapons," he ordered, pointing to Jannet and Joe.

"I don't give them orders. They make their own decisions." Through the Connection, the human Watchers agreed it was best to look defenseless. Joe and Jannet discarded their weapons.

"Before we finish," Aidan started, "I want to satisfy my curiosity. How are you able to activate the Talisman or to communicate with the other world? *I* need this ring."

"I'm special," I said blandly.

Aidan snorted. "Maybe so. The black dragon knew the queen was trying to reach a human in this world. He determined your bloodline, a descendant of the first possessor of the Amulet, and approximate location. It took a few days to track the genealogy of the people in your neighborhood. Once I narrowed it down, we watched."

"You rented the house down the street to spy on me?"

"Yes. We watched for unusual visitors. When no one showed up, we started trying to intercept your mail. I wasn't able to get into the delivery company's database fast enough to stop the shipment of the note which told you what to do, but I did get access to traffic cameras, airline databases, and your financial records. The digital world can be so accommodating."

His speech confirmed he did not know about the bracelet and how he had tracked me around the globe.

"We thought you would lead us to a Talisman. You have exceeded our expectations. You have also found the Amulet."

He held out a hand and licked his lips with anticipation. Pulling the Kinetic Talisman out of his breast pocket, he laid it in the palm of his outstretched hand. "Such a small thing which has so much power. And now, I shall have two."

Aidan stood in front of Wizard, "I want you to walk very slowly to me and give me the Conceal Talisman. If you don't, your friends or someone else will have new holes in their bodies. Oh, and call off your mutt."

I signaled to Wizard to settle on his haunches. Pulling up my sleeve, I clicked the silver tile from the indentation on the arm band. With a bitter look, I reached over Wizard and dropped it into Aidan's open hand. It made a metallic sound when it fell on top of the other Talisman. He looked at them greedily resting in his palm.

"Now, the Amulet," he said putting out his other palm.

I reached to undo the clasp. After a couple of seconds, I adjusted to get a better grasp. The moment my elbow came up, Wizard jumped and knocked Aidan's hand. The tiles went flying over his head. Iolani pulled out of her dive and snagged them in mid-air. She pirouetted, flew above me, and dropped them. I Pulled them to my hand. Quickly, I reached around to the arm band. They both attached to it as if they were magnetic. The defense field activated as soon as Iolani had let them fall out of her talons.

"Shoot them," Aidan bellowed in rage.

"No!" I shouted. I spun and swung my arm as if to bat at the guns. I didn't know what I was thinking because they were too far away. Everyone was surprised when the guns flew out of the men's hands as if someone had hit them with great force. When one man tried to retrieve his, Iolani attacked and left deep scratches down his arm.

Wizard yelped. When I wheeled to face the noise, I saw Aidan had picked up Wizard by the scruff and was about to plunge a knife into him. Without thinking, I stepped forward and punched Aidan in the chest with both fists. He flew back and landed almost ten feet away. When he left his feet, he let go of Wizard.

The second man behind us went to pick up his gun. Joe was there in two strides, stepped on it and held his blade ready to strike.

"Enough!" I thundered. The men melted back into the trees.

Joe stood guard over Aidan while Jannet and I put on gardener's gloves, picked up the guns and took out the clips. People had fled the area earlier so we were alone. Iolani and Wizard let us know Aidan's helpers were truly leaving. Aidan was sitting and rubbing his chest when we finished with the guns.

Now, we had to figure out what to do with him.

Chapter 27

When I approached him, Aidan stood; Joe was tensed, ready for any physical attack. Instead of swinging at me, Aidan spit. I was close enough for it to hit me. Joe put his knife up to Aidan's throat. The look on Joe's face scared me almost as much as anything we had experienced to this point. Jannet put a hand on Joe's other arm. He looked at her. She held his gaze and shook her head the tiniest bit. He pulled the knife back.

In classic bad guy style, Aidan wasn't going to relent or repent.

"You won't find the other three Talismans," he said tauntingly.

"Maybe or maybe not. The more important thing is making sure you won't keep them if you do," I replied.

His eyes fell to the Amulet. He spoke more softly, but the hardness in his eyes stayed. "Do you even know what kind of power you hold there? You could change the world. Think about it Nadia, you could make the world safer for other species and keep humans from destroying this planet. You could help restore balance and end the wars over resources. The power is hanging around your neck."

I stood unmoving and silent so he continued. "The queen dragon is a master manipulator. She wants mankind weak. She wants the dragons in slavery. She knows we could help ourselves with this power, but has deceived you into thinking it will hurt us.

"The black dragon wanted to communicate with you to find out what lies she has been telling you. She kept him away so he contacted me to help you. Together, we could rule this world. Maybe we could even bring the dragons here to help. Let me help you see the truth."

Jannet shot me an uncertain look. I cocked my head to one side and regarded him cynically. "My parents often told me you could tell what a person really wanted by what they said. Thank you for telling me what the black dragon and you want."

Iolani did a fly by and let us know we were not going to be alone much longer. I told the Watchers to get ready to leave.

"He has killed others. Something should happen to him." Jannet said.

"It isn't our place," I replied. "I wish we could make sure he wasn't going to continue to be a menace, but I don't believe taking justice into our hands is the right thing."

Joe smiled broadly. "I am glad we are people who do the right thing because it is the right thing instead of doing it just to accomplish our goals."

"You are going to let me go?" Aidan asked incredulously.

"Not exactly," I replied, "We are going to let you speak to some people about why you were threatening a group of tourists with guns."

Jannet stepped forward with the rope we found in the groundkeeper's cart. We trussed him up a bit and tied him to a nearby bench. Iolani kept buzzing us with updates of the police's arrival. We went back around the bend in the path and activated the Conceal Talisman right before the police arrived. It was a comical sight to watch Aidan try to assert his innocence while the police trained their guns on him. When they found his knife and a gun strapped to his ankle, he sputtered and began asking for the French Consul, in French.

On the way to the airport, I touched base with Mahrah. She rumbled in satisfaction when she learned we had succeeded in getting the Kinetic Talisman.

"Did you doubt us?" I asked.

"I did not doubt what you could do. I was unsure of how well prepared your adversaries were. We are happy you have been able to complete your tasks. You are a credit to your kind. We will remember this day, you, and the Watchers."

I figured it was as close to getting knighted as I was going to get.

***

It was almost a week later before we could organize a celebratory dinner. Jannet used her connections to help Joe get his visa processed more quickly as we bounced through Europe and back to the States. Iolani and I endured the long flight across the Atlantic; afterwards, it was nice to sleep in my own bed. I had emails and phone calls to return dealing with site location requests. I beamed when one of the requests dealt with looking for villages in southeast Georgia.

We had just finished a meal of barbecued ribs, corn on the cob, potato salad, and baked beans. Ben said it would be a great way to introduce Joe to American cuisine; Ben forgot to mention he loved barbecuing. Jannet and Ben's backyard was greening nicely. While we were away, leaves had popped on the trees and some of the flowers had begun to bud.

"Jannet told me you have a request to look for prehistoric villages in Georgia," Ben said.

I shot Jannet a look, then turned back to Ben. "There is evidence people have been living there for thousands of years. It is possible I would find a habitation that is older than almost anything in this part of the world," I replied evenly.

Ben cleared his throat, "Is it purely professional interest which would have you accept the contract?"

Now, I knew I was being taunted. "Purely professional," I said as straight-faced as I possibly could. It was two seconds before I was grinning like a fool.

Everyone laughed loudly. The animals woke up and wondered what the matter was. When they determined we were just doing our primate vocalizations, they went back to their naps.

"Joe, how is the job search going?" I asked.

"It is very well. I have a part-time job in town and I will be doing marketing for a computer business."

I looked at Ben suspiciously.

"When I told him about what my small company does, he came up with some great ideas to get its products into people's hands. It is a win-win for us," Ben replied.

"The best part is I can still serve my village," Joe continued. "By staying here, I am protecting the Chosen which is my job as Watcher given to me by the maker of the Talisman. I will be able to send money back to my village which will help them financially which is the job of my birth position."

"Do you think you will miss your people?" I asked with concern.

Joe thoughtfully took a sip of his beer. "I am not with my people in body, but my heart is with them. It helps there are ways to speak and see them. It was harder when I went to University and technology was not as developed."

"Is there anyone in particular you might miss?" Jannet asked as delicately as possible.

"Oh, Jannet," he said grinning, "I had not yet picked a bride. It was my father's greatest concern. Because of my vision, I knew it was not time to marry. Maybe I will look now. There are women from East Africa who live here, yes?"

I laughed, "Yes. But, you may want to be careful. Most of them are very independent. They will not get married to someone just because they were picked."

"This I know. I will need to show them I will be a fantastic husband like my friend, Ben." He clapped Ben on the shoulder.

Wizard stood up and shook himself. He inserted himself under Joe's hand. Joe obliged and began to pet him.

"There is one thing I do not understand," Joe said as he fondled Wizard's ears. "How did Wizard get out of the cage?"

"Wizard is very well named," I began. "He is a service dog because he gets severe separation anxiety."

Joe looked puzzled.

"When he was young, he would scratch at doors, carpets, and windows to find his human who he thought had gone missing. His first owners tried putting him in a kennel while they were gone from the house. When they returned, he met them at the door. Then, they tried a wire cage with clamps that spin shut. Again, he met them at the door. They figured he used his tongue to undo the clamps."

Wizard knew we were talking about him and sat gazing at us with a wide dog smile. "That dog can get out of any cage he is put into and he can do it quickly. He is an escape artist. 'Houdini' didn't quite fit so I called him 'Wizard'," I finished.

Jannet and Ben cleared the remains of dinner and brought out dessert, apple pie. It was another new taste for Joe. He exclaimed it was sweeter than he liked. In spite of his declaration, he ate three pieces. We sat with cups of coffee or hot chocolate as the night became full. After a bit, Ben sensed the three of us needed to talk and excused himself.

We spoke of the confrontations we had in Georgia.

"It really was a gamble to give Aidan the Conceal Talisman," I reflected.

"I was totally against it until you told us about what Mahrah said," Jannet confessed.

"I am glad she knew about being able to use the Amulet to pull the Talisman back. It meant Aidan would not have gotten far even if he had decided to turn and run the moment I put it in his hands."

"The look on his face when Wizard knocked them out of his hands and Iolani caught them was worth the trouble we went through," Joe proclaimed with a laugh. "In the beginning, I was very unsure about those two as Watchers, but Mahrah was right to pick them."

"She was right to pick all of you. The Talismans and Amulet would not be safe if it weren't for your actions. You have given up where you live and what you do with your life. You may have to give up more of your time and put yourself in harm's way again. I am honored to call you Watchers and friends."

I had connected with the non-human Watchers during my short speech. Iolani poked her head out from under her wing. "Yes, all of you," I said looking up at her.

A reflective silence fell.

"We really didn't give those three much consequence for their actions," Jannet said.

"I think the Devlin Duo will be able to get themselves out of trouble easier than Aidan," I said.

"I agree," Joe said, "It will be easier for the brother and sister to lie about why they were locked in the chapel and have people believe them. I hope the man they hurt is okay and remembers enough to contradict their story."

"The police probably will not go lightly on someone found sitting next to two weapons and carrying a third. Especially not in a country which has had recent turmoil. Aidan is going to have to talk quickly to get out of that mess," Jannet said.

"Or hand out a lot of bribe money," I added.

"Which reminds me, how did you know he stole from his uncle's shop?" Jannet asked.

"The news photo we saw showed the name of the jewelry shop on the window. When I found out it was from the same part of the world we suspected our dark-haired man to be from, I looked into the ownership of the shop right before we left Wales.

"My brother found the owner had a nephew who had once been a partner. A document to dissolve the partnership indicated the nephew had stolen a precious piece of silver jewelry from the shop and refused to return it. The owner was able get dissolution of the partnership in lieu of sending the nephew to jail."

"There had to be several people with the last name on the window. How did you know his first name?" Joe inserted before I could take a sip of my cooling hot chocolate.

"When I first met Kelly, she mentioned she had a husband and told me his name. When we first met Bryce, aka Buttercup, in Nairobi, I thought he was her husband."

"But you knew differently when she introduced him as her brother," Joe concluded.

"I kicked myself when we saw Aidan, who we were calling Reginald, on the video from London. I had let all the other events distract me from the guy who was following me around Colorado. Anyway, when I saw the pictures from London, I knew he was Kelly's husband. What I didn't know was if Kelly had kept her maiden name or not. Since she had, it made finding him a little more difficult. The jewelry window sign was a godsend."

Bats flew overhead catching the biting bugs. I wished them good hunting. A breeze picked up. Since it was late spring, it had a chill to it. We spent a couple of minutes contemplating and sipping our beverage.

"I hope we never see Kelly again. Do you know if they moved out?" Jannet asked breaking the silence.

"Yes," I replied, "I happened to run into the owner of the house today while walking Wizard. The owner lived there until about a year ago and always said hello to Wizard."

"Maybe I can rent the house and then I will be even closer if I am needed," Joe said hopefully.

"Possibly, but don't expect any furniture. The owner said there was very little. He told me he received a call they were breaking the lease. He expected the worse for the property, but when he went over, the place was really clean. He found one cot, three camp chairs, and very little in the way of food."

"Good," Jannet said firmly, "I do not want to tell you what I was going to do if she showed her face around here again."

"I could lend you a spear if she does," Joe joked.

"Such strange events we have been through the last few weeks. I guess things will never quite be what they were since we have some powerful devices to guard," Jannet reflected. "What are we going to do about the other three Talismans?"

"Aidan has been looking for them and hasn't found them yet. Maybe we can beat him to them," I said.

"But, you are not convinced we can get there first?" Joe chimed in.

"He has been looking for them with Bryce's help for some time. Which means, they must be well hidden. We might be able to find some clues in the manuscripts Kelly mentioned, but I think we are more likely to get a lead from oral traditions, something which won't be easy."

"What makes you think so?" Jannet asked.

"Many indigenous people do not tell others, particularly rich white people, their most treasured stories. Joe only told us about a ritual site. It wasn't until I found the site that he told us about the Talisman."

"I think I would have told you where to look," he said. "I was almost certain you were the right person because you wore the dragon bracelet."

"Which brings up another thing I have been wondering about," I said, "Who exactly can see the bracelet and why?"

"Ben can now," Jannet said bluntly. "He said he didn't see it before our time in Wales."

"Why then, could Michelle see it?" I asked slowly.

It was a question to which we only had theories, but I knew who I was going to ask.

Chapter 28

After the White fell, the Red mourned. The rawness of her grief terrified the people. Before the humans had overcome their fear enough to come out of their houses, the Red disappeared and was never seen again.

Because of their fear, the people created stories about the beasts they thought were gods. In their stories, the beasts were crushed and the people were not afraid.

***

Being back in the mountains helped settle me even further. Wizard loved being off leash. He tracked ground squirrels and lapped out of the frigid stream we hiked by on the way in to a rocky crest, overlooking the still snow-capped peaks.

I saw and listened to the birds, felt the warmth of the sun, and breathed in the scent of awakened pine. Even though the bad guys were at large and there were three missing Talismans, I felt at peace. When we arrived at our destination, Wizard found a soft spot on the forest floor and began to snooze. I reached out to Mahrah.

"Greetings, Chosen. I thought you would not contact me for some time."

I was perplexed. "Why wouldn't I?"

"Because you do not need me currently. You have honed your skills and have accomplished your tasks. When you did not contact me in the last several days, I believed it was the way of your kind."

"Mahrah, I apologize. I now see it has been some time since I have spoken to you. I did not mean to ignore you. It is not how humans are."

Mahrah was relieved. After a few moments, she said, *"You have questions."*

I laughed. "I do. I seem to have a lot of them. You have endured many over the short time we have known each other."

"It was uncomfortable at first. You are a very inquisitive and somewhat impatient being. It is our nature to sit with our questions for a time and see if they will be answered."

"How long?"

"In your time reckoning, years."

"I don't think I could remember a question that long let alone wait for an answer."

"Then, we should proceed," she said playfully.

"How did the black dragon escape?"

"His color allows him a special skill, which is known only by a few. With effort, he can change the color of his scales. Very few know of his ability. He tricked the guard into thinking he was another, who let him leave. The black dragon has since hidden."

"Will he be able to contact me or his Bearer?"

"You have rightly determined he has his own agent in your world. The black dragon's access to you and the Watchers will be no more. I have been able to block it. However, I cannot keep him from speaking with his person."

"Will he be able to reveal anything else to Aidan?"

"The black dragon will be able to help Aidan understand what abilities you have with handling energy. I hope. . ." Mahrah stopped. She had a profound sense of dread, *"I hope he will not have planned on providing his Bearer with the same instruments and skills you have. The abilities of the Watchers cannot be recreated but it may be possible Aidan will learn more about handling energy."* Her answer was disconcerting.

"How long have you been planning on recovering the Talismans and Amulet?"

"My plans began the day I left your world. Our actions had not gone as we had planned. I knew it was only a matter of time before your kind would find and reactivate the Talismans. I observed your world for many years to find one who would become our ally in protecting the humans from our mistake."

"It is only a mistake because we have used them for our own gain rather than to help our species and others." The magnitude of Mahrah's effort hit me. "You have been monitoring people on the earth for years?"

"It was a small number of you. The next Chosen needed to have the same energy signature as the first Chosen. It was fairly easy to find you among all of your kind."

"How many of us are there?"

"A few thousand."

"So, I wasn't your first choice." I was disheartened at the idea.

"Chosen," she addressed me with affection, "*You are my first choice of this age. I hoped fervently at least one Talisman would be discovered during your lifetime. You have been our best hope of recovering them, ever."*

"Why didn't you just have one of my ancestors start looking for them?"

"We believe it is better to let events happen in their own time."

I smiled. "We have an expression about that too. 'Let sleeping dogs lie.'" Mahrah chuckled with a rumble at the image. "I have always been the proactive type. Maybe I should allow things to happen more often."

"Hopefully, not in many things." With the sentence came the image of Michelle.

"Did you arrange for Michelle and I to meet?" I asked suspiciously.

"The meeting was of your arrangement. I found it fortuitous for introducing you to another."

"You contacted her?"

"Not in the same manner as I have you. She too has the first Chosen as her ancestor so I knew of her. I determined she had similar interests you did. Since she shared your energy signature, it was an easy matter to reveal your bracelet to her. She was quite perplexed about the subconscious thoughts she had when she met you. To her credit, she determined an agreeable course of events."

"You set me up on a date?" I couldn't believe it. This was the most outlandish part of the entire escapade. A dragon was playing match-maker.

"Why?"

"You have not had a mate. There was great happiness and contentment when I had my mate. You have committed to help your world stay at peace. It is a difficult path. I hoped you would find another to share the burden in a way the Watchers will not be able to do so."

When I did not reply, Mahrah added uncertainly, *"I hope I have not offended."*

I sighed and let go of my objections. "You have not. Humans do the same thing all the time. I thought I had a mate years ago. When she left, it made me afraid to take the risk of revealing so much of myself to another. I didn't even want you to know much about me."

"Truth. I, too, did not want to reveal much of myself to you."

"Yet, we have stumbled upon dark moments of our pasts in just a short amount of time of knowing each other."

"Your gentleness and comfort as those events came to be discussed rekindled a desire to befriend and love my kind."

I examined my own heart, "For me too. Though, I am afraid Michelle won't like me as she gets to know me."

"Does that mean you should not try?"

A question. The agreement between us was to answer them.

"I should," I said with resignation, "I am just so afraid of being alone again."

"You will not be alone. You have the Watchers. You have me." She sent me an image of herself. I looked at her strength and beauty.

"I will try again. But, you must promise me something."

Mahrah radiated uncertainty.

"Is it permissible for you to look for another mate?"

"It is," she said with some hesitation.

"Good. I would like you to look for another mate. I do not want you to be alone either."

"Nadia, I am no longer alone. I have you, my friend."

"Truth," I replied.

Acknowledgements

Like so many worthy endeavors, this book came in to being through the effort and support of far more people than can be named individually. Thank you to Kristin Holtz for her valuable feedback, her unwavering support, and graciously taking time out of countless days to handle my inquiries. Thank you to my early readers, whose close reading made this a much better book.

My students have convinced me to pursue my dream by pursuing theirs. They have inspired me as I have watched them believe in their potential and take risks. Thanks to all of you for your interest and unflagging support as I have nurtured my ideas into a novel.

And, most of all, thank you to my colleagues, family, and friends who have allowed me to bore them with yet another detail about writing and publishing, have listened to my triumphs and frustrations, and have reminded me about the Oxford comma, among other things. I could not have done this without you. To Monika, thank you for all you have done to help me. Barb, Elizabeth, and Susan, you are the best.

CPSIA information can be obtained
at www.ICGtesting.com
Printed in the USA
FSHW020121140619
58994FS

9 781733 899413